About the Author

Mark Hayden is the nom de guerre of Adrian Attwood. He lives in Westmorland, England, with his wife, Anne.

Mark has had a varied career working for a brewery, teaching English and being the Town Clerk in Carnforth. He is now a part-time writer and part-time assistant in Anne's craft projects.

He is also proud to be the Mad Unky to his Great Nieces & Great Nephew.

THE
13th WITCH

The First Book of the King's Watch

MARK HAYDEN

**PAW
PRESS**

www.pawpress.co.uk

First Published Worldwide in 2017 by Paw Press
Paperback Edition Published 2018
Reprinted with corrections 07, June 2020

Cover Design – Rachel Lawston
Design Copyright © 2017 Lawston Design
www.lawstondesign.com
Cover images © Shutterstock

Paw Press – Independent publishing in Westmorland, UK.
www.pawpress.co.uk

ISBN: 1-9998212-1-1
ISBN-13: 978-1-9998212-1-0

To Elle & Esmé,

Mini-Niece and Nano-Niece

THE
13th WITCH

Prologue – A Phantom at the Roadside

Did you know that the gods can use mobile phones? No? Me neither.

It had been a hell of a day already, and I knew that it would get a lot worse when the police caught up with me, especially if they caught up with me while I still had the gun. Why they were looking for me and how I got shot is another story completely, the story of Operation Jigsaw. You can look it up, if you want.

The body armour had saved my life, but my shoulder was throbbing so badly that I was sure it was cracked. I really needed a medic, and I needed one sooner rather than later.

But first, I had to get rid of the gun…

It was the early hours of the morning, and I was piloting my trusty Land Rover Defender down the M40 towards London and away from a trail of bodies that led back to Morecambe Bay.

I was only doing fifty miles an hour, because that's the maximum speed at which the Defender will behave like a normal vehicle. Above that, the wind noise deafens you, the steering wheel vibrates like a pneumatic drill, and the whole thing bounces like a roller-coaster in an earthquake. My leg was hurting, too.

I hit a bump and the shock went straight through my collar bone. Reflexively, I jerked my arm, and if the motorway hadn't been empty, I'd have caused a pile-up. I couldn't risk that happening again, so when I saw the sign for an exit, it was time to find a quiet spot, dump the Kalashnikov and surrender to the authorities. It had been a hell of a day, and it was about to get a lot weirder.

I drove half a mile off the motorway and pulled into a lay-by next to a wood. It was barely above freezing inside the cab, and well below freezing outside. The thought of digging a hole one-handed in frozen ground was too much to bear. Perhaps I'd have a coffee and a fag to get me going. I reached for the flask, and my phone pinged with a message.

My hand stopped in mid-air. I'd turned off my phone at St Andrew's Hall…

Was it true what they said? That GCHQ can turn on your phone remotely? I looked at the message, from someone calling themselves *Allfather*. What?

I didn't pause to wonder, because the message said: *The Police will be here in 10 minutes. Look for a pile of logs 200m inside the wood.*

I had never been so flummoxed, or had so many quandries slung at me so quickly, and that's when my training, my experience and my well-honed survival instinct kicked in.

I used to be in the RAF. I used to fly helicopters for Queen and country, and I've flown them into some of the world's most inhospitable places. Knowing when to act and when to assess can make the difference between life and death. Now was the time to act.

I climbed out of the Land Rover, every joint aching, and grabbed the AK47, a blanket and a torch. I set off through the trees, dragging my left leg – the one with the titanium tibia. There was a lot of snow lying in the wood, dazzling me with reflected LED light as I scanned the torch around looking for a pile of logs. When I found it, right where the message had said I'd find it, I wondered how this Allfather character knew such an obscure corner of England so well.

The pile of timber was covered in fresh snow and looked set to be undisturbed until the spring. I used the last ounces of strength in my good arm to ram the Kalashnikov into a gap, cover the gap with the blanket and cover the blanket with snow.

Panting with the effort, I dragged myself back towards the lay-by, keeping my eyes on the glare of headlights summoning me back to the warmth. Half way there I froze. Standing behind my vehicle was him. The Phantom.

Earlier this year, I'd suffered a head trauma. Ever since then, a shadowy, cloaked figure had been popping into my vision at odd moments. I'd gone privately to see a neurologist, and she'd told me that I had a, "short circuit in the visual wiring. Nothing to worry about. Probably."

There was no light at the back of the Defender, but I could see the Phantom clearly, more clearly than ever before: rough trousers, long cloak and hood over the face. In every previous appearance, it had just stood there. Tonight, it raised its hand in a salute, at the exact moment my phone pinged again.

I had to blink away tears from the Arctic air, and when the tears had gone, so had he. I checked the message: *Well done. We'll meet again after the Solstice.*

I was numb. Numb from cold, numb from pain, numb from what I'd seen and done in the last twenty-four hours, and numb with the thought that I might be losing my mind, because if I lost my mind, I'd lose the prize I'd fought for, killed for and been shot for: a clean slate, with all my sins forgiven.

I'd acted, and now it was time to reflect. That lasted about two seconds, until the cold sent a shiver up my spine and into my collarbone. I cried out with the pain, and that gave me enough energy to get back to the lay-by and pour myself a coffee. I lit a cigarette and saw blue lights flashing in the distance.

1 — *Christmas in Gloucestershire*

When the hospital had patched me up, and the police had spent three days taking my statements, I was released to start my new life. Hah.

Talk about baggage – as well the long and short term physical problems, I now had mental health issues to worry about as well. The Solstice had been and gone, and I'd had no more contact from the Phantom, so I focused on the here and now.

I walked out of the police station with my arm in a sling and no transport. I was in London, home was in Gloucestershire, and the woman I love was in Lancashire. One day I hope to have home, Mina and me all in the same place. Until then, I did what I could.

Mina was my immediate priority, and our future, if we have one, faces some challenges. The biggest one right now is that I can only see her for ninety minutes at a time, and I had to travel 250 miles even for that. It was worth it, though.

After we kissed goodbye, I got a taxi back to the station and it was time to relax. It was Christmas Eve, and I was heading home for Christmas.

You can't imagine the relief I felt when I got off the train at Cheltenham Spa and saw Dad puffing away on a cigar. He looked the same as he always does: well-cut suit, expensive overcoat and a tan from his retirement villa in Spain. He looked me up and down, mostly up, because I'm 6'4" tall.

'What happened, son?' He pointed to my left arm, pinned up in the sling. 'That wasn't the Taliban. Not this time.'

'You should see the other guy. He's dead.'

Dad gave me a dark look. 'Do I want to know?'

'You've got no choice, because I'm going to tell you anyway. Any chance of a lift?'

He spread his arms. 'That's what I'm here for.'

'No. I mean the case. I can't pick it up. It was bad enough lifting it on to the train.'

He stubbed the end of his cigar into some snow, carefully saving it for later (no smoking in the car: Mother's Orders). He huffed and puffed until the case was in the boot, then we were on our way out of Cheltenham towards the village of Clerkswell, where I was born and where I grew up.

I haven't lived there since I was eighteen. I'm now thirty-seven years old, and home is still my parents' house. Mind you, it's now got my name on the deeds.

While Dad huffed and puffed again to unload the case, I stood before the front door. Elvenham house is not ancient by any means, the oldest part dating back to the 1840s when my great-something grandfather James Clarke decided that a solid, successful provincial solicitor needed a solid, successful house for his growing family.

I only mention this because I don't want to give you the impression that I grew up in a mansion, although it does have two staircases and servants' rooms in the attic. Not that we had servants. We've always had a cleaner, and more recently Mrs Gower from the village has become a sort of part-time housekeeper. You might meet her later.

The most striking part of the house is the Gothic mini-tower which faces the road. It's the oldest part, and over the door is a worn block of limestone, carved with a dragon. Family legend says that the carving is much, much older than the house, and that you have to salute the dragon whenever you return from a journey. I said a big hello to the beast and limped round the side. Dad followed, struggling to wheel my case over the gravel.

'Hello, dear,' said my mother. She was standing in the middle of utter Christmas chaos. A roll of wrapping paper was next to the turkey, as if she'd only realised it wasn't foil at the last moment. Two pairs of socks were dangerously close to the hot plate on the Aga (that would be my Christmas present, then), and a Waitrose Luxury Pudding was holding open the pages of *Delia Smith's Christmas*. It's not that my mother is a bad cook – far from it – she's very good at everything she focuses on: the trouble is getting her to focus. Right now she was towering over the chaos, holding an iPad in one hand and the house phone in the other.

When I say *towering over the chaos*, I mean that literally – Mother towers over everything except me. Some very cruel girls had nicknamed her *the Stork* at Cambridge, and the name had stuck all through her years at GCHQ. Retirement suits her in a way that it doesn't suit Dad, which is why he pretends he hasn't retired.

'It's Rachael,' she said, staring at the iPad and completely ignoring my injuries. As usual. 'I can't get hold of her. I don't know if she's coming, or who she's bringing if she is coming.' She gave me her full attention. 'Conrad, dear, do you really think she's gay, or is it just a phase?'

My sister was a surprise to my parents and is ten years younger than me, which makes her twenty-seven. I joined the RAF when she was eight, so I don't know her very well, but I do know that she's not gay. Even I picked up that much. If she didn't come home, it's probably because she'd heard that I was coming.

Dad had dumped my case in the hall and appeared in the doorway. 'Do you need a hand, Mary?' he said, with the clear expectation that she didn't.

'If you don't, I was hoping to catch up with the boy. He's been through a lot, you know.'

'Later, Alfred. I need you to finish the tree if Rachael's not going to arrive and do it for you.'

Dad looked forlornly in the direction of the village pub and started to take his coat off.

'Do you want a hand, Mum?' I asked, pointing to the chaos.

'Go and unpack. You'd only be under my feet. What am I going to do with you, Conrad?' She put the iPad on the kitchen table and tucked the house phone into her apron. 'Can I hug you, or are you too broken for that?'

I wrapped my good arm around her and kissed the top of her head. It was the most concern she'd shown in years.

I dragged my case up the main staircase, which is thankfully quite shallow, unlike the Mont Blanc pitch of the servants' stairs. I dumped the case and collapsed on to the bed, exhausted from having to tense every other muscle to stop my collar bone and ribs moving. I'd barely gone *Whoof* before I got a text.

I hoped it might be Mina – she'd said that she'd try and borrow a phone over Christmas, so I struggled upright again. No. It was this Allfather character. *Meet me by your well. 10 minutes.*

Whoever was creating/manipulating this Phantom knew enough about my family to refer to it as 'our' well. I was beginning to get uneasy.

The Clarke family has lived here for at least three hundred years, possibly longer. It's well documented that the village used to be a monastic grange farm, and that it takes its name – Clerkswell – from a spring that some monkish clerk turned into a water supply for the villagers. In due course, a bigger, deeper well was dug near the church, and everyone thinks that that one is the Clerk's Well. It isn't. The original well is at the far end of our grounds, where the land slopes up to the limestone plateau of the Cotswolds. It's in exactly the place you'd expect a source of water to be found.

The Parish Council weren't keen, but my father managed to convince them that Elvenham House has the original Clerk's Well, so the impostor was re-named Church Well. It cost Dad a packet to prove that we own the original well, and the first thing he did was to install a pipe direct to the village pub so that they could brew their own beer, "With water from the Original Clerk's Well." It's what I always drink when I'm in there, and very nice it is, too.

Thinking about all this was a good way to put off meeting the Phantom. Now I only had five minutes.

I limped back downstairs. Dad emerged from the sitting room with a large box of Christmas decorations. 'I'm going for a walk up to the woods,' I said.

He looked at my leg, the one with the titanium tibia. 'Are you sure you're okay to walk?'

I'd been in a helicopter crash last January, but I wasn't the pilot. The actual pilot had died, and I'd got a double compound fracture. I also got a Distinguished Flying Cross and a medical discharge. Dad had flown over from Spain to visit me in hospital.

'Honestly, Dad, the more I walk, the easier it gets. It means I won't be limping when we go to the Inkwell later.'

'As long as you're sure.'

I stopped in the scullery to put on an old pair of boots and collect some backup. I may have left the AK47 in a pile of logs, but I'm not without resources. I had two shotguns in the gun cupboard but you can't fire a shotgun one handed. On top of the cabinet (where only I can reach it) is a wooden box labelled *String* – it was the most boring thing I could think of. Inside the box, under copious amounts of string, is an old .22 target pistol left over from the 1996 handgun ban. I avoided the kitchen and headed outside.

There is a formal garden at the back of Elvenham House, sadly neglected, then some trees, then a tennis court (overgrown), more trees and finally a path through rough grass to the well. The light was already fading as I stopped by the last tree to scope out the ground. There was no one there that I could see.

I took out the gun and walked up the path to the well, scanning the woods ahead of me constantly. Nothing. I arrived at the well, sat on the ledge, rested the gun on my lap and took out my cigarettes.

'Good afternoon, Squadron Leader Clarke,' said a voice from behind me.

'What the fuck...?'

On the other side of the well was the Phantom, barely six feet away. I scrambled up, taking hold of the gun and dropping the cigarette packet.

I tried to stop my voice shooting up an octave. 'It's Mr Clarke, now.'

The top of the shadow moved slightly, as if it were nodding. 'Very well. I want to offer you a position.'

'Oh?'

I looked around the edges of the shadow, trying to see if it might be a hologram. Someone could easily have set up a projector at the back of the well using the power supply for the water pump, and the Phantom's next remark confirmed that it wasn't really there.

'I wouldn't bother with the gun. It won't do me any damage. I've had my eye on you for some time, Mr Clarke.'

15

'You can call me Conrad, if it helps. Do you mind if I smoke?'

'No.'

I stowed the gun in my coat and picked up the fags. I slipped one in my mouth and reached for my lighter.

'I'd rather you didn't take out that lighter,' said the shadow. 'I don't want to confuse things.'

This illusion was too real. I grinned. 'You don't mind me smoking, but I can't use a lighter?'

'Here,' said the shadow.

It stepped forward, round the well, and a gnarled hand emerged from a long sleeve. A very realistic looking hand. No hologram, no virtual reality kit or any technology can mimic a physical presence like that, just a few inches from your nose. My stomach lurched.

Then the hand clicked its fingers, and its thumb burst into flame.

I jerked back, and my collar bone screamed in pain. My stomach heaved, and I scrabbled to get away from the well before I threw up. I just made it to the bushes in time.

If the Phantom were just a man, I'd deal with him. If I was having a brain seizure, someone would find me soon and ring for an ambulance. I straightened slowly and turned to find the Phantom standing behind the well. A battered silver cup, like a chalice, stood on the ledge in front, next to the packet of fags I'm sure I'd dropped on the floor.

I pointed to the cup. 'May I use that to get a drink?'

The Phantom nodded, and I took the cup to the pump that sends our water down to the Inkwell. The pump has a tap for testing, and I used it to fill the cup, then gave my mouth a good rinse. I took a drink to dilute the acid in my stomach and took out a cigarette.

The Phantom slowly lowered its hood. The hand that had burst into flame had been white, but now its hands were black, and the face underneath the hood was black, too. Its features were old and wizened, with white hair curled tightly to the scalp and an old-fashioned pirate patch over its right eye.

'Shall we try again?' it said. There was no trace of a recognisable accent in the voice.

I glued my eyes to its right hand and leaned forward. The fingers snapped, a flame appeared, and I lit my cigarette. I was going to enjoy the smoke.

'You're worried about the head injury, aren't you?' said the Phantom.

I nodded.

'If it weren't for the trauma, I'd still be invisible to you. I've always been around, here and there, but that injury opened up a part of your brain. Gave you a chance to see me.'

I took the Phantom's words at face value. 'I've been shot recently, but I don't remember hitting my head again, so how come you're talking all of a sudden, not just lurking in the shadows?'

'Because it was my choice to appear in the flesh, and it's costing me a lot to be here, so I don't want to hang about.'

'Me neither. It's too cold. Costing you a lot of what?'

'Lux. You'll see what I mean if you accept the challenge.'

I've been in shock a few times in my life. You don't remember it, really. Not most of it, anyway. From what I could remember, this wasn't anything like the beginnings of medical shock. It was pretty damn peculiar, though.

I picked up the conversational thread I'd dropped when I vomited. 'Is it a challenge you're offering or a job?'

'A position. Well, two positions, really. You have to accept the challenge to get them.'

'Now that I've destroyed my employers, I'm going to be at a loose end. What's the job? Jobs?'

'Positions. One position is working as my agent. The other position is with the Crown. They are compatible.'

I zipped my coat all the way up to the top, and fished my other glove out of the pocket. Whatever he/it was, I wasn't going to be anyone's client unless I knew who they were. 'Who are you?' I said simply.

The Phantom nodded, as if we'd crossed some sort of line. 'I am Odin, son of Bor. I am many things, but most call me the Allfather.'

I am a thirty-seven year old former RAF officer. I have killed and nearly been killed on many occasions, but I confess that all I could do was laugh like a hysterical hyena. 'I thought you were supposed to be white.' The words shot out of my mouth before I could stop them. The Phantom blinked its one eye.

'I'm neither white nor black. This appearance is for your benefit. Next time I might be more Scandinavian. I've had more practice at that.' The smile at the end was definitely not that of a phantom. This was definitely some sort of Him.

He nodded again. 'You think all this is illusion. That's a sensible attitude. I can prove it isn't, but only if you accept the position. Humour me for a moment.'

I sipped from the cup and dredged through my memory for everything I knew about Norse mythology. *Yggdrasil ... Loki ... Valhalla ... The Valkyries ...*

'Do I need to be dead to work for you? I can't say that's a great incentive to sign up.'

He shook his head. 'No. Not any more. I used to collect dead warriors; now I prefer the living.'

'Won't you need them for ... what was it? Ragnarook?'

'*Ragnarok*. No, because it's already happened. They weren't much use then, in the end.'

'Right. I thought you were supposed to die at Ragnarok.'

'I did. Someone put me back together.'

I frowned. I could go on asking questions like this until Christmas morning and it wouldn't prove anything. There was one more, though, that I just had to ask. 'What about the creation of the world? Are you claiming responsibility for that?'

He looked pained. He rubbed the skin around his eye patch. 'No. Of course not. I have no idea how the universe was created. That's not the problem: the problem is that I remember creating it just as vividly as I remember Ragnarok. I'm sure the other Powers have similar memories.'

The thought of *other Powers* was too much to swallow. I promised myself one more cigarette before I did something – phone an ambulance, maybe, or my mother. Something like that. I leaned forward to get a thumb-light. This time I stared closely at the Phantom's thumb: the flame seemed to hover above it with no hidden tubes, just a little blue flame.

'Okay. Fine,' I said. 'What does being your client involve, and what's this job with the government?'

'Client is an old-fashioned word. Look on it as being my agent. You're familiar with that line of work.'

I was. It was what I'd been doing for Sir Stephen Jennings until he shot himself a few days ago.

'The other position is with the King's Watch.'

'Which King would that be?'

'James the Sixth and First. You'll find that the world of magick hangs on to old titles. And old spellings. Don't bother to look them up.'

'I presume this is dangerous.'

'Oh, yes. Very dangerous.'

The cold had penetrated my coat, glove and scarf again. It was time to wrap this nonsense up. I had one last question, just to see just how consistent this Phantom could be.

'What about Mina? We've not even been on a date, yet, and I'm not giving up on her.'

'I have no objection. I can't speak for Ganesh, though.'

Now that was alarming. I thought of my cigarette lighter – it's a fake Zippo, with an image of Ganesha on the side. It was a present from Mina, the only one she's given me so far, and she bought it when she was going through a really tough time. I know that she was praying to Ganesha a lot during that period, but how did the Phantom know this?

'Ganesha will expect a price,' said the Phantom. 'But it won't be excessive. Ganesh likes a deal.'

According to Mr Joshi, Ganesha likes nothing more than a deal. Mr Joshi is a Hindu priest, and the only other person who's got Mina's back 100%. I stubbed out my cigarette. 'Go on, then. How can you prove that you're not an illusion?'

'You need to take off your coat and expose your back. Don't worry – I'll make it more comfortable.'

He moved his hands like the conductor in front of an orchestra during a really intense piece of Mahler. Suddenly, I was sweating. The air around me had warmed up by twenty degrees. My breath wasn't steaming any more.

I unfastened the thick coat and unzipped the fleece. Finally I unbuttoned my shirt and shrugged the three layers down my good shoulder. I turned round to face the well.

'It's customary to kneel,' said the voice from behind me.

I braced my feet in a standing position, mostly because my leg hurt too much to bend.

'Do you accept me as your Patron and bind your fate to mine?'

'Yes.'

I felt the back of my neck prickle, then he put his hand between my shoulder blades.

The whole kneeling thing is because you collapse at that point. The pain was like being shot, but without the kinetic punch of a bullet, and I felt him grab my arm to stop my head hitting the side of the well. He eased me into a sitting position, his arms as real and as physical as the cold stones against my back.

'What the fuck was that?' I said through gritted teeth.

'I've given you an upgrade. They call it Enhancement at the Invisible College.'

'I'm not a phone or a computer. I don't need extra chips. What have you put in my back?'

'Get yourself a scan. It won't find any chips or electrics. Sometimes the Old ways are the best.'

'So what did you do?'

He shook his head and held out his hand to help me up. I'm not proud – when I need help, I always take it. He lifted me up like I was a rag doll. The temperature started dropping again, so I zipped up my fleece and coat, leaving my shirt unfastened. Doing buttons with one arm in a sling is not easy.

Instead of answering my questions, he lifted the plastic cover from the well, opened the box next to the pump and took out the rope and bottle we use for taking deep samples. He slung the weighted bottle over the edge, then pulled it up and carefully decanted some water into the battered silver cup. 'Watch carefully,' he said.

He held his hand over the cup and it sort of glowed. I say *sort of* because I don't know how to describe the colour. It wasn't really a colour, it was more like the feeling you get when you stand next to a really, really hot radiator. The closest analogy I can get is the footplate of a steam engine – you can sense the flames, heat and power even when the door to the firebox is closed. If you've never been on the footplate of a steam engine, just use your imagination.

The Phantom nodded, pleased with his handiwork. 'If you get that sort of feeling again, and you aren't expecting it, watch out. I'll say no more for now. Drink.'

I drank. I gagged. Instead of well water, I got a mouthful of Inkwell Bitter. Now that's a trick I'd like to learn. I swallowed the beer and the same sensation of glowing spread inside me. My collar bone burned and itched like hell for a second.

'Go on,' said the Phantom. 'Try to move your arm.'

Anyone who can turn water into Inkwell Bitter without malt, hops and yeast deserves listening to. I eased my arm in the sling and there was no more pain. 'Thank you. I think. How am I going to explain this to my mother?'

'You'll think of a lie. You usually do.'

Aah. He must have been watching me closely.

'What do I call you?'

'Allfather. I won't be watching you all the time. In fact, now that you've got my rune on your back, you'll actually be able to tell when I'm watching. You can text me if you like, though I don't always reply. As I said, it costs me a lot to be here.'

I should make it very clear at this point that there was no part of me which believed that I'd just made a deal with a god. No part at all. Yes, I was willing to believe that *someone* had just cured my shoulder, and that I now had an undetectable implant in my back, but I was not willing to believe that I was in the presence of divinity. That was just silly.

'Enjoy your Christmas, Conrad. I'll text you soon with your instructions.'

'Have you any advice?'

'Always carry a packet of dried worms if you go underground.'

Great. That was such a help.

'One last thing, Allfather,' I said politely. 'If this is costing you a lot, you must have a reason. Not even my mother thinks I'm that wonderful. Especially not her.'

He smiled again. I looked him in the (one) eye. It didn't blink once.

'I owe a debt. Two debts. Your success will pay off both of them.'

'Christmas?' I said, trying to keep the conversation going. 'Do you…'

'Another time, Conrad,' he said, cutting in to my question. 'Your mother will be worried. Go well.'

And with that, he was gone.

I walked back to the house very slowly. What had I done? Either I had been through a psychotic episode, or I'd just done a deal with someone who could … what, exactly? I stopped by the tennis court and unzipped my coat. Carefully, I eased my left arm out of the sling – nothing. No pain, no grinding of bones, just a little stiffness. I extended it fully. Ow, that hurt my ribs. They weren't cured, and the level of pain from them told me that the Phantom/Allfather hadn't just slipped me a powerful painkiller. The improvement in my collar bone was local, instantaneous and impossible.

I put my arm back in the sling and carried on walking, navigating by memory and the beacon of light from the kitchen. What did I know for certain? A person calling himself after an old god had approached me. He wanted me to believe that he was real, and I certainly did, but what sort of "real" was he?

He was capable of sophisticated illusions (the vanishings, the jet of flame, the turning of water into beer), yet he also possessed some powerful technology. My collar bone was evidence of that, and, yes, I did feel different after he'd touched my back. He also wanted something, and I wasn't going to find out what by going round in circles. I guess I'd just have to wait.

I replaced the pistol in the box of string and heard my mother shouting from the kitchen, calling Dad and me with excitement in her voice. We arrived together, and she announced with a beaming smile that Rachael was coming – for New Year.

'Alone?' asked Dad.

'Do you remember Carole, from school and college?' said Mum.

Dad nodded; I looked at the cracks in the ceiling. I didn't like where this was heading.

'Rachael met up with her a while ago. Carole said that she was coming home for New Year, and did Rachael want a lift. She wanted it to be a surprise.'

'Who wanted it to be a surprise? Rachael or Carole?' I asked.

Mother gave me one of her looks. 'It's not all about you, Conrad.'

Ever the diplomat, Dad stepped in. 'That's lovely. When are they coming?'

'Not until Thursday evening. Now that I know it's just going to be the three of us for Christmas dinner tomorrow, I'm going to do a late supper tonight.'

'Even better,' said Dad. 'I can take Conrad out for a drink.'

Mother paused. She wasn't happy. She thought about objecting until she realised that there was nothing she could say that wouldn't look spiteful. She settled on the old favourite. 'Can you mix alcohol with strong painkillers?' she said to me.

I looked theatrically at my watch. 'I can in ten minutes. Now that I've got the train journey over, I shouldn't need the strong ones any longer.'

'Stay off the whisky, Alfred,' she said, turning back to her bowls and packets. Dad and I beat a hasty retreat.

Clerkswell isn't a huge village. It did grow a lot when the Great Western Railway built an extension from Birmingham in the 1900s, and it's managed to keep the Holy Trinity of village life – shop, pub and school, with the church as a bonus. Despite our alleged ancestry, none of the Clarkes are churchgoers, and in the very unlikely event that I really had made a deal with a Norse god, I doubt I'd be welcome there anyway. It made me smile – as did the thought of seeing Mrs Clarke's Folly again.

William Clarke (an ancestor) married a girl with an enthusiasm for religion, and she believed that it was her mission to build a Methodist chapel in the village, to which end she donated a piece of land. She gave up Methodism when she became pregnant, and the land lay unused until William persuaded her that it could be used for other communal purposes. Ever since, the home ground of Clerkswell Cricket Club has been Mrs Clarke's Folly, and yes, that's the official name.

'You look more cheerful,' said Dad. 'The walk must have done you some good.'

'More than you could guess. It's good to be home, Dad, even with Rachael coming and Carole back in the village.'

Dad slowed down. Elvenham House is on the road south from the village green, a road that doesn't really go anywhere. We were approaching the centre of the village, and soon we'd have the church on our right and the Church Well on our left. Dad stopped by the railings of St Michael's churchyard, well before the lychgate. No one would come this far down.

'Dumping Carole like that wasn't your finest hour, son, but she got over it.'

That wasn't the whole truth. What had happened between Carole, Rachael and me was complicated. Dad was about to start walking again until I touched his arm. 'Look, Dad, I've got a lot to tell you, but there's one thing that means more to me than anything.'

He turned properly towards me. 'Go on, son.'

I took a deep breath. 'Speaking of relationships, I don't know whether Mum will be pleased or horrified, but I've fallen in love.'

'Oh dear. Are you sure you don't want to sit in the nice warm pub to tell me this.'

'I've got to tell you why I shot someone last week and I need a drink for that, but I need to tell you about Mina first.'

He dug out the remains of the cigar he'd been smoking at the station. 'There must be a problem, son. What is it? She's got six kids? She's a journalist? She's a Mormon? Whatever it is, it can't be as bad as when you fell for that Amelia girl.'

The church organ blared out the introduction to *Away in a Manger*. The bass sounded very wrong and the organist stopped. He or she started again, even more shakily, then subsided forlornly.

'Aah. I've got some news about Amelia, but that's for later.' I took a deep breath. 'Mina *was* married, but her husband was murdered. On Valentine's day, of all days.'

'Blimey. You didn't have a hand in that, did you?'

'No. I was trying to save his life, and I shot the bastard who killed him. Mina finished him off. That's one of the reasons she's in prison.'

'Bloody hell, son.' He took a puff on his cigar and studied the end. 'Mina? I know you had a thing for a German girl once. Is that short for Wilhelmina?'

Dad was in the antiques business for years. He's very sharp when it comes to things like that.

'No. Her name's Mina Desai. Her family are from Mumbai, originally. Her husband was English. They didn't have children.'

Dad grunted. The lack of children dodged another of mother's potential objections. 'What's the other reason she's in prison? And how long is she going to be there?'

'Money laundering. She should be out in late spring.'

Dad nodded. I lit a cigarette and we started walking slowly towards the green. 'Did you start your relationship before or after her husband died?' he asked.

'After. If you can call it a relationship. We'd only known each other a few weeks before Miles was killed, and we've only seen each other a few times since she was arrested. It's mutual, I know that much.'

'Then that's all that matters. If she's a good person, and you love each other, you'll work it out.'

That's Dad for you. Ever the optimist – one of his great qualities as a father, and one of his biggest weaknesses as an antiques dealer.

He stopped again. 'Have you got a picture?' he asked with a grin.

I slowly took out my wallet. Others would have a slew of snaps on their phones, but I didn't. Just one picture, printed in glossy colour. I angled it to catch the light.

Dad looked up sharply. 'Prison won't be the problem, son. She's gorgeous.' He nodded slowly to himself. 'How old is she?'

The same thought had occurred to me many times. 'She's Rachael's age.'

'Whisk her away from those prison gates and get a ring on her finger quickly. That's what I'd do.'

And that's more or less what he'd done with my mother, and thirty-eight years later, they're still together. The church was receding behind us. A different, more confident pair of hands attacked the organ. Somewhere, perhaps, the Herald Angels were singing. I Harkened, but heard them not. Neither did I hear the Ride of the Valkyries, Bollywood music or any other sign of divine intervention.

The official name of the village pub is the Clerk's Well Inn. At some point in the nineteenth century, the landlord had decided that this was too boring, so he got a sign showing the tonsured head of a monk leaning over a manuscript. In the foreground of the painting is a large inkwell – get it? The food is so-so, but since they started brewing their own beer – and especially since they started using water from our well – people flock from miles to try the Inkwell Bitter and Inkwell Gall Ale.

We were early enough to have a choice of seats, and I used the five minutes Dad spent schmoozing the other punters to make a phone call. Nothing to do with Phantoms; this was closer to home.

Dad returned with the drinks, and I started my story. I was into my third pint of Inkwell Bitter before I finished.

'Time for a smoke,' said Dad. 'I'll go first so you can save the seats. It'll give me a chance to ring your mother and warn her about Mina. She sounds like a special girl.'

'Woman, Dad. She's a woman, not a girl.'

He shrugged on his coat. 'Are you really telling me that you've killed two people as part of a global money-laundering scheme, and that you've walked away scot-free?'

'Apart from the leg, the arm, the ribs, the collar bone and the head trauma.'

He patted my good shoulder. 'I always said you were a chip off the old block. Well done, lad.'

I settled back to see if I knew anyone in the pub. I used to play for the village cricket team, and many of the kids I went to primary school with are still around, though not all of them would be pleased to see me. Especially Carole's brother, Ben Thewlis.

At the time, Carole had maintained a dignified silence, but Rachael hadn't. She'd put a lot of rubbish around the village, and that was one of the reasons I didn't come home for a long while. Ben had threatened, on behalf of his sister, to do all sorts of damage if I showed my face in the cricket pavilion. We were in the pub, not the pavilion, but here was Dad coming back with Ben in tow.

He came straight over to me, firm of gaze, and held out his hand. I shook it, and he said, 'I hear you're a bit of a war hero, Conrad. Saw your picture in the rag when you got that medal.'

'I wouldn't say that, Ben,' I replied. 'Good to see you. Catch up next week?'

'We're having a session on Monday night, and if you're up to it, we could use your leg spin in the summer.'

'I'll look forward to Monday, but we'll have to see whether I play again. My next visit to Mrs Clarke's Folly might be as an umpire.'

He snorted. 'You? An umpire? There's no team in Gloucestershire that would trust you.'

I placed my hand on my heart. 'You wound me. I'm a changed man.'

From behind him, Dad pointed to his watch and the door.

'I'll see you Monday,' I said. Ben clapped me on the shoulder (the good one, fortunately), and that was that. Friends again.

On the way back, Dad said, 'What have you bought your mother for Christmas?'

'Some jewellery for her, and I've got a present for the whole family. I've just been on the phone to get Rachael included as well.'

'Oh?'

'That job at Fylde Racecourse I've just told you about?'

'The illegal job which nearly got six people killed, including you?'

'Yes, well, apart from the risk to life and liberty, I really enjoyed it, so I've booked us a suite at Cheltenham Races for the Boxing Day meeting. Champagne reception and lunch.'

Dad stopped and lit up the lane with a big grin. 'Welcome home, son. It's going to be a good Christmas.'

2 — The Tower of London

Dad was right. It was a good Christmas.

I had a great time, thank you very much, until just before I met up with the cricket team on Monday, when I got a text from this Allfather character:

Report to Merlyn's Tower on Thursday morning. It's in the Tower of London.

I didn't bother to reply. I went out and enjoyed myself with the lads, because one of many things I learnt in the RAF was to take each day as it comes, especially when you've had your movement orders.

The next morning I tracked Mother down to the formal dining room. She'd gone into overdrive on Boxing Day and was currently wielding an extendable duster to eradicate the spiders' webs adorning the chandelier. I know that makes it sound rather grand, and I suppose it is. Rachael hadn't been to Elvenham for nearly two years, and Mother wanted to make it look as homely as possible. Yesterday, I'd been forced to chop half a ton of firewood *now that your shoulder's better, dear.*

I coughed to get her attention. 'If you're wondering why Rachael doesn't come here often, it's because your swimming pool in Spain is a lot more enticing to her than the waters of Elvenham Well.'

She stopped attacking the cobwebs. 'I've never heard you bang on about that blessed well as much as you have this holiday.' She pointed the long handled duster at me. 'Just because you own the house, it doesn't give you carte blanche to start scheming. You're as bad as your father.'

A terrible thought struck her. 'He hasn't been giving you ideas, has he? He once talked about bottling the water. Please don't tell me he's trying to talk you into it. It took years to make back the money we spent on that pipe to the Inkwell.'

'But it's worth it for the beer they brew, Mum.' I smiled at her. 'Dad hasn't said anything about the well. It's a damn good idea, though.'

'Conrad!'

'Perhaps I'll look into it if this job falls through.'

She looked relieved that I had no immediate plans for the well. Bonus point. Then she twigged. 'What job?'

'Not sure. It's for the Crown, I know that much. They've asked me to go for a chat. On Thursday.'

'Oh.'

My mother is good with *Ohs.* This one meant something like: *I want you here doing the cleaning, but I'd rather you got a job.* Because it was Mother, she wouldn't ask awkward questions, accepting that Crown business has to stay secret. Good. For once, I was being honest when I said that no idea what the job – sorry, *position* – might entail.

'I'll go up on Wednesday. If you can talk Dad into lending me the Jag, I should be home on Thursday evening to help you get sorted for Rachael coming. You'll need help killing the fatted calf for her, won't you?'

'Stop being facetious. I'll talk to Father.'

Of course Dad lent me the Jag. He didn't have much choice, did he?

On Wednesday night I stayed at my flat in Notting Hill. I bought it a few years ago at the right time, which was either good luck or good judgement. I've never lived there properly, and a succession of fellow officers on postings to the Air Ministry have paid the mortgage, or their expenses did. It even became known as *Clarke's Mess*. My tenants had to let me sleep there whenever I needed it, and sometimes I got the spare room, sometimes I got the couch. The story of how I got to own Elvenham House is a lot more complicated.

The current tenants of Clarke's Mess had gone home for Christmas, so I grabbed a takeaway and put my feet up with a bottle of red and my laptop. The Internet has plenty of info on the Tower of London, and plenty on possible sites for Merlyn, but nothing at all on the two together. Shakespeare used to think that Julius Caesar had built the Tower, apparently, but no one has ever suggested a link with King Arthur or his magician. The only clue I got was that the Devereux Tower was previously known as *Robyn the Deville's Tower*. Perhaps locating Merlyn's Tower was the challenge. I doubted it.

The crisp frosts and lying snow of Gloucestershire had become mud and cold drizzle in London, the worst weather for my bad leg. To fortify myself for wandering around outside, I dropped in to a cosy, family-run café in Moorgate. There are lots of family businesses in the City; few of them are run by English families.

'Quiet today,' I said after ordering the Full Monty breakfast.

'Yeah. Early rush is gawn and most of the offices are shut for the week. Dunno why I bothered to stay open. Still, it keeps me out of trouble and stops me having to have look after the kids. 'Ere, do I know you? Didn't you come in with some of the Motorhire crowd? I'm sure I saw you with that Mina. You was on crutches, then.'

I went a deep shade of red. The café is over the road from a dodgy limousine company where Mina was the chief accountant and money-launderer. The trouble with being six foot four and then breaking bread with someone as distinctive as Mina is that you make memories.

'Mmm. Yes,' I said.

The matriarch passed my order through to the kitchen and made me a pot of tea. She wasn't done yet. 'Poor kid. I heard about Miles, and about her going down for GBH with Intent.' Miles was Mina's husband.

'Yes,' I said.

She held on to the pot of tea, reluctant to let me off the hook. 'And you're walking around? All the others are still banged up.'

Translation: *You must be a grass.*

'I hadn't been there long enough to get caught in the net. The police had nothing on me. I'll give your regards to Mina.'

She passed over the tea. 'Is she out of prison, then?'

'Not yet. Some good has come from it: she's had surgery on her jaw. Finally.'

'Good for her. Food won't be long.'

I chose the same table that Mina and I had used before, to remember being close to her. My food was brought by a girl who looked barely big enough to carry such a large plate, and I worried about the safety of my beans and her blouse all the way from the kitchen. There was no mistaking who she was.

'Has your mum made you work in here over the holidays?' I said.

The girl looked over her shoulder. 'Bleeding slave labour, that's what it is. I'm only here so the proper staff can go back to Poland for Christmas. She only pays me half what they get.'

The food was very good, and just what I needed. I drank my tea and left the daughter a big tip.

I walked down Moorgate to digest the very generous breakfast, and the café matriarch was right: the City of London was very quiet. I strolled along, enjoying the freedom that having a purpose gives you, until I got to Threadneedle Street, between the Mansion House and the Bank of England.

Waiting to cross the road, I got *that* feeling, the one I'd felt when the Phantom did his thing with the well water. I backed up to the fortress walls which surround the Bank and stared hopelessly around. Some new, sixth sense was trying to tell me something, and I had no idea what it was. I edged along the wall and waited until there was a gap in the traffic, then I bolted across the two roads. Nothing attacked me, and the feeling was gone when I got to King William Street. All I attracted was some funny looks, quite an achievement in London.

Ten minutes later I was standing in the big plaza between the ticket office and the Tower of London, clutching my guidebook and remembering the last time I'd been here, twenty years' ago.

Dad had suddenly found himself on emergency childcare duties because the village school had closed unexpectedly for a week. Something to do with asbestos, they said. I'd just finished my GCSEs, and was at a dangerously loose end.

Dad had bought the contents of a local artist's studio when the poor woman was killed in a car crash. He had to sell as much of the work as he could before the bank – or Mother – realised what he'd done, and he had to do it in London with Rachael and me in tow.

Those three days in London were the one and only time that Rachael and I were alone in each other's company. She was six, and I wonder if she remembers much about it. After the Zoo, the London Dungeon and the Planetarium, I thought the Tower would make a good day out. Well, I enjoyed it.

The City of London is ancient, one of the oldest continually inhabited settlements in Britain – it's much older than the idea of 'England', for example. There are parts of London which feel alive in a way that's got nothing to do with the people who live there. The Tower is one of those places.

From the moment you walk through the Gatehouse, you feel watched. There is no dark corner in that place which is not overlooked by some door, window or embrasure (arrow slit to you and me). I'd felt it when I was sixteen and I was feeling it even more strongly now.

The Tower is also very big. You can walk for ages and not get anywhere, or if you stop to examine every nook and cranny you can lose an hour trying to cover a hundred yards. I decided to make an inside circuit towards the Devereux Tower and see if anything leapt out at me.

I passed the New Armouries, the Hospital and the Fusiliers' Museum. Nothing. No spooky tingling, no signs saying *Interview Candidates this way*, and no creepy figures holding a sign with my name on it. The next obvious place was the Waterloo Barracks, home to the Crown Jewels. If the Phantom liked a joke, *working for the Crown* might have been a literal clue. I dodged into the old barracks and took a look.

You pass the regalia on a moving walkway, to stop you standing and gawping at the loot. If you want to gawp, there's a raised platform behind the travellator. I moved along, I admired the bling, then I stood and gawped. No one approached me or tapped me on the shoulder. I even examined the tapestries for mysterious cloaked figures. You never know, there might be a secret door behind one of them.

To check every tapestry, painting and poster in the Tower would take at least a month. Merlyn's Tower was somewhere I was expected to find in a morning. I left the Waterloo Barracks and lit a cigarette, turning through 360 degrees and looking for inspiration. I'd nearly come full circle when I saw three cages down by the Wakefield Tower. Of course – the ravens.

The old legend requires that six ravens be present at all times, lest the Tower crumble and the monarchy collapse. Everyone knows that this is accomplished by clipping their wings and having seven ravens in case of death, escape or attack by urban fox. I had deliberately resisted further research into Odin, because I refused to believe that it mattered. What I did remember was that Odin had two ravens. I limped over to the cages to see if I were on the right track.

The information board informed me that one of the ravens was actually *called* Odin – along with Hugin and Munin, Odin's Thought and Memory. Ravens are big birds, but shy: you don't get to see them up close in the wild. Even with their wings clipped to keep them onside, you can sense their power and menace. You can also see how intelligent they are.

'Right, you lot,' I said loudly to the assembled birds. A startled Asian tourist looked round in fright. One of the ravens hopped on to a closer perch and stared. 'Come on, beaky. Give us a clue. My leg's aching and I want a coffee.'

I jumped back when the bird let out a double *caw caw*. Like formation dancers, all seven ravens hopped on to perches, turned to their left and nodded. Twice. They held the pose for a second, then hopped and jumped around like normal birds.

'You make them do a trick?' said the tourist.

'I wish,' I replied, turning to follow the direction the ravens had shown me. It pointed towards a blank piece of curtain wall.

'Let's hope it's on the other side,' I said, partly to myself, partly to the ravens. The one who'd first looked at me closed its eye. I'll let you decide if it was winking.

Which came first, the raven or the egg? Was I good with directions because I'd flown choppers, or was I a good pilot because I had a strong sense of direction? Either way, when I skirted the wall, I knew exactly where the imaginary line that the birds had shown me continued. It pointed just to the right of a building called … I looked it up: the Well Tower. That sounded promising. Unfortunately, it was in the off-limits zone and there was another wall in the way.

There are a couple of cafés within the walls, so I picked the quietest and ordered a cappuccino to warm me up. I'd chosen the quieter place so that I could try pumping the staff for clues on what happened in the off-limits areas. I discovered that there was a mixture of private housing (for the Yeoman Warders), offices and store rooms. 'But you can't get in without a pass,' said the waitress. I smiled and took my coffee outside to finish it off.

One day I'll write a book called *How to Blag your way through Security*. This one was a doddle. I left the Tower and picked up a cardboard box from a dumpster. There was a profile of one of the Warders in the guide book, saying that he was married with children, so I walked up to security and said, 'Package for Mrs Jefferson. Needs her signature.' I showed my driving licence and they waved me through.

Inside the restricted zone, I picked up the ravens' line and stared. From left to right I identified the Develin Tower (more devils?), the square Well Tower, a series of Georgian looking houses and a squat round tower that barely rose above the outer curtain. This last one was on no map and was missing from the aerial photo I'd printed off the Internet last night. That sixth sense was tingling again.

There was a short staircase to an unmarked, unprepossessing door. I took a deep breath and pushed, expecting to find it locked. It wasn't. Beyond the threshold was a landing with stairs spiralling up and down and a door facing me. The door was most definitely locked, and even had a hi-tech security system. In every organisation I've ever come across, ever, the most important people have the highest rooms. I turned right and limped up the staircase.

I reached another landing, with another locked door. The stairs up from here were not only straight, *but they had carpet*. I was definitely on the way to the boss's office.

There was no landing on the top floor. Instead, the stairs opened to a reception area. Facing the only window was an unoccupied desk, covered with papers and hosting a computer. To the right of the desk was a pair of very elaborate oak doors with two signs. This was it. The Phantom had sent me to work for...

The King's Watch
Office of the Peculier Constable

I tried not to snigger. Mother says my humour hasn't moved on much from school. Perhaps she's right, but who wouldn't snigger at a Peculiar Constable? I've drunk enough beer in Yorkshire to know that *Peculier* means something different from *Peculiar*, but I'm not sure what. Underneath the larger sign was a more recent addition. It seems that the current Peculier Constable is *Colonel Dame Hannah Rothman, DCB CGC PC BSc (Hons) MA RMP.*

For those not familiar with our weird honours system, this meant that the PC (Peculier Constable) had been given a top knighthood (Dame-DCB), had two university degrees (BSc and MA), and had been awarded a Conspicuous Gallantry Cross. That's a serious medal and it puts my DFC to shame. I wondered how she'd earned that and become a colonel in the Royal Military Police (RMP)?

So, my potential new boss was a soldier, and a senior officer at that. There is only one way to approach such creatures – with trolley loads of bullshit. I squared my shoulders and gave a commanding knock on the door. The right hand one seemed to be slightly ajar, perhaps because the

PC's PA was inside, or because the doors were so thick I wouldn't be able to hear her if they were closed.

'Come in,' said a not unpleasant woman's voice.

I pushed the door fully open and marched four paces into the room. On my way forwards, I got a quick impression of a large office with antique fixtures including a substantial desk. Behind the desk was the Peculier Constable, reading a document. She was a much younger woman than I'd expected: in her early forties and with a huge mane of glossy red hair which exploded most unmilitarily in all directions.

I came to attention and was about to salute when she looked up, and panic shot across a lined face. Straight away I felt her glow with that weird feeling, much more intensely than in Threadneedle Street.

I started to salute. The second my hand rose, she dropped her fountain pen and made a stabbing movement towards me as she dived to her left. The air shimmered in front of her, then I was smacked by the blast of a silent explosion. It lifted me off my feet and threw me at the wall. I just had time to brace my head for the impact before my back smacked into the ancient masonry.

I felt a *thud* rather than a *crack*. Hopefully I wouldn't have any more broken bones, but I didn't have any breath. I collapsed in a heap and struggled to get air into my lungs. I rolled on to my side to see what the hell was happening, and found the PC peering at me from round the corner of her desk. Not just peering, but doing the tingly thing and giving me a bug eyed stare. At least she wasn't pointing at me.

I managed a breath, and croaked, 'Don't shoot, ma'am!'

Her eyes stopped bugging out and she raised a hand to her mouth, mortified with embarrassment. She used the desk to pull herself up, and as I felt my bones for breakages, I got my first good look at Hannah Rothman. She wasn't particularly tall, nor noticeably under or overweight. It was difficult to tell exactly what was lurking under the starched white shirt, heavy blue skirt and brown knee-length boots. What I could see was that her hair was a wig, and that it had slipped badly. Underneath I could see bare skin, angry and scarred, with none of her original hair left at all.

'I'm so sorry. So, so sorry,' she said, taking a step forward, then another, then holding out her hand to help me up.

I didn't want to pull her over, nor to have my ego diminished even further by discovering that she was incredibly strong as well as possessed of advanced technology. I smiled at her, then rolled on to my front and got up slowly by way of my knees and the wall.

'You must be lost,' she said.

'I hope not, ma'am,' I said. 'Otherwise that was a bit of a waste. Is this Merlyn's Tower?'

She took a step back, and I felt her guard come up again, only I had no idea why I thought that – I just sensed that she was now protected in some way. She also raised her hands and turned the palms towards me. That did not look good.

She had taken my salute as a threat, so I didn't try again. As best I could, I stood to attention. 'I was told to report here by ... someone calling himself *The Allfather.*'

A look of profound sadness, mixed with anger, disfigured her face. She half turned away from me and clenched her fists. 'Damn him. Damn him to hell, the bastard.' She turned back to me and lifted her hand in a totally unthreatening gesture of sympathy. 'You poor thing. You poor, poor thing.'

That was not what I was expecting. I wondered if this was my biggest mistake since agreeing to join Operation Blue Sky.

I was still at attention. 'Sorry, ma'am. Why is that?'

She sighed. 'Because you're going to die a horrible death soon. He didn't tell you that, did he?'

'He didn't tell me anything at all, ma'am. Literally nothing. Not why I'm here, not what the position entails, nothing. He certainly didn't tell me who he really was.'

First, she looked appalled. Then she shook her head, sending her wig even further askew and revealing more scar tissue. Perhaps this was how she got her CGC. 'You really don't know who he is?'

'No, ma'am.'

I thought that *you're going to die a horrible death soon* was the worst thing that she could say to me. What she said next was much, much worse.

'He's Odin Allfather, king of the Aesir, god of Valhalla, one of the Greater Powers. And a bloody menace.'

'Sorry? Ma'am.'

She tilted her head to one side. I couldn't take it any longer. I nodded towards her head. 'If you'll excuse me, ma'am ... Your hairpiece?'

'Shit.' She grabbed her wig and yanked it back into place. We both turned to the door at the same time as we heard footsteps crossing the stone flags outside (the carpet stopped at the top of the stairs. Maybe they'd run out of money).

The Peculier Constable looked through the open door and said, 'Tennille, how's my hair?'

A motherly black woman stepped into the room, a bundle of photocopying under her arm. She gave the PC's hair a slight adjustment. 'Are you okay, honey?' Her accent spoke of a childhood in the Caribbean.

The PC pointed at me, and said, 'Another one from the Allfather. Poor sod.'

I assumed that Tennille was the PA from the outside office. She looked me up and down, shook her head and left, closing the door behind her.

The PC turned her attention back to me. 'Why are you standing like that?'

Really?

'I'm trying to stand to attention, ma'am, but you flattened me against the wall. My back hurts.'

'Why are you? ... Oh, are you a real soldier?'

'RAF pilot, ma'am.'

'You can stand how you want in here. I'm not a real colonel, you know. I was a Detective Inspector, once. I'd offer you a seat, but you'll be leaving in a second.'

That explained a lot. Clearly the rank and the knighthood came with the job. It didn't explain the Conspicuous Gallantry Cross, though. I took a step back and leaned against the wall. I'd been happy to think about military ranks and about her hairpiece because it meant I could avoid thinking about what she'd said: that the Phantom was actually a god.

I tried to think about it for a second. No good. 'A real god, ma'am?'

'Stop it with the "Ma'ams" already, Mr RAF pilot. Call me Hannah until you leave.'

'It's former Squadron Leader...'

'...Stop. Don't tell me your name. I don't want to know.' She took a deep breath. 'Did he – the Allfather – do something to you? Are you seeing, or smelling, or feeling weird things when you didn't before?'

'Yes. Yes, Hannah. You sort-of glowed before you smacked me with your force field.'

She looked down at the scuffed toes of her suede boots. 'It wasn't a force field. What you're sensing is magick. With a "k". The Allfather has Enhanced you so that you can feel magick, but I can tell by looking that you have very little of the Gift. Just enough to find Merlyn's Tower and get yourself killed.'

The Allfather had said he was going to Enhance me. I thought it was a bonus. Clearly I had a lot to learn.

'Are you going to be doing the killing?' I said, trying to smile.

'No. That will happen when you go for gold.'

I was getting very lost here. *Keep up, Conrad*, I tried saying to myself. 'Go for gold? He really did tell me nothing, only that I should apply for a position and that I should report here. Oh, he did say it would be very dangerous.'

'Terminally. Well, to be fair, it's not *certain* death, but with your level of Gift, and no training, you've got no chance.'

'He also said that I didn't have to go through with it.' I stopped and backed up a few sentences. 'Did you say *magick*?'

'Yes. It's real. Get over it. And no, I'm not going to do a demonstration. Clear?'

'No. But I can see you're not happy. If you could just tell me...'

'The position he was talking about was Watch Captain, previously known as Witchfinder. They work for me.'

'Aah. Sort of like...'

Her blue eyes lit up with fire. 'Don't you *dare* say *Ministry of Magic*.'

'Right. And no references to *Muggles*,' I added.

'They're called people. In context, we refer to their world as the mundane world.'

I nodded in agreement. Hannah was in a mood of epic proportions, and I wanted as much information as I could get. 'How do I get to be a Watch Captain?'

'You have to turn up and take the oath. You have to take the oath on your own sword, which then carries your Badge of Office. A sword endowed with magick. You don't have one, do you?'

'Sorry. We don't get issued magickal swords in the RAF.'

'Ha ha. The only creatures who can make the sword are Dwarves. Yes, Dwarves. No Tolkien references, either.'

'Dwarves. Got it. Where do they live?'

'Where do you expect Dwarves who hoard Alchemical Gold to live?'

For the first time since I'd taken the Allfather as Patron, I had a tiny inkling. 'Would that be underneath the Bank of England? I felt something there this morning.'

She gave me a sharp look. 'Yes, actually, but you won't have sensed the Dwarves. Probably the Invisible College.'

I couldn't cope with that, so I ignored it for now. 'And the Dwarves don't just give this Alchemical Gold stuff away, do they?'

'No. They'll demand a price, but that's not the problem.'

Dwarves. Magick (with a 'k'). Alchemical Gold. None of this was the problem, apparently. What on earth could it be? I raised my eyebrows.

'You can't use the front entrance without your Badge of Office. No one has survived using the rear entrance for some time, including the last three *shnooks* who the Allfather sent to try it.'

Shnook? Hannah's Jewish heritage was coming out all over. I didn't know what a shnook was, but I could guess. 'And how do I...?'

'Go to Bank tube station. You'll find the entrance down there. Just keep going down. And no, it's not on Platform nine-and-three-bloody-quarters. It's in a service corridor. Now, get out. Seriously, get out.'

3 — *Talking to Strange People.*

(includes family)

I opened the door to leave and discovered that Hannah's PA hadn't shut it fully. From our very brief acquaintance, I guessed that Tennille had done so out of concern for her boss rather than out of nosiness. She was seated at her desk, sorting papers.

'Don't take it personally,' she said in that rich accent.

'Trinidad?' I enquired.

'Barbados,' she laughed. 'Don't try to sweet-talk me. It don't work. The Constable gets upset at what that man's been doing and she don't want to know who you are because it hurts too much. I want to know, though.'

'Very kind.'

She held up a piece of paper. 'So that I can notify your next of kin when you vanish without trace. The Constable is worried about you; I'm worried about your family.'

I took the form and jotted down a few details. When I'd finished, I folded it and held it just out of her reach. 'I'll swap you for Hannah's business card. In case I do survive.'

She fished in a drawer and held out a card. We swapped. She read the form and gave a sigh of relief. 'At least you're not married.'

I was going to say *not yet*, but held my peace. It would be very presumptuous to think that Mina might marry me.

Tennille brought out an ID badge on a lanyard and handed it over after copying down its number on the Next of Kin form. The badge bore the Transport for London logo and had *Contractor* written on it. 'That will get you into the service area. It's got a built in chip. Don't worry, I've got plenty, and I'll know from the log that you've been inside.'

'I was just wondering, if you've got a moment. About this magick thing…'

She laughed. 'Don't ask me. I've got no Sight at all. Unlike my girl.'

'Oh? Is she a Watch Captain?'

'No. Goodbye, Mr Clarke. And good luck.'

'You've been most kind, Mrs…?'

She shook her head. 'Unh-huh. No names. Goodbye.'

When she shook her head, I noticed a small cross on a chain around her neck. If Tennille were a practising Christian, and the Constable was Jewish, and the Allfather had talked about the *Other Powers*… what was going on, cosmologically speaking? Could my brain even cope with that? Not now. Maybe tomorrow.

I stowed the badge and left. Outside, it was raining. Of course.

Forsaking the Tower of London, I bought a large coffee from the nearby Costa and sat on a bench in the shelter of a bare tree. The first thing I did was light a cigarette. The second thing was to take out my phone and send a text to the Allfather. The ravens should have told him that I'd appeared, so he might be expecting to hear from me. The conversation went like this:

Me: *I'm not doing a suicide mission. What sort of CO sends in a totally unprepared volunteer? And what's with the Minimally Gifted rubbish?*

Him: *It's not a suicide mission. The previous volunteers were young, very Gifted and very enthusiastic. You're a survivor.*

Me: *What's down there?*

Him: *I can only see what the raven can see. They don't fly well underground.*

Me: *And if I decline?*

Him: *Sooner or later, someone will spot you and decide you're a threat. They will definitely kill you without my patronage. Or I can remove your Gift. You'll regret it for the rest of your life.*

I doubted that very much. The Allfather might think he knows me, but he doesn't. Not that well. I could walk away from this without a backward glance.

Me: *How long have I got to decide?*

Him: *See your family for a few days.*

Perhaps he did know me. A few days with my family would drive anyone to undertake an underground suicide mission. Only joking, Mum.

I dumped the empty cup in a bin and looked around. I wasn't going to risk walking back past the Bank of England, so I took a cab to Charing Cross Road, where Foyle's Bookshop provided me with copies of the Eddas. Apparently there are two of them, poetic and prose. After that it was lunch, another cab, and then the drive back to Gloucestershire.

I had a lot to think about on the way back to Clerkswell. It felt like I'd been watching a play, gone out for the interval and returned to find a completely different set, actors and script. Yet it was still the same play – my life. How was I going to make sense of that?

What worried me most was that I might be mad. Completely lost touch with reality and any sense of what "real" might mean. I tried to think about it. That made my head hurt, so I let my mind drift.

Soldiers in the army – squaddies – don't have much time for the RAF. According to them, we sit in heated luxury being waited on hand and foot while they squat in muddy holes in the ground being shot at. They also claim that we only work two hours a day "because they're not allowed to fly more than that."

In the Cold War days, that might have been true, though I was still at school when the Berlin Wall came down. I did several tours in Afghanistan, which is more than most squaddies, and believe me, flying a huge unarmed airborne target like a Chinook into hostile territory is one of the most frightening things you can do. And when you get there, what thanks do you get for rescuing a bunch of Neanderthals who've allowed themselves to be surrounded? None. It's more like, "Where've you been, flyboy? Having a massage?"

I'm telling you this because it puts some things in context. There is, in fact, a lot of sitting around in the RAF. This is not because we're lazy, it's because our planes are so expensive, and their Airships (the senior officers) don't like their toys being risked more than necessary. Over the years, I've used the downtime to read a lot, I've watched some films, I've refused point-blank to get interested in football, and I've had a lot of weird discussions. One of the weirdest was upcountry in Afghanistan. There was an Englishman, an Irishman, a Scotsman and an Afghan...

We were in a Lynx, flying north to the headquarters of a local leader. The press refer to these guys as "Warlords". The truth is a lot sadder and a lot more nuanced. In those provinces, society is a lot like Europe was during the middle ages. They aren't "Warlords", just "Lords", and they run the show, for good or ill. It was the middle of summer, and we'd almost made it to our destination when the gearing on the tail rotor overheated. A lesser pilot would have crashed, I told them when I made a forced landing in the middle of a rocky gorge. At least there was plenty of shade to sit in while we waited for a spare part and an engineer to be flown out.

Being the Englishman, I started to brew some tea. Our Irishman was an intelligence officer from Coleraine (so that's Northern Ireland), and he started talking to our translator (the Afghan). The Scotsman was an air gunner who didn't trust the Irishman until he'd established that the guy wasn't a Catholic. And they say that Afghanistan is a tribal society.

The Irishman was having a polite discussion with the Afghan about the Quran, which was a polite way of finding out where his loyalties might lie. They were talking about the Prophet's *Miraj* (his night-time visit to Jerusalem), and whether or not it was a dream. They hadn't got very far when the Scotsman chimed in with, 'Have you seen *The Matrix*?'

I would have told him to butt out, but the Irishman was too polite. The Scotsman got into his stride. 'That's kind o' like a dream, you ken? Everything we see about us is all an illusion. It's all put in our heads by this all-powerful computer. We've got no idea what's real or not.'

The Afghan looked mystified. The Irishman said, 'You mean the all-powerful computer could be like God?'

'That's right. You only get to see reality if you get to take one of they pills. You only get to see God if He wants you to.'

I passed mugs of tea around and joined in. 'What if the pills are fake? What if they make you dream about an underground world? How could you tell?'

The Scotsman added some sugar to his tea. 'Well, you'd just *know*, wouldn't ye? It would be more real than reality.'

'Biscuit anyone?' I said. At that moment, we got a message calling off the mission: our contact had been killed in a palace coup.

And that was the best I could do when it came to Merlyn's Tower, Hannah Rothman, Alchemical Gold and the Allfather. I just *knew* that they were more real than reality. I stopped at the services near Swindon and bought myself a muffin to celebrate.

I had a plan once, before I met the Allfather. I was going to recuperate, buy a helicopter and start a charter business. I was going to ask Mina to be my business partner when she left prison. This was still an option – the Allfather could take his Enhancement and give it to someone else.

Mina has lost her father, her brother and her husband to violence, as well as suffering life changing injuries herself. She might fancy settling down as mistress of Elvenham House and being the first Ethnic to join the Clerkswell WI. Then again, she might grow out of it very quickly.

There was no one I could turn to for help. Not directly. I was no nearer an answer when I got home and braced myself for a Rachael shaped onslaught, only to discover that she was going to be late. Something to do with Carole's fiancé giving them a lift. That meant...

'Can I take the boy to the pub?' said Dad. 'Find out what he's been up to?'

A man after my own heart. Or I'm a man after his: that was what I wanted to find out. I enjoyed the walk to the Inkwell, especially when we passed St Michael's. I stopped by the lychgate to see if I could sense any magickal activity.

'Are you all right?' said Dad.

'I'm fine. I was just working out if it was safe around here.'

Dad gave me a funny look and strode ahead.

Business was brisk in the pub, and we had to settle for squeezing into a corner by the door to the kitchen. The smells would help me work up an appetite.

'Well, how did it go? What's it all about?' said Dad. 'Have MI6 recruited you?'

'Something like that. Dad, can I ask you a question?'

Father looked very wary. The last time I said that was before I asked him whether he'd been faithful to mother all their married lives. I'm still waiting for a straight answer.

'If you must,' he said.

'Why did you do it, Dad? Why did you get into the antiques trade, and why did you keep at it for so long? You weren't born to it.'

He laughed, relieved that I hadn't reopened the other conversation. 'My father was a solicitor, as was his father before him and his father before that. I blame my mother.'

'Granny? How come? I can't imagine a woman who looked more like a lawyer's wife than Granny.'

'Exactly,' said Dad. 'And I don't think she was ever happy. She made my father's life a misery for decades until he dropped dead. I didn't want that for me. Or my future wife, if I found one. And I did. Your mother wouldn't have married a lawyer, son.'

That was food for thought, all right. I'd seen Mina and Miles together. He was even older than I am. Were they happy? Hard to say, because they met when Mina was in hospital after having her face smashed to bits by the man who killed her brother. Now she's had her face fixed…

'So who was it?' said Dad. 'In London.'

'An arm of the security services, Dad. One of those whose budget gets lost in the Secret Vote, I imagine. They want to recruit me because I don't play by the rules.'

'Will you take it?' he asked.

'I've got a few days to think it over. There's a stiff entry test to go through. When are you two heading back to Spain?'

'Middle of next week. Once term starts and the flights get cheaper. Hang on. I think that's my phone.'

He checked his messages. 'Drink up. We've been summoned. I'll just pay a visit to the Gents.'

While he was gone I forced myself to think about Rachael and Carole.

My mother is a maths genius. It was very unusual for girls to get the encouragement to pursue such 'hard' subjects when she was at school, and if Grandma (a very different creature to Granny) hadn't been so keen, Mother wouldn't have had the confidence to go to Cambridge. Her roommate was a language specialist, and in their second year, now firm friends and sharing a flat, they were given the metaphorical tap on the shoulder by the security services. Not MI5 or MI6 and the glamorous world of spooks for those two. No, it was tea and scones in Cheltenham at GCHQ.

My mother and her friend stayed overnight in Cheltenham for their preliminary visit to GCHQ, and they went into a nice looking pub for a meal and to talk over what they'd seen. Propping up the bar was a handsome devil (in his own words), who bought them both a drink and offered to show them his collection of original Beardsley prints.

No one was more shocked than my mother when he wrote to her a week later at college. As I've said, they've been married thirty-eight years. Mother became a cryptographer, her friend a translator.

I'm good at maths, but I'm no genius. My sister, on the other hand, is as clever as Mum. After St Michael's school in Clerkswell, I went on to a sporty private school in Gloucester, partly to get me out of the way. I didn't take it personally.

Rachael was sent to a very competitive girls' school two years' early. She did take it personally. Mother insisted that Rachael went to Oxford, not Cambridge, because Oxford is only 40 miles away and Rachael was only seventeen, poor kid. Her saviour was a postgrad engineer from our village, Carole Thewlis, who took Rachael under her wing. They were thick as thieves for a couple of years, and that may be where Mom got the idea of Rachael being gay. After Oxford, Rachael was headhunted by a financial firm in the City and Carole joined the oil industry. Carole and I started a relationship soon afterwards.

When I was assigned to my first tour in Iraq, I had told Carole that I was being sent to preserve the Iraqi oil fields for her to exploit. It was a joke. Sort-of. She didn't see it that way, so we had a row. A real humdinger. We couldn't patch it up because I was out of the country the next morning. There was no relationship to come back to.

And now she was engaged, and her brother had bought me several pints the other night. Perhaps Rachael would move on, too.

'Hurry up, daydreamer,' said Dad. 'We'll be on jankers if we're not careful.' Dad was too young for National Service. On the other hand, his childhood was dominated by old war films, and his parents' generation had fought the second world war. He uses more military slang than I do. I got my coat.

Sitting in the pub after driving down from London had done nothing for my limp, and progress was slow. We were half way down Elven Lane when a big car roared past, blowing leaves in its wake. We saw it slow, crawl, then pull in to our drive. Before we got there, it roared out again. Rachael was waiting next to her case, underneath the dragon. I'd seen her waving to it as we approached.

Dad wrapped his arms round her in a big hug, and was hugged in return. When they'd kissed, he said, 'I'll take your case in.' It was his way of being diplomatic.

She brushed her hair away from her face and stared at my leg as I limped towards her. It's really true: we hadn't met since before I was blown up. She sighed, shook her head and allowed me to embrace her. It wasn't a hug. Not yet.

'Am I forgiven?' I said.

'Who by? Me or Carole?'

'Both, of course. No point in only one of you forgiving me.' Years ago I would have added, *Not that I've done anything wrong.* I've grown out of that.

She stuck out her right leg and examined the toes of her boot, checking for damage from the gravel. Rachael spends a lot on clothes, and I think she looks good in them. What I'm trying to do is find a safe way to say that my sister is very attractive. Don't tell her I said that.

'Yeah. You're forgiven,' she finally said. 'You can even keep the house.'

Too bloody late for that, Sister, I said to myself.

'Good,' is what I said to Rachael. I offered her my arm, and we crunched round to the kitchen. 'We've got a lot of catching up to do.'

'Yes. We have,' she replied, almost cheerfully. I decided to take a risk.

'What's he like? Carole's fiancé?'

She stopped. 'You know, Conrad, I have no idea. I've never met him.'

'Didn't you just…'

'… Drive down from London with him? Yes. Except that Caro and I sat in the back and gossipped. She put my case in the boot, and the car has differential courtesy lights. He's not bald, I can tell you that much. He's older than her, and Carole loves him. He's some sort of oil guru, I think, and she met him through work. Anyway, what have you got me for Christmas? It had better be good if you want to stay forgiven.'

'It's a shared present. I've booked the whole family a suite for the New Year's Day races at Cheltenham. Box. Champagne. Lunch. Just the four of us.'

'Wow? What brought that on?'

'I've rekindled my interest in the sport of kings. It's one of the many things I need to talk to you about.'

'Join the queue,' said Rachael as we arrived at the kitchen. 'Mother gets first dibs on my time today.'

No change there, then. She ran in for more hugs while I brushed my boots on the mat.

New Year's Eve was a day spent catching up. My leg hurt like hell in the morning, and I decided to go for a walk *before* breakfast. I would have preferred to go riding, a form of exercise that suits both my temperament and the specific nature of my leg wound.

It was sunnier than yesterday, so I took a brisk hike round to the Inkwell, up the public footpath into the woods, then slowly down the private track to the back of our grounds. I took it slowly because I was out of breath and the track is very uneven.

In the woods, on the slope down, I got really hot. Without thinking, I unzipped my coat and fleece. The cold air stung, and I stopped to think. It wasn't hot at all: I was feeling that magickal tingle. Not actively, like before, but like an echo of heat. If that makes sense. If it doesn't, sorry, but that's what I felt. I zipped up and waited. In five minutes, nothing had changed.

I left the woods and sat on the well. It was here, too, but perhaps fainter. I'd lived with this here all my life, evidently, so it wasn't a threat. I could give up my Gift and carry on. Maybe.

As I said, the well is slightly higher than the house, and it's a good vantage point in winter. I'd spent last summer abroad, on a contract, and we'd rented out the house to holidaymakers. A local firm had kept the gardens tidy, but no more. If I took up permanent residence here, I'd need to spend a lot of money refurbishing both house and grounds. On the other hand, we still had the original stables. They'd become garages for motors, then a lock-up for Dad's business. I could keep a horse there. Always girls in the village desperate for part-time work mucking out in exchange for riding practice.

Feeling better, but no nearer a decision about the Allfather's offer, I walked back to the house. Rachael was standing in the hall, waving an envelope.

'We have got a lot of catching up to do,' she said.

'Oh?'

'The postie's just delivered a letter for you. A real letter, like you read about in books. A woman's handwriting, too. But that's not the best bit. The envelope is franked *HMP Cairndale*. What have you not told me, Brother?'

'Oh, it's part of my charity outreach work. I volunteer a lot.'

'That's not even remotely credible.'

'OK. My new girlfriend is a criminal. She's doing time for killing someone.'

'That's better. Much more outrageous, and theoretically possible. Here.'

I took the letter and headed for the kitchen. Over my shoulder I said, 'I'll tell you the truth over a pint. She's an accountant.'

'Right. Yeah. She's an accountant, and I'm the Duchess of Cambridge in disguise.'

'Laters, Your Royal Highness.'

Rachael does bear a passing resemblance to Prince William's bride. They're both tall, white, thin and have long brown hair. Dad thinks Rachael's better looking.

The kitchen was quiet, so I read Mina's letter over breakfast. It was in two parts. The second part is of no immediate concern to you, as you'll see when I tell you what she wrote:

Dear Conrad,
When I did my GCSE English, we had to write letters. Did I tell you I got an A? I*
thought 'We're never going to write letters'. How wrong was I! Or should that be How

wrong was me!? Only joking. This is the third time I've started. After the second go, I borrowed a dictionary from the library. They should let us use computers.

You can write as many letters as you want in here. Most of the girls don't bother, because they really do have problems with writing. Or the people they want to write to can't read. Or both. Why should they write anyway, when they can text?

The Prison Officers (POs) can read this, and if you write back (please), they will read that too. They'll enjoy that. I have to be careful, but they know it's true. Anyone can get a phone in here. I promised I'd text you over Christmas. I hope you weren't disappointed. It would be against the rules to text, but that's not the problem because they won't catch us. The problem is that I would have to owe someone if I borrowed their phone. That would be dangerous. The POs are all on leave so we have more time in our rooms (cells). I'm bored, and I've wanted to write to you for ages. I didn't before because of all the Stuff. You know what I mean.

Anyway. I want to tell you about life in here, but you don't know anything, because it's all about the people. Whenever we've met, we've talked about my jaw, or us, or you, because you've been trying to stop doing the Stuff. I like talking about us. I loved our kiss before Christmas. I want to kiss you again. Please bring me more winter clothes soon. It's bloody cold in Cairndale. Tell me about what you did at Christmas. Tell me about your family.

I am going to write about all the other girls so that you know what I'm talking about. I'll put it on another piece of paper so the POs can censor it if they want. It will give me something to do.

Christmas in here was very sad for everyone. I missed you so much, then I felt guilty for not missing Miles. It was another Mina who married him. I'm a different person now. I think. Maybe I'm not. I don't know. It's hard to know who you are when you're in here – you're not a number or anything like that. It's just that you're not You. Or I'm not Me. Or something.

Tell me everything about what you've been doing. Or don't, because you promised never to lie to me. Don't put anything in a letter that you don't want Lisa the PO to read. Just write to me.

The Assistant Governor is going to see me next week to talk about his budget. He says I'm the only one in the whole prison who understands asset depreciation properly.

The Christmas turkey was tough, but I chewed every bit of it, because I could. You've no idea how that good that made me feel. I hope your mother's cooking was good. Or your father's. Or your sister's. You do have a sister, don't you?

I'm going to stop now and start on the other part. Maybe I can be a writer one day. It's a good job I'm barred for life from accountancy. Gives me an excuse.

You promised never to lie to me, Conrad. Then you said you loved me. I love you too. Happy New Year,
Mina.

I saved the soap opera-sized other letter for later, and carefully folded the one I've just quoted. I used Mother's printer to photocopy the bit about the assistant governor and *You do have a sister, don't you.* I passed through the sitting room and dropped it into Rachael's lap while she was talking to Mother. I'd reached the hall before I heard her scream, *'Oh my God, Conrad!'*

If you're wondering what happened on New Year's Day, we had a great time, and the family made over £200 profit from the bookmakers. I'll just relay one short conversation I had with Rachael:

'Do you work in the City of London itself?' I asked her.

'No. Mayfair, actually. We have very, very rich clients and we need to be near them. Why the sudden interest? It's welcome, but…'

'I just wondered. I might be getting a job based near Tower Bridge. Hush-hush and all that. If it comes off, I thought you could buy me lunch.'

She stared at me for a second. 'I think I preferred the old Conrad. It was easy to hate you when we weren't speaking. If you're going to be nice, I'll have to work at disliking you.'

'I can make it easy for you for you to dislike me. I'll ask pointed questions about your love life and tell Mother you're gay.'

'Shut up, Conrad. The next race is due to start soon.'

I sent a text to the Allfather, telling him I was going underground next Thursday. If you're wondering why, it's because of Mina's letter. The person who wrote that letter was not going to be interested in being the business manager of a helicopter charter operation. If I gave up my Gift, Mina would leave me. I could live without one, but not both. It was a simple choice in the end.

4 — Going Underground

My preparations were straightforward. I wasn't going to carry a gun around the City, because I didn't think it would do me any good underground, and because no one would vouch for me if I got arrested. Ditto the body armour. I wrote a long letter to Mina hinting that I was up to no good again and telling no lies. I bought two new torches and read the Eddas. If I ever got out of this alive, I had some serious questions to ask my Patron.

On Wednesday afternoon, I dropped Mum and Dad at Luton airport and drove the Jag to her brother's place. Dad can't afford to keep a car in Britain, so he usually scrounges one, and my uncle had been abroad for Christmas, hence the luxury transport. The Defender was still being processed by the police, so I took the train to Notting Hill and next morning I took the tube to Moorgate. The condemned man was going to eat a hearty breakfast.

I made one last detour, to an outdoor shop, before heading to Bank Station. I bought some gear, including a hunting knife, and got them to pack it up. Nothing illegal in carrying a blade that's wrapped up. On my way out of the shop, I saw a display labelled *Bushtucker Treats*, and I remembered the Allfather's advice: *Always take dried worms when you go underground.*

In the middle of the display were bags of Giant Curried Worms. Surely no one actually *eats* dried worms — surely they must be jelly sweets or something, so I examined the ingredients. No, I was wrong. The list began with *Megascolides australis*, and the small print said that they'd been *raised on a farm in sterile conditions*. I bought a packet and shoved them in my pocket.

I had done a little research into Bank Underground Station: it's a complete nightmare of tunnels, tubes and platforms. As if that weren't enough, it's connected like a conjoined twin to Monument Station. Go with what you know. Hannah had said *Bank* Station, so there I was.

I started above ground, making a slow circuit round the big junction of five City streets. It was slow because there were a lot of roads to cross and a lot of traffic lights to wait for. I got the same tingle in the same place as last week. That was good. It meant a static source of magick rather than a moving one. I got nothing near the Bank of England itself, so I crossed round the front of the Mansion House. Was that a whisper, or just my imagination?

I finished in front of the Royal Exchange, by a rather spectacular equestrian statue of the Iron Duke. It was the only place in the whole of the plaza/junction with benches. Time for a last fag.

It was also the only spot with any greenery – a couple of dormant flower beds. A rook flew down and landed in one of them. That was wrong. Very wrong. On the wing, only a twitcher can tell the difference between a rook, a crow, a jackdaw and a raven. On the ground, it's obvious. The rook has a pointy grey beak, the raven's is black and hooked at the tip. It was wrong because rooks are almost never solitary, they hate people and they loathe cities.

It was hopping around the soil, as if it were waiting. I stood up and walked towards it, not taking my eyes off the bird, trying to look at it in the way that Hannah Rothman had looked at me. As I got closer, it shimmered. The beak became black, the end became hooked and the bird just … grew. It was a raven. I stopped.

'Yes?'

Caw Caw said the Raven, then it took off and flew away. I somehow knew that it had said, 'Go well.' Time was up. Conrad Clarke is going underground.

I took the Threadneedle Street entrance and found myself in the Central Line ticket hall, just underneath the busy roads above me. A couple of tourists were trying to figure out what to do, but all the natives were rushing through the barriers, slapping their Oyster Cards on the reader as they entered or lifting their bags as they exited. I got no immediate tingle.

Working for Sir Stephen Jennings had taught me a few things about subterfuge. If I just lingered, someone in security would be feeling my collar in minutes. You have to have a purpose, so I set off down the corridor. Purposefully.

This was taking me away from the Bank, but deeper underground. In a few yards I came across a short side tunnel which ended in a security door. I ducked into the opening and pressed the Visitor's badge which Tennille had given me against the lock. It opened. Bingo.

The corridor on the other side of the door led me towards the Mansion House, but this was definitely the right place. I was soon descending more steps and came to a pair of doors covered with *Danger of Death* signs and labelled as *High-Tension Switch Room No 3*. I didn't fancy that, and both doors were secured with old-fashioned padlocks. The corridor continued for another twenty yards, and I could see from the state of the floor that no one ever went down there, especially not the cleaners. After all, there was no reason for anyone to go down there. No doors, no openings, nothing. Just a dead end.

I wasn't going to be disturbed down here, and there was no CCTV camera to watch me pace up and down feeling the glossy bricks. Again, nothing. No hollow section, no brick out of line – and above all, no magickal tingle. I stopped and scratched my chin, and let my mind wander. How had I found Merlyn's Tower? By being pointed towards it by the ravens. I had gone looking, and there it was.

Ravens. Could the appearance of the raven this morning have been a hint? I paced back out of the dead end, then walked forwards, staring at the walls like I'd stared at the rook. It worked. Just like the rook shimmered into being a raven, a section of brick on my left shimmered into being a solid metal door. A door with no handle or keyhole.

I stopped myself feeling depressed by saying out loud, 'You've just done your first magick trick. Or spell. Or whatever. Come on, Conrad, you can do this.' I've done the same in tight spots before. Often with a co-pilot listening. It usually works.

Perhaps there was no lock at all. I pushed the door hard, and got a sore shoulder. I stood back, took out a small torch and examined the door closely. It was old, but not that ancient because it was a piece of machined steel, so no older than 1900. It was a lot older than me because I recognised the paint. It was a sort of deep green, and used by the British military in bucketloads until the late 1950s. Great chunks of MOD property are still painted that colour.

Close examination had revealed no mechanism, so the answer must be magick. I couldn't *see* anything, so I closed my eyes and tried to *feel* for magick. There. About chest height, I got a tingle. Keeping my eyes closed, I touched the door.

Ouch. That was *hot*. I touched a lower part. Cold. I slid my hand slowly up the metal until it hit something hot. This time I didn't flinch. The metal was hot, but no hotter than a radiator. I'd come across something in relief, standing out from the door. I traced it with my fingers – letters? A message?

I made the mistake of opening my eyes and the letters vanished, as did the tingle. Another lesson. I screwed my eyes shut and tried again, finding the beginning and working to turn the shapes into letters.

Five minutes later, I was laughing. If Hannah ever found out about this, she'd go mental. At some point in the past, whichever wizard had been given the job of securing this door had made a very bad joke combining two loves of public schoolboys from the same era as the green paint: *The Lord of the Rings* and *The Goon Show*. The message in magickal writing said:

Speak Bluebottle and Enter

It took me another five minutes, but when I said *Friend* in a Bluebottle voice, the door opened. If you've never heard the Goon Show, take it on trust.

On the other side was a steep, stone staircase going down. I took a last look round the Bank Station corridor. It might be the last thing of the mundane world I saw.

I switched on the big torch and descended the steps. The door closed behind me all on its own. To be expected, I suppose. I unshipped the package from the outdoor shop, took out the knife and put it in my pocket.

My sense of direction was still working, even underground, and when the steps ended in a passage, I knew that I was below the Central Line, but above the Northern Line, and even further above the DLR, and when I felt a rumble a few seconds later, I had no idea which way it came from. The passage was a T-Junction running left to the Mansion House and right to the Bank. I turned right.

And got about thirty feet before the tunnel dead-ended in a collapse. Were my unlucky predecessors buried under the rubble? I scooted back a few feet in case more of the ceiling came down, then got busy with the torch. I'm no expert on tunnels – they hold few attractions for chopper pilots. I shone the torch on the rubble and heard another train coming.

Hang on. I shouldn't *hear* trains, I should *feel* them. This wasn't a train, it was something in the corridor behind me. I wheeled round and shone the torch ahead. Barrelling down the passage was Death, in the shape of a giant mole. I didn't know whether to laugh or cry.

Moles have enormous upper bodies compared to their back legs. They can shift a huge amount of soil for their size, and this one was almost as big as me at the shoulder, which meant that it was about twelve feet long. It moved quite quickly, flicking its head constantly around the passage, brushing its huge snout against the walls.

I may not know tunnels, but I do know moles. We had a plague of them once, and they ruined Rachael's tennis court. I had a lot of sympathy with them for doing that. They're almost completely blind and their eyes do very little, but their ancestors could see, and had brains with a visual cortex. That capacity was transferred to the myriad nerve endings in their snouts, so if a mole touches something, it *sees* the object.

All of which is to say that my plan of action consisted in preparing to smack it on the nose. If that didn't hurt it, nothing would. And then I saw the teeth.

It was getting closer. I could hear the hissing noise of its breath over the scrabble of its paws. Claws. Hands. They would bat me aside like a bull tossing a matador. I had no idea why, but I felt that the mole was a *him*, not an *it*. I put down the torch and picked up a loose rock, then I hurled it over the mole to clatter behind him. He stopped for a second to listen. There was something about that mouth and those teeth…

He came at me again, and the answer came to me. Moles eat worms and bugs. They have small mouths. This mouth was huge, and it had lips. It could speak.

'Stop! Wait!' I shouted. I also took out the knife.

The mole did stop. Then it came at me, moving at twice the speed as before. I raised my arm ready to strike it with the knife. His nose moved like a sabre. It touched the ceiling, the floor, my legs and my arm. Before I could strike, his left paw smacked down my right arm and he head-butted me back into the soil. The knife flew out of my hand, and I tried to roll away. The right paw pinned down my left arm and the nose descended, more slowly this time.

It was only at that moment did I feel the magick. Obviously this creature wasn't natural. It defied every law of nature I've ever come across, and all the others, too. Yet it *behaved* like a mole until it touched me.

Just like the Peculier Constable, this creature was scoping me out. Not my physical talents, my magickal ones. And like Hannah, the mole found me severely wanting. I grabbed a rock with my right hand. I was about to sacrifice my left arm in the hope of getting in a blow with my right when he lifted his nose and backed off a fraction. He also breathed over me, and I got a foul wash of mole-breath. A twelve foot long creature which eats worms has very, very bad breath. Ugh.

He backed up again. The mouth worked for a second. I scrambled to my feet. Then he spoke.

'Where is your Luksh, little man?'

Luksh? Ah – Lux. His voice rasped, and he had difficulty with the 'S' sound, as if his tongue were too big for his mouth, but I could understand him. The words anyway: I had no idea what he meant. Lux? The Allfather said his manifestations cost him *Lux*. Must be something to do with magickal power. Clearly, I had very little of it.

'Nowhere. Very short of Lux, I'm afraid,' I responded. 'And what little I have will cost you a lot, Mr Mole.'

He snorted. He clearly wasn't afraid of me, but he didn't attack. Yet.

'Can't we do a deal?' I said.

'What can you offer me that I can't take for myshelf?'

'How about these?' I dug out the bag from the survival shop. 'Here,' I said, dumping the contents of the bag on the floor, half way between me and the mole. I stepped back, picking up the knife as I did so.

The mole stepped forwards, brushed his snout against the worms and sneezed. 'Gheegsh,' he said, in what presumably is Moleish. If they have a language. Then he stabbed his mouth down and ate the lot. Just like that.

'You bring me offeringsh. That ish good.' The curried worm did nothing for his halitosis, I'm afraid.

'Yes. I really would prefer a deal to a fight. I'm sure you would, too.'

'You want to shee the dwarf, don't you?' he stated.

'Yes.'

'If you had shomething for him, you would ushe the other door. You have nothing to offer me. I can take what little Luksh you have and eat your inteshtines.'

'Just my intestines?'

'The resht is too chewy.'

He was getting restless, flicking his snout around and reading the passage. Hang on. *Reading the passage.* I had a desperate idea.

'I can bring you something that no one else will offer you. Something that will change your life for ever. I just don't have it here. I've given you the curried worms. I don't want to hurt you.'

'Let me noshe you again. Put the knife away firsht.'

Nose. Another new verb in my dictionary, along with *Enhance.* I'd lost track of the new nouns. I put the knife away.

He came up to me and flicked over my whole body, both physically and magickally. He told me to turn around, and I did. His nose stopped between my shoulder blades.

'I noshe Odin'sh Rune. You are hish creature.'

'We could argue about that, but yes, he is my Patron.'

'Then shwear. Make an oath in hish name to return today with shomething for me.'

'Tomorrow. I can't do it today. What happens if I break the oath?'

'Didn't he shay? An oath made by a client ish binding unto death. If you're not back by shundown tomorrow, you will die. If I don't like what you bring, you'll die ash well.'

Something about the way his mouth spread out at the end looked different, and his nose twitched in a way it hadn't before.

'You're smiling at me,' I said. 'All the *You will Die* stuff. It's a joke.'

'Yesh. To me. You won't be laughing when I eat you. Gheeh.' I think *Gheeh* is Moleish for *Ha Ha, you sucker.*

'Where do you live?' I asked. 'This is a dead end, and there are no worms around here.'

'Too close to the Dwarf,' said the mole. 'I nesht under the Mansion, and roam where the wormsh are fattest with Luksh. They crawl out from the shewer. They have namesh, I think, but they mean nothing to me. Why do you want to know?'

'It will help me decide on my offering.'

Not only is there a giant mole living under the streets of London, it eats magickal worms. I didn't want to know about that. 'How do I make this oath?'

'Keep it shimple,' said the creature.

'Do you have a name?' I asked.

'The Dwarf callsh me Mole. I am Mole.'

There was a quiver in the nose again, different to the smile. A hint of self-doubt, perhaps? I moved on.

'In the name of Odin Allfather, I swear to bring to Mr Mole an offering worthy of my life before the sun sets tomorrow.'

As I said the words, I felt my shoulders tingle where the Allfather had touched them. If he didn't know now, he'd know about the oath when I got to the surface.

'Go,' said Mole.

I went.

Could a raven fly in to the ticket hall? In theory, I mean. After returning through the service door, I had a moment to collect my thoughts before I returned to the magickal grid and returned to my Patron's field of view. I wondered if I could turn off the rune on my back like I could turn off my phone. It didn't matter, really, because the clock was ticking anyway. I grabbed a takeout coffee from a small stand underground and returned to daylight.

My shoulders tingled half way up the steps, and my phone got a message almost straight away. Two messages. The first had been sent some time ago, by Rachael. I'll come back to that. The other message was timed *just now*, from Odin:

Mole?

Me: *Don't tell me you didn't know about the Giant Mole. That's why you tipped me off about the dried worms. Stop being so fucking obscure.*

Him: *Don't swear at your Patron. It doesn't help. I thought it might be a Dragonling. There are eggs all over London. I've never, ever, come across a Giant Mole. What have you promised him? Well done, by the way.*

Me: *Sorry. I won't ask about the Dragonlings. Thanks for the help. Wait and see. Sorry again, sir.*

I drank my coffee, smoked a fag and read Rachael's message.

Is your new girlfriend called Mina Finch? I Googled all accountants in prison for killing someone. If you buy me lunch, I might let you tell me the story.

Dad had bottled it over Christmas. He had decided that the best plan for telling Mother about Mina was to wait until they were back in Spain. On reflection, he was actually being brave, because when the shit hit the fan, he would have to take it all himself. I'll give Rachael her due, because she'd said nothing to Mother either. Perhaps she didn't think it was important. I text back: *How about tomorrow? You book the table.*

I crushed out my fag and lit another. Time for a plan. I had a good idea what might save my life, but whether I could pull it off in a day was another matter. I've mentioned my phone a lot in this story; you may have noticed it's only in connection with calls and texts. I ditched my smartphone after Operation Jigsaw folded. Too many people wanted to track me, and too many of them had the technology to get round a smartphone. They're not as secure as you think.

Not having a smartphone, I couldn't Google my next destination, so I hailed a black cab and asked the driver if he knew. He did. You don't get that with Uber. As he drove, I called my friendly electronics shop. For trusted clients, they offer all sorts of kit you can't buy over the counter.

'Kajan. Hi. It's George Baxter here,' I said.

Sorry about the fake name. Long story.

'Hi, George. Happy New Year. What can I do for you?'

'How can I get an Internet connection in a tunnel thirty metres underground?'

I could hear the sucking of air through his teeth. 'That depends.'

'On what?'

'How much bandwidth you need, how long for, what the access is like, how secure you want it to be. Whether you can run a cable anywhere. That sort of thing.'

'Hang on.'

We'd arrived at our destination. I gave the driver a hundred quid and told him to wait until it ran out. I knew he'd be there when I'd finished, and you don't get that with Uber either. I stood on the pavement and picked up the conversation with Kajan.

'About 8mbps should do it. Six at a pinch. I can run a cable to a tube station, but it might be over 100m. Half an hour max. Oh, and totally secure.'

'When do you want it for?'

'Tomorrow morning.'

'No problem. It'll cost you, though.'

'I know. And that's not all I'll need. See you soon.'

I disconnected and ran in to the charity offices. They had what I wanted, but not in stock. Nor could they get one overnight. In the end, I put a five figure sum on my debit card and walked out with the manager's entire personal set-up. I insisted on a receipt. If I wasn't dead tomorrow, this was going on expenses.

'You've got twenty quid left,' said the cabbie.

'Tottenham Court Road, please.'

I spent the rest of the afternoon with Kajan Desai trying to make everything connect together. He's no relation to Mina. Apparently it's a common name in Gujarat . After a couple of hours, it became clear that I'd need a second person if I were going to pull this off, and they had to be someone I could trust. Someone who would have my back. There are a couple of people in Clerkswell who would do it, and a few Up North, probably even a few in the RAF. None of them were any use for tomorrow. I decided to turn to someone I'd roped into a highly illegal operation abroad, and whom I'd nearly got killed. Why did I choose him? Because he'd enjoyed it.

His house in west London looked even more dreary than the last time I'd seen it. The occupants had made some attempt at Christmas, but they didn't really get it. They are French, after all. A young woman in a very tight pair of jeans answered the door. She didn't remember me. I'll have to get used to that now that I'm well past thirty.

'Bonjour, Amélie,' I said.

She frowned. 'Monsieur?'

I do know more French than *Bonjour*, but not much. They all speak English, anyway. 'Is Alain at home?'

'*Oui.* Come in.'

She assumed that I knew where the sitting room was and trailed off into the kitchen after shouting upstairs for Alain ('Who is it?', 'A man.' At least she didn't say *An old man*).

Alain bounced down the stairs with the energy of the truly young. The truly young who don't have titanium tibias. He stopped dead in the doorway.

'*Merde.* Georges.' Along with Kajan, Alain also thinks I'm George Baxter.

'Happy New Year, Alain.'

'You promised me that you'd leave me alone.'

You'll notice that he didn't tell me to get out. Probably because he was scared of me.

'Any chance of a cup of coffee?'

'If it means you will go away, yes.'

As he moved towards the kitchen, I said, 'Make sure it's Amélie's coffee. Yours is shit.'

He turned back. I liked that gesture, it showed that he'd grown up a bit. 'I used some of the money you gave me to buy a new machine for the 'ouse. All our coffee is good.'

'That sounds great. Thank you.'

He nodded an acknowledgement and went to get two very French coffees. Just the ticket. Another good thing about Alain's house is that they all smoke.

Alain put the cup down in front of me. 'What do you want, *Georges*. No one in England is called George except the little Prince.'

I shook my head. He didn't need to know who I am. Much safer for him. 'How are your studies coming along?'

'Do you care?'

'Yes.'

'They are good. Next week I am on placement with a bank. A good one.'

'Excellent.' I meant it, too. If he is doing well at university, then he will have spent a lot of money over Christmas celebrating, and he'll need a new suit for his new job. 'Do you know Bank Station?'

He jumped back in horror. 'You are going to shoot someone in London? Non. No.'

'Relax. No guns. No danger to you. All I need is some help with communications. Like last time.'

'And will that mad man turn up again? Like last time?'

'No. He's dead. I shot him.'

If Alain hadn't watched me do something similar to some French gangsters, he might not have believed me. He just went quiet instead.

I took out some twenty pound notes, crisp and new from the cashpoint. 'One morning's work. Here's five hundred pounds. The same again on completion.'

It was Alain's turn to shake his head. 'I want it now. You know where I live, but I know nothing about you. If you get killed, who will pay me?'

A fair point. I wasn't going to put him in my will, was I? Talking of wills, I should have updated mine *before* going underground this morning. Another job for the to-do list. I counted out the balance of his payment, and added another two hundred. And a shopping list.

He studied the list. 'Where do I get these things?'

'Your problem. Just meet me by the statue of the Duke of Wellington at eleven o'clock tomorrow.'

He waved the note at me. 'Always, you go on about Waterloo and the Duke of Wellington.'

'Only when I'm talking to Frenchmen. See you tomorrow.'

I went back to Notting Hill and spent the rest of the night learning a language I hoped I'd never have to use again. And charging batteries. A great many batteries.

There was enough time before my meeting with Alain for me to start worrying. I don't like to worry. It does no good. My coping mechanism is to think of stupid things to do to other people. Not very grown up, I know, but it's better than worrying. On the way to Bank Station, I stopped at Covent Garden and spent another two hundred quid on a piece of tat. It took my total spend on this project to nearly fifteen thousand pounds. At this rate, the helicopter charter business wouldn't be an option for very long.

Alain was on time. He arrived with a big bag, a coffee and a fag in his mouth. This boy will go far. He opened the bag and passed me a hard hat.

'I got size extra large because you 'ave a big 'ead.' No question. He'll definitely go far.

'Thank you. And the rest?'

He passed over gloves, a tool belt and a Hi-Viz vest with the TFL logo on the back. We kitted up.

The RAF officer training course was my university (shorter, cheaper and with better job prospects), and learning to fly was only a small part (though not a very easy one). The RAF needs pilots who can fit seamlessly into a combat operation, and know when to use their initiative and when to follow orders to the letter. In fact, the Initial Officer Training has very little to do with flying at all.

We did some strategy and some tactics, little of it very memorable. None of us was ever going to re-fight the battle of Waterloo (for French readers, please substitute your favourite battle here. If there is one). One thing that did stick with me was How to Plan.

The course leader had a thing about the difference between Risk and Luck. I'm good at statistics and probability theory, and I thought I'd be able to shoot this guy down in flames. Not for the first or last time, I was wrong.

The instructor put it like this. *Risk* is something you can work out. Risk is the likelihood of the enemy responding effectively to your plan. Good officers minimise risk; great officers know when the prize is greater than the risk. Napoleon was a great officer. See? I can be nice about the French.

Luck is something you can't work on. Good luck means the enemy have an outbreak of norovirus the night before a battle. Bad luck is different. Your plan should not be reliant on good luck nor vulnerable to bad luck. If *your* troops get norovirus, don't attack.

There was considerable risk in my plan. The reward – my life – was worth it. The only element of luck concerned Alain's part of the operation. I gave him the kit he needed and went over the plan again. Despite hearing it twice before, he listened carefully.

'We are contractors, yes?' I said, as a test.

'*Oui*. We work for Universal Telecommunication Testing.'

'Good. I'm the boss. You are only a trainee. You know nothing.'

'This is true.'

'Your job is to hold the door open so that I can get a mobile signal.'

He nodded.

It may reassure you to know that security on the London Underground is quite good. The visible and invisible security staff would be checking our passes, and possibly checking us against a list. My saving grace was Tennille's Visitor Badge. Alain would be standing in full view. If he had this pass clearly visible, he'd be safe enough. No one would check it against a list. Unless my luck ran out. If I had the bad luck for an inspection to take place, or a bomb hoax to be called in, the plan was toilet water. Nothing I could do about that.

What I could do was give him an out. I showed him a piece of paper.

'*Qu'est-ce que c'est?*'

'It's your get out of jail free card. If I disappear and you get arrested, say nothing. Nothing at all. You will be given one phone call. Ring this number and mention my name.'

'Georges Baxter.'

Of course. Tennille would know nothing about Mr Baxter. I added my real name underneath. 'No. This name, on here.'

I sealed the note in an envelope and signed over the flap. 'If everything works, give me this back unopened.'

'I understand.'

'Right. Follow me.'

We walked purposefully and quickly down the steps, turned left in the ticket hall, and without a hitch we arrived at the service tunnel. Alain opened the door.

'Wish me luck,' I said.

'Good luck, Georges.'

I clapped him on the shoulder and walked down towards the secret door. Alain was carrying a very sensitive and very illegal mobile phone repeater. It would get a signal down to the end of the corridor. I had no wish to experiment with drilling a magickal door. See? That's minimising risk. My instructor would be proud of me.

Today, I could see the door without having to concentrate. Another small detail noted. I placed an even stronger repeater on the floor, used the silly voice and pushed the door open. My Bluebottle noises made Alain turn around and look down at me as if I were utterly mad. Then he remembered that I was English. He shook his head and returned to keeping an eye on the concourse.

Another repeater inside the door, then I did my Theseus impression, rolling out a data cable down the stairs. Now you know why I needed all the batteries. I got to the bottom.

'Hello?' I called. I thumped the wall a couple of times and shouted again. If Mr Mole didn't turn up within half an hour, I had no idea what would happen. Would that be his fault or mine? This was a risk I hadn't quantified.

Two more thumps on the wall, and I heard him coming. Showtime.

I stood still and let him nose me all over. It's only polite.

'What ish your offering, little man?' were his first words.

'My first offering is a name. Or at least a title.'

He hissed at me aggressively, but I saw the twitch in his nose. He was interested.

'My name is Conrad Clarke. You should have a name, too. Feel this.'

I took out the piece of tat which I'd cobbled together in Covent Garden: a big chain of silver links with a medal on the bottom. Mole dropped his head and nosed over it.

'What do I want with thish?'

I picked it up. 'I'm going to put it round your neck.'

'If you hurt me, the Allfather will kill you.'

'I know. I wouldn't hurt you even without the oath. I'm not like that.'

I carefully draped the chain around his neck. It looked good in the light from my camping lantern. 'You live under the Mansion House, don't you? Do you know who lives inside it?'

'A human. With no Luksh. One time a lot of human came. Too many to eat. Many of them had Luksh.'

That was interesting. The Lord Mayor's Banquet had magickal people at it. Very interesting.

'We call that person the *Lord Mayor of London*. I think you should have a title. Lord Mayor of Moles.'

He hissed. The snout waggled. He lifted his neck. He liked it, even if he did look like he'd won *Child of the Day* at nursery school. I breathed a sigh of relief. 'Can we go to your nest? Is it far?'

'Why?'

'My next offering needs to be set down.'

He squeezed his body round in the tunnel. I picked up the gear and followed him, until the tunnel turned right, turning away from Mansion House. He carried straight on, through a great hole in the wall which was undoubtedly his handiwork. Or paw-work.

Through the hole, the tunnel was narrower and lower. I had to duck my head, then nearly vomited when a never-forgotten smell smacked me in the nose. It had first hit me years ago, wafting over a field in Iraq when I was standing next to the chopper. The squad I'd brought were digging a hole, so I went to see what they'd found. Nothing on earth smells like a mass grave of fresh corpses.

'You shmell the meat?' said his Worship the Lord Mayor.

'Yes. It smells human.'

'It ish.'

He pushed past a small side opening, and I couldn't help but shine the light into the void: four bodies were laid out in the chamber. None of them had heads. All of them had been eaten. Three of them were women. That shouldn't have made it worse, but it did. I knew they were women because Mole had ripped open their clothes to get at the abdomen, and I could see their bras. The man had no legs, and had been eaten more than the others. I had to lean on the wall to stop myself falling over.

'Why did you do it?' I knew the answer, but for the sake of my predecessors, I had to hear it from the Mole himself.

'They attacked me.'

Oh. I hadn't been expecting that. I'd been expecting him to say that he was hungry.

'Can we go?' I asked, swallowing heavily.

A little further, the tunnel became an open space. The Lord Mayor's Nest. The only thing inside it was a large pile of straw for a bed. Where on earth had that come from?

'Won't be long,' I said. I started to set up the kit next to a wall. 'While we're here, I wondered how you learnt to speak English.'

'They taught me.'

'Who's "they"?'

'The onesh I ate.'

I stopped connecting things. That was a lot to digest. Sorry. His words had put a very unpleasant image in my head. And then a worse one came to me.

'Did you need to eat any … specific part?'

'The brain. It'sh where the Imprint ish shtrongesht.'

'What's an Imprint?'

He hissed, and his nose twitched. I can now identify a Moleish laugh with 90% accuracy.

'Esshence. Shoul. Pershonality. They are all wordsh to deshcribe an Imprint.'

I turned to face him, leaving the kit on the ground. I couldn't wait long, but I had to know a little more.

'How did you get here? Where did you come from, Lord Mayor?'

'The Shpirit brought me. He picked me up from the marsh and brought me here. He fed me my first Luksh worm. He helped me grow.'

Small differences can kill you. The cabin of a Chinook helicopter comes in many flavours, from fully computerised to steam gauge only. Between some models, they'll move a knob. Just an inch. That can kill you.

'Sorry to be boring,' I said. 'Is Spirit another word for Imprint?'

'No. A Shpirit ish a creature. It brought me here and fed me. Then it shent little men to hunt me and chain me. I heard their noishe, and when I ate one, I shucked it clean. The other little men tried to kill me. They had more Luksh. I learnt very little from them.'

His words begged far more questions than they answered. I hastily plugged everything together. The rig had worked in Kajan's shop, and it had worked in my flat. I crossed my fingers because this was a risk element I couldn't avoid. I closed my eyes. It beeped. It worked.

'What was that noishe?' said Mole.

'Your Worship, would you like to nose all of these items?'

I watched him carefully as his snout flicked around from the ethernet cable to the repeater, from the phone to the laptop and from the laptop to the terminal. I wondered what he'd say.

'What are theshe things? I noshe the heat. The little men had bokshes like theshe. They have the heat of Luksh but faint, sho faint. What ish it?'

'I'm sorry. I have no idea. There must be a connection between electricity and what you call Lux.'

'What is *electrishity*?'

I paused to consider, to consider his question, not my answer. When Mole learnt English, the new words must have mapped on to ideas he already understood. *Lux*, for example. And Imprint. But the whole world of technology was clearly alien to him.

'Electricity is like Lux, I suppose. It's power. It's energy. It makes things move. And you don't need a Gift to use it.'

'What good are theshe thingsh to me?' His snout went up and down. I think it meant he was disappointed.

'Could you place your nose on the one nearest to you?'

He did as I asked. It was the first time his snout had been truly still. Even when his head wasn't flicking about, his nose moved on its own. What looked like a pointy snout was made of little boneless fingers, all aquiver. It made me feel worse than seeing the bodies. The disembowelled bodies were gross, but natural; these nose-fingers were just plain *wrong*. I shook my head and pressed a key on the laptop. The screen reader software was an upgrade on the manufacturer's version, with a rather rich woman's voice.

'Hello Lord Mayor,' said the reader.

Mole hissed and lifted his nose. This was something new for him.

'Could you put your nose back. It's going to say the same thing again.'

He returned his nose to the terminal. A very expensive, variable-display Braille terminal. I'd bought it from a charity for the blind. If ever there was a creature designed for Braille, it was the Lord Mayor of Moles. I clicked on the laptop to engage the terminal, and the reader repeated its greeting, this time with the words coming up on the Braille terminal as well.

The Mole shot back six feet and hissed, baring his teeth. 'What wash that?'

'Writing. Special writing. The bar under your nose makes different shapes for different words.'

A hiss. A shake of the snout. 'Again.'

I repeated the procedure. His snout twitched, but he kept it on the reader. 'Again.'

I checked my watch. 'I'm sorry to rush you, but I need to know if you can press the buttons – the shapes – next to the words.'

He tried. His nose could exert just enough pressure to depress the keys. The reader attempted to turn his random presses into sounds. He hissed.

'Sir, can you find the box with the ... sticky-up lid?' I said. How else would you describe a laptop to a blind Mole?

He nosed the laptop. I'd fitted it with Braille overlay stickers. I had no idea such things existed until yesterday.

'It ish the same thing,' said Mole.

'Can you find the one with *no* markings? Remember where it is, but don't press it.'

His snout hovered over the F1 key. When he pressed it, a teach-yourself Braille program would start. I had a feeling that he'd be a quick learner. Having located the key, his head moved around again, back to its constant rhythm.

'There's something else electricity can do. It can make waves, and send information over a long distance. This box. It's called a computer. It can read anything to you. Let me demonstrate.'

I had thought about getting it to read the Wikipedia page for *Talpa Europaea*, the common mole. That would have been a bit rude, so I opted for the Mansion House.

'*The Mansion House is the official residence of the Lord Mayor of London...*' began the cultured voice.

'...And of the Lord Mayor of Moles,' said His Worship, interrupting, and impersonating the voice. Somehow, his tongue seemed to fit better in his mouth: was coping better with 'S' sounds. I pressed the Pause button.

'Can you feel the small box to the right. It's a phone. You can talk to me with it. Or send messages. You can talk to anyone if you know their number.'

'It has no Luksh,' said Mole.

'No. It doesn't need any.'

He hissed. 'Without Luksh, it can't talk to the Shpirits, or the Powers.'

'Well... I'm not sure about that. The Allfather sends me messages. He has a lot of Lux, I suppose.'

He nosed over all the gear again. 'This is a great offering, little man.'

'Call me Mr Clarke.'

'You have earned it.'

I breathed a huge sigh of relief. My first mission. Accomplished. 'Excuse me one moment,' I said. I sent a text to Alain: *Safe. Close the door and go. Wait for me at the statue. Oh, and get coffees.*

'Sir,' I said, 'there is a problem...'

'Wait,' said Mole. He nosed the ground, twisted in half and shot off towards a tunnel leading east. For want of anything else to do, I followed him.

Mark Hayden

He barrelled down the tunnel, nosing as he went. At one point he twisted round a sewer pipe and I caught a glimpse of something underneath him. Before I could take it in, I saw the grossest thing I've ever seen. So far.

A big fat worm was oozing into the tunnel like toothpaste being squeezed from a tube. Golden, wriggly toothpaste that glowed in the dark. When Mole pounced on it, there was about four feet of worm in the tunnel. He pulled another three feet more from the wall, then started to eat it. All of it.

'The best,' he said. 'Praed's worm.'

My mouth was already hanging open from the sheer ick factor in the worm; it dropped further when Moley made his announcement in a squeaky voice, as if he'd been sniffing helium balloons. Wow – there must be something special in those creatures.

I shook my head and focused on what he'd actually said, and not just the way he'd said it. 'Do you mean that worm came from Praed's Bank?'

'Yesh.'

I've got a lot of money in Praed's Bank. Why was my bank creating giant magickal worms in its basement? Another problem for another day.

I retreated towards the nest. 'Sir, I've shown you the basics of this equipment. You can learn more by pressing that key with no letter on it. Unfortunately, the connection to the outside world is lost, and the electricity will run out in a couple of hours. That's the problem I mentioned.'

'Now I know what it is, I can go to the Dwarf. He has many such bokshes. It was him who bought the bokshes from the dead men. I thought these bokshes were experiments in Luksh that had gone wrong. The Dwarf are always making, always dying. I will work for him, they will give me electricity.'

I opened my mouth to say something about His Worship's grammar: he was having great difficulty in sorting out the number agreement regarding Dwarf/Dwarves. I changed my mind, not only because Mole is still quite scary, and it would be rude, but also because he might be giving me a message.

'Oh? That sounds good. What will you do for them.'

He hissed. His nose laughed. 'Dig tunnels.'

'I thought Dwarves liked digging tunnels.'

'They don't like to get their hands dirty.' He waved his snout around and moved towards the laptop, anxious to play with his new toy. 'I will remove the dirt from the tunnel. You can pass freely in four days. After that, you can pass any time, Mr Clarke.'

'Thank you. Excuse me asking, but how good is your sight? I'm sorry if it's a sensitive question.'

He hissed. Annoyed, but not angry. 'No better than my brothers'.'

'I'm going to take an image of you. I could have done it without asking, but it's better if you know.' He didn't object. Nor would he sit still. I'd brought a compact camera because, as you've probably guessed, the camera in my phone is rubbish. I can't send pictures either. This picture was by way of an experiment. I'd already tried a quick snap of the secret door. The camera's display showed only bricks. Whatever magick had been used on the door, as on Merlyn's Tower, was having an effect on the physics of light. Yet I could see through it. What was that all about?

I checked the display. There was Moley. Grinning. Or baring his teeth. 'Thanks again. On my way out, may I look at the dead people? They have family who may wish to have a reminder of them.'

He hissed. Moles are not big on family. Turning away, he pressed F1 and began his tutorial on Braille. It would be followed automatically by one on Windows 10. I was rather pleased with that.

I didn't have any last word for the Lord Mayor. He wouldn't be listening, and I'd see him again soon. At some point Moley was going to have to rethink his attitude to family. I thought he was a he. He thinks he's a he. When he turned round in the tunnel, I clearly saw a row of teats. Mr Mole is going to get a shock in the spring.

I lit my lighter in the tunnel outside Mole's mortuary. The flame flickered. I don't know where the fresh air was coming from, and I didn't want to think about it because I'd end up imagining a giant mole hill appearing in St Paul's Churchyard, and London is not ready for that. However His Worship did it, there was enough air in here for me to light a fag. It was the only thing that would stop the smell.

I ducked inside the chamber. It was bad. I sucked hard on the cigarette and shone the torch around. Mole had made a pile of their belongings in a corner, including the contents of their pockets. That was a neat trick. I quickly sifted through the sad remains of four young lives. The Dwarves had taken the electronic devices, but not the other valuables. I picked up a wallet and three purses, shoving them in my pocket without looking. They were probably covered in blood. Something glinted in the torchlight. An engagement ring. Poor woman. Poor fiancé. I took that, too.

My last act underground was to bring the repeater down from the magickal door and leave it in the tunnel. The camping lantern I left on the stairs, ready for my next mission.

5 — Of Moles and Sisters

The London air smelled very sweet after Moley's tunnels. Alain was waiting patiently on the bench. Well, he was on his phone – you're never bored in the twenty-first century, unless you choose to be bored. He looked up when he heard me limping towards him, and I came to a decision.

'Conrad Clarke,' I said. 'Pleased to meet you.'

'Conrad? Is this your real name? I 'ave never met a Conrad before.' He shook my hand happily enough.

'Yes, it is. My mother was a fan of Joseph Conrad. Famous author.'

'Never 'eard of him. Your badge, your letter and your coffee, Conrad.'

'Thank you.'

I sat next to him and lit a cigarette. Alain went back to his phone. An hour had passed since we sat here making our final preparations. An hour in which I'd saved my life, discharged an oath and learnt a little more about the mad, mad world of magick. I'd learn more when I went back to see the Dwarves. Until then, I could afford to forget about it and rest my head. Except for one thing.

'Alain?'

'Hmm?'

'Which bank are you going to?'

'A little bank called Praed's. It's very near 'ere.'

I thought about warning him off the basement. I'd looked at Alain this morning. Really looked at him. There was no trace of Gift, or of magickal activity. He should be safe enough.

'I hope it goes well for you.'

'Thank you. Are we finished?'

'We are. You've been part of saving my life again, Alain. Hence the high rate of pay. If I have any more jobs, the rate might not be so good.'

He shrugged. I wonder if the French exaggerate their shrugging when communicating with Brits, just as we speak more loudly when talking to foreigners.

'Have a nice weekend.'

'You too, Conrad.'

He left me to it, returning to Bank Station with an enviable nonchalance. I got out my phone to talk to the Big Boss.

Me: *How did the Mole know about you?*

Him: *He read it in the Rune on your back. It has all my details.*

Me: *Thank you. If I had your email address, I'd send you a picture.*

Him: *Just stare at your camera.*

I got out the camera and stared at the display, scrolling in and out. The Rune on my back heated up, almost burning, then quickly chilled. I received a message.

Him: *This is very interesting.*

I waited for a moment. Nothing more. I put the hard hat and vest in my now nearly empty bag and went for a cab.

'My God, Conrad,' said Rachael. 'Either you've been digging up the road, or you're going for a radical reinterpretation of *lumbersexual*. I'm surprised they let you in here.'

'If the elegant, sophisticated and rich Miss Rachael Clarke hadn't made the reservation, they probably wouldn't have.'

'Shut up, Conrad. Stop changing the subject. What have you been doing?'

'A security op on the Tube. No one died, which is a good thing.'

'Oh. Are you drinking? I don't at lunchtime.'

'After the morning I've had, I'm definitely drinking.'

'Good. Let's order.'

The food was good, but not as good as the final bill warranted. And she made me pay. Sisters. Who'd have 'em, eh?

She also made me tell her about Mina. I enjoyed that part, but something made me hesitate when it came to the financial part of her crimes. I glossed over it by saying that she'd become mixed up with some bad people and changed the subject by showing Rachael the picture, she peered closely at it.

'How big is she?'

Rachael had always worried that she would grow up to be as tall as Mum. When she topped out a little shorter, she worried that she'd put on weight like Dad. When she asked how big Mina is, she probably meant *What size is she*. I chose to misinterpret her.

'She's five foot two. Not that it matters.'

She grunted an acknowledgement, and went on to finish her main course. We weren't going to be doing pudding. When she'd laid down her knife and fork, she put her elbows on the table.

'I said last week that I'd forgiven you. About the house. I might unforgive you. I'm still not sure I'm ready to move on.' I picked up my napkin, ready to throw it on the table. It took a heroic effort not to.

Raitch was making an effort, so I had to try, too. We've never been close and we'd drifted further apart after Carole and I split up. We fell out completely a few years ago when she discovered that I'd bought Elvenham House from Mum and Dad.

'What can I say, Rachael? We've been over this so often, I don't know what to say any more.'

'Why did you do it?'

I moved the napkin around. I topped up my wine. 'I did it because I could. I did it because I had the money and you didn't. I did it because Dad asked me to. I did it so that they could buy the villa in Spain without having to sell Elvenham House on the open market. I did it because I wanted to keep it in the family.'

What I said next, I only said because we were on her territory. She'd waved to several people when she came in, and I knew she wouldn't risk a scene. Not here. I leaned forward. 'What I didn't do was buy the house to spite you, Rachael. Your inheritance is secure. You got enough from the deal to put a deposit on your first flat. Because of that, you've actually made *more* money, because London prices have rocketed. I paid over the odds for Elvenham.'

Her lips screwed up, and her brows knitted together. 'Why did they need the money so badly? Mum won't say.'

She deserved to know, I suppose. 'It was Dad. He'd made a bad decision. He could have ridden it out, but that would have meant staying in the business. He wanted to get out and be with Mum.'

She sighed. 'Useless bloody man.' As Dad wasn't around, she picked on his nearest representative. Me. 'Why didn't you put my name on the deeds, too? I could help you out with the restoration. I know you've been plotting it.'

'Because we need to go our own ways, Rachael. Look, if it helps, you're still in my will, and you will be until I have children. If I die, Elvenham house will be yours.'

She sat back. 'What about Mina?'

'She's in my will, too, or she will be soon. She got cleaned out by the Asset Recovery Agency, and all her hidden stash went on private surgery and dental bills.'

Rachael nodded. I could see her trying to swallow the metaphorical pill. I finished my wine with a prayer that it cured her.

'You're bloody impossible, you are,' was her considered response.

'I blame our parents for that. It's something we have in common.'

'About the only bloody thing we have in common.'

'Let's find out, shall we? I might be spending more time in London, and I don't want to lose touch again. For my sake and yours. You never know when you might need a big brother.'

'I'll think about it.'

'Good. I'm going to catch a train later and sleep all the way to Cheltenham.'

She wrinkled her nose when we kissed goodbye. It reminded me of the Lord Mayor.

That night was the first I'd spent in Elvenham House on my own, as its master. I was too shattered to think about that when I collapsed on to the bed, and too groggy to appreciate it when I first got up. The strangeness of it all hit me after I'd had a shower. Going downstairs, I was walking into utter silence. No Radio 4, no kitchen noises, no sounds from the garden. I stopped half way down the staircase and listened to the silence.

I could hear the sounds of an eye-wateringly expensive boiler keeping me warm. I could hear two of the loose windows rattling in the wind. I could hear, just, the hum of the freezer in the scullery. Freezer. Food. Was there any? Mother doesn't like to waste anything, and I'd be surprised if she'd left anything behind. She hadn't. For breakfast, I had a black coffee, a fag, and a lesson in househusbandry. I now have to buy my own milk.

The whole thing was very strange. Even stranger was the message on my phone:

The Spirits are hiding from me. I will nose them out.

That could only be one person. I added Lord Mayor of Moles to my contact list, and sent back: *Thank you for getting in touch. If you ever need my help, just message me. Perhaps one day I can help you find the Spirit. I take it you don't want to shake its hand.*

Mole: *No. I wish to chew on its Imprint and bury it under 2.4 tonnes of rock. Tell me, Mr Clarke, why does your Internet have nothing about magic?*

Me: *I don't know. Yet. I wish it were that easy. Try to tell your computer to spell magic with a K. As in magick. Do you have email? Can you make voice calls?*

We exchanged email addresses. The Lord Mayor said that he was working on voice calls.

I needed a new plan. I needed breakfast more, so I treated myself to the All Day Breakfast at the Inkwell. It was full of Locally Sourced this and Organic that, but it didn't taste as good as the one in Moorgate. Probably wasn't their speciality.

The village shop provided enough basic rations to last a few days. Then I tried to carry them. I forked out for two Fair Trade jute bags with the shop's logo on the side and was able to get home without plastic handles cutting through my fingers like cheesewire. I stowed the bags in the scullery next to four others, exactly the same. Today's first resolution was not to forget my bags again.

The second resolution was to remember that it was now *my* job to contact Mrs Gower and ask her to get the supplies in, not my parents'.

I found a hire car company who would deliver a Korean 4x4 to Clerkswell, then I went for a walk to clear my head. I returned to the Inkwell for a few pints and a natter. I went to bed.

On Sunday, I started making two lists. The first was headed *Dwarves;* The second was headed *Elvenham House — Long/Short Term.* I spent the rest of the day wandering around the house and grounds, jotting down ideas on both lists as they came to me. By supper time, I'd filled several pieces of paper for Elvenham, but had only three items on my plan for the Dwarves.

That made me scratch my head, which told me I needed a haircut, and also brought the words of my Cranwell instructor crashing back from my subconscious. *You've no intelligence, laddie.* He wasn't actually Scottish, but it sounds much fiercer in a tartan brogue. He was right: I had no intelligence. My encounter with Mole had taught me that this was a very dangerous business to be in. The Allfather had told me. Hannah had told me, and I'd believed them, too.

The problem had been that my many brushes with death at the hands of the Taliban, Iraqi insurgents and the Operation Jigsaw crowd had seemed much more real. I hadn't thought I was in any genuine danger in the magickal world. I wasn't going to make that mistake again.

My ignorance was no longer total: I had safe passage to the Dwarves; I had a working relationship with the Lord Mayor of Moles; I had Odin's power behind my word of honour.

I started a fresh piece of paper and put everything down. The one thing that struck me was Hannah's attitude to my journey. She had predicted the danger in using the back entrance to Dwarfland, but she hadn't seen the Dwarves themselves as a risk to me. Mole was happy to work for them. They weren't his natural enemy. Good. The more I thought about Hannah, the more peeved I became. She hadn't done anything to hurt me, but she hadn't made any effort to help, either. I finally came up with a plan.

Satisfied, I sent a message to Mole, a message to Clarke's Mess and called my parents before going out. They were fine. Dad always answered the phone, because he still does a bit of business occasionally. He likes to pretend that Mother doesn't know.

I told him about some of my plans for the house. He gave some names of local tradesmen, and passed me over to Mother. She told me that she'd made the semi-final of the bridge club's annual cup (for the fifth year running), and then she paused.

'I've had a funny phone call from Rachael,' she said eventually.

'Oh?'

'She said that she's going to be seeing more of you in future. Not that it's any of my business.'

Only my mother could consider her children's relationship as *none of her business.*

'We'll see. You never know, we might find we have things in common.'

'I doubt that,' said mother. Did I detect a smile over the phone? I think I must have, because she continued, 'Who knows, dear, she might even have a boyfriend before your girlfriend gets out of prison.'

'Aah.'

'I'm not going to approve or disapprove of someone I've never met. Your father likes her already because she's young and exotic. I have more exacting standards.'

'Rachael might have a girlfriend herself by then. You never know.'

'Conrad! What are you not telling me?'

'I had lunch with her on Friday. She didn't say anything about romance, so you're probably right. She's never told me anything.'

'I'm not sure I follow your logic, dear. Well, we'll see, won't we?'

'We will. Good luck with the competition.'

What do you say when you run a secret magickal operation and you have to answer the phone? It rang three times and I had my answer.

'OPC. Tennille speaking.'

'Good afternoon. This is Conrad Clarke. I'm alive.'

'Thank the Lord,' she said, with a rush of enthusiasm. She really believed; there was no doubting it. 'I checked the records,' she continued, more evenly, 'and I saw you'd been in twice. I thought you were taken the second time. Congratulations, Mr Clarke. What did the Dwarves say to you?'

'Nothing yet – I'm seeing them on Wednesday. There's something your boss needs to know. It's quite complicated, and I don't think it's what she's expecting.'

'I see. What happened?'

'I'd rather explain it to her myself. Can she fit me in tomorrow morning?'

'Hmm. Let me see. Eleven o'clock suit you?'

'Great.' I looked at the business card which Tennille had given me. The phone number was clearly Hannah's office, but what about the email?

'Just one thing,' I said. 'On the card. Is that the Constable's personal email?'

'Yes it is. I check it too, but that's her account.'

'Thanks. I'll see you tomorrow. How do I get past security at the main entrance?'

'Say you have an appointment with Mr Bunbury at the Records Office. They'll ring through, and Records will confirm it. You know your way after that.'

'Thanks. There's something I need to speak to you about, too. After I've seen the Boss.'

'She ain't your boss yet. Goodbye, Mr Clarke. I'll see you tomorrow.'

The ruse with Mr Bunbury worked like a charm. Perhaps it was a charm. Perhaps it was a magickal spell that would get me through any security barrier in the country. Perhaps not.

Tennille stood when I got to the top of the stairs, and came round the desk to give me a warm hug. That was nice.

'Tea or coffee? She won't be long.'

I opted for tea and took a seat by the window, because I wanted to make sure I got a mobile signal. She left the tea to brew for a long time. The more I saw of Tennille, the more I liked her.

I heard footsteps on the staircase: two sets, one with heels. The first sign of life in Merlyn's Tower that wasn't Hannah or her PA. Tennille didn't seem bothered about me being there, and didn't look up until two people got to the top of the stairs.

Just in front was a man, about thirty, of Chinese extraction. He was wearing a smart suit and his black hair was gelled to within an inch of its life. One stair behind him was a much younger woman. Interesting. This staircase was wide enough for them to have walked side by side.

The man walked towards Tennille's desk, and I got a good look at the woman. She was wearing an outfit which did her no favours: the white blouse and grey trousers leached all the colour from her face. Next to Tennille's rich black skin, and the Chinese guy's healthy glow, she was the very image of washed out whitey. Even her mousy hair, worn long and loose, looked like it could do with some tlc. She glanced at me on the way past, and managed to simultaneously smile and frown. I liked her already.

'We'd really like to see the Constable,' said the Chinese guy. His accent was worth at least £20,000pa of school fees.

'Lee, you could have called,' said Tennille. She pointed at me. 'As you can see, Hannah's busy this morning.'

Lee (or was it Li?) turned in my direction. He frowned, with no trace of a smile.

The young woman smiled at me properly. 'Sorry to interrupt,' she said. A Geordie. This really was the United Nations of Magick.

'No problem,' I said, smiling back. I resisted the urge to introduce myself.

'She can fit you in at two,' said Tennille. 'Oh, and Vicky, could you make sure you bring the full report.'

'Yes. Of course,' said the young woman, hereinafter known as Vicky. She was the first to leave. Lee/Mr Li nodded *at* rather than *to* Tennille, and followed Vicky down the staircase.

I'd noticed that the door to Hannah's office was firmly shut, which is why she rang through when she was ready. While Tennille poured the PC a coffee, I sent a text which I'd prepared earlier. Tennille led the way, and put the coffee down on Hannah's desk. On her way out, she shut the door firmly behind her.

The Peculier Constable was reading a file with a familiar cover: it was RAF blue and had my name on it. She stood up to shake my hand. No hug, but an improvement on blasting me across the office. Presumably she'd washed her shirt, but otherwise she was wearing exactly the same outfit as the last time we'd met.

'Welcome back. I thought we were the secret organisation until I read this.' She lifted the file off the desk. 'The last four pages are so redacted I've got no idea what you were up to. And they were dated *after* your medical discharge.'

'What can I say, ma'am? Man of mystery. If you give me a job, I'm sure they'll play nicely and tell you the rest.'

'Stop calling me *ma'am*. No one does that. Anyway, Tennille said you had something important to tell me.'

'Could you check your inbox.'

'Now?'

'Now would be the best time, yes.'

She leaned towards her monitor and moved the mouse. Then she blinked. 'What's this.'

I couldn't resist it. 'It's an *Emole*.'

'E-what?'

'An Emole. Read it.'

She read it aloud. '*To the man in charge of little men with Lux. If you wish your men to pass through my territory, we will need to agree a price. This does not apply to Conrad Clarke. From the Lord Mayor of Moles.* What in God's name is this?'

'My opponent turned out to be a giant, magickal mole. I did tell him you were a woman, but moles have real gender issues. He was going to eat me, but we reached an understanding in the end.'

Hannah shot back her chair on its casters and stood up. I thought she was going to blast the computer. I even detected a surge of magick from her. Instead of taking it out on the machine, she turned to me.

'Oh my God, Clarke. You don't know what you've done. You've unleashed a Particular. One of our jobs is to keep them away from modern technology, and it looks like you've handed it to him on a plate. What were you thinking?'

I stood up and put my hands on her desk. Even leaning forwards, I was a lot taller than her. It was one of the few advantages I had. The other was anger.

'That's the problem. Ma'am. I have no fucking idea at all what I've done, because you wouldn't tell me. I do know that I'm alive, and that I found three corpses with no heads on them down there. I know that much.'

She went bright red. Almost as red as the wig. She also stood her ground. 'Sit down, Clarke. I've faced down bigger men than you.'

Score one point to the woman. I stood back, but I didn't sit down. 'I hope for their sake that Li and Victoria get better briefings from their CO.'

She went from red to white, and had to swallow before she resumed the attack. 'How dare you come in here and talk to me like that. You're not a Watch Captain yet, you're just Odin's patsy.' She picked up the folder. 'You managed to get three reprimands for insubordination on one tour of duty in Iraq, and you were investigated twice for alcohol smuggling. I'm surprised they didn't kick you out a long time ago.'

I pointed to the file. 'How many crew did I lose? How many squaddies died when I was their pilot? None, because if the chopper pilot dies, everyone dies. Call the HR department and ask them what happened to that wanker who reported me, the one who accused me of insubordination. They sent him to look after the Air Cadets in Wales. I bet his file is stamped *Not fit for Operational Command*.'

I stared at her, leaving the accusation hanging. Was she fit for operational command? She kept eye contact with me, then lifted her hand, and I braced myself for a magickal assault. The hand went to her hair, and she pulled off the wig. There wasn't just scarring on her head, the left hand side was sunken, as if a bit were missing. I could see why she wore such a full wig.

She pointed to the depression in her head. 'I'll see you one broken leg, and I'll raise you a shattered skull. It looks queer because the titanium plate is thinner than the bone. I know all about the dangers out there.'

A hint of guilt flashed across her face in the tremble of her lip. Her head looked horrible, and I wasn't going to win a pissing contest based on facing danger, but she hadn't answered the question. She'd lost someone in whatever business had led to her trauma. Now was not the time to press the point.

'I'm sorry,' I said. I pointed to the wig. 'That thing must itch like hell.'

She managed a smile. 'You don't know the half of it. I only see visitors in the morning, usually, because I can't wear it for more than a couple of hours.'

She dumped the hairpiece on the desk and opened a drawer, pulling out a blue and white bandanna which she knotted quickly around her head. 'This is how my team normally see me. You've got five minutes to drink your tea and ask any questions.'

She sat down and picked up her coffee, keeping an eye on me over the cup. I stayed standing.

'What's a Particular?' I asked, to start the ball rolling.

'A Demi-Power. A living creature, with heart and lungs and an appetite, but one that's both magickal and individual. The most famous one is the Coventry Unicorn.'

'Not that famous.'

'It is in our world. Don't ask me about the Great Powers, like the Allfather. You've already used up one minute.'

'Dwarves. What do I need to know. In one minute.'

'They're *Animate*, not living. You'll see for yourself. They're the oldest and wiliest of the Creatures of Light. They are the only creatures who can make Alchemical Gold, which is ordinary gold with Lux stored in it. Yes, a magickal battery. They also make Artefacts. Your goal is to get them to make you a sword, so you can join my happy band.'

'If you'll still have me. Ma'am.'

'Not my choice. If you make it that far, you'll meet another Power. It's up to her who gets to join the Watch.' She sighed. 'I might have to force myself to get used to being called *Ma'am*. Technically, all the King's Watch are in the Army, because that's how we get paid. If you join, you'll be the first real soldier for over two generations. I was a copper, before this. All the kids have come straight from the Invisible College.' She put her cup down before I could open my mouth. 'Time's up. You'll be going to the College if you pass the test, so you'll find out all about it then.' She stood up and pushed a button on her phone.

'I'm not a soldier, ma'am,' I said. 'I was an Airman, and if I come back again, I'll be resuming my commission. If that's acceptable. No sense in buying another uniform.'

She laughed. 'I'll look forward to seeing you in that. I only wear mine when absolutely forced to, and that's too often. Good luck, Clarke. I'm now going to open negotiations with a giant mole. All in a day's work for the Peculier Constable.'

Tennille opened the door and stood ready to escort me out. I started to leave, slipping in one last question. 'You're not going to nuke him out of hand, then?'

I'd made up enough ground with Hannah for her to answer. 'No. The problem with Particulars is that they need a lot of Lux. Unless he starts raiding out of his tunnels, he can dig in peace.'

'Or until he meets a Dragonling. That might be worth watching.'

I'd reached the door and was about to leave when Hannah shouted, 'What do you know about Dragonlings?'

'Nothing, ma'am, except that there are eggs under the City. That's all.'

'Shit. That's all I need. Go away, Clarke, before you tell me that you've got faeries in the garden.'

I left. That was not a topic to explore today.

'You wanted to see me?' said Tennille after she'd closed the door.

'Please.'

She waved me to a seat. 'I heard voices,' she said, pointing to the PC's office, 'In there.'

'I like to have my disagreements in the open. Clears the air.'

'Hmm. You don't know how hard her job is, Mr Clarke. She don't need you making it harder.'

I held up my hands in surrender. 'I've seen her head. I know she's earned the right to her position.'

'Don't say that until you know the full truth. The fractured skull has healed; the other wounds may never get better. Now, what did you want?'

I got out a piece of paper and unfolded it. I slid it across her desk. 'Do those names look familiar?'

It only took one glance before she looked up sharply. 'These are the three poor creatures that your Patron sent to their deaths. How do you know their names?'

I took out the three purses I'd found in Mole's Mortuary. I'd checked them and found nothing you wouldn't expect to find in a young woman's purse. No membership cards for secret societies, no list of spells. The stains on them were blood, so I handed them over in a clear plastic bag. 'I don't know whether it will help their next of kin or not. There's this as well.' The engagement ring was in a smaller bag. It looked like an expensive one.

Tennille sighed from the bottom of her ample chest, and rubbed a hand against her eye. 'Thank you, Mr Clarke. That was a noble thing to do. I won't ask how you got them, and I won't be passing on the purses. I'll make sure the ring gets home.'

I stood up. 'Three women. All a lot younger than me. Does the Allfather have a thing for young women?'

She stared at me. 'You have so much to learn.' She pointed at the sign on Hannah's Door. 'They wanted to call the first Constable by the name *Witchfinder General*, because the men priests were afraid of the wicked women. Three quarters of all children with a Gift are girls, and always have been. It's only now that they're getting a chance to show what they're worth.' She paused. 'Did the Constable warn you not to come back?'

I'd reached the top of the stairs. 'In what way?'

'Once you've spoken to the Dwarves, you may not enter Merlyn's Tower until you complete the task. Or die.'

'What about email?'

'No contact with the Constable at all.'

'Then goodbye for now. I'll be back.'

'Goodbye, Mr Clarke.'

I'd said nothing about the fourth body deliberately. The Lord Mayor had said that the Spirit had sent *men to chain me*. If Hannah was going to leave Moley alone for now, I was going to keep everything I knew about him to myself, including his origins. Interestingly, the three women had thought nothing of toting their everyday IDs around whilst on a magickal quest. The man had been different. All he had in his wallet was a tourist's Oyster Card and £500 in cash. There's a trick to getting bloodstains out of bank notes. When I get back to Elvenham House, I'm going to try it out.

The builders of Gloucestershire were swinging back into action after Christmas, as much as the bad weather would let them. The frost and snow meant that there wasn't much happening outside, so they had time to go out pricing up jobs, and Mrs Gower let them in to Elvenham House in my absence. On Tuesday afternoon I had long phone conversations with two of them about the state of Elvenham House and whether or not it needed repointing at the back. One of them said it did, and that the roof was fine. The other one said that the pointing could wait a few years but the roof was in need of remedial work. Dad had slaved away when I was young to afford a completely new roof, but that was a long time ago.

Because the second builder had actually been on the roof, I was more inclined to believe him. I told him to email me a quote. Both of them said that converting the old stable block would be relatively easy because no humans were going to live there.

So far, so domestic. The third call was from a gardener. We talked about a few things in general, then he said, 'Of course, you'll need to deal with the mole problem first.'

'Mole problem? I didn't have a mole problem when I left the house on Monday.'

'You do now. Six mole hills on your lawn. It was quite odd, actually. I've never seen them arranged in a circle before. Never.'

This could not be a coincidence. 'Oh. Thanks for telling me. I'm quite keen to restore the gardens to what they were like when the house was built. I'll try and do some research when I get home. For now, don't do anything about the moles. Is that clear?'

I must have overdone it, because the guy left too long a pause before replying. 'Yes, mate. It's your lawn. Are you sure about having the gardens landscaped?'

'I'm sure. Yes. It's not urgent, but now that I've moved in permanently, I want to start a programme of renovation. Including the gardens. I'll get back to you soon.'

This was not a conversation to have with His Worship by Emole. I'd ask him about it tomorrow. I spent the rest of the day trying to hack the tourist Oyster Card which I'd found with the body. Despite much trying, without the guy's email address I was going nowhere. Neither was he.

The only thing I took with me next morning was the big torch. Until I knew a lot about my new life, it seemed safer to travel light than to prepare for the unknown. That huge combat knife had done me no good at all, though it did remind me where I'd bought it. I went to Bank Station via the outdoor shop and bought all their curried dried worms. I told them it was for a party.

I was thinking about the Dwarves when I put the Visitor badge up to the security reader outside the door which led off the station concourse. It stuck to the plate, and the door didn't open. I tried to pull the badge off, and leaned forwards to see if some idiot had put superglue on the reader.

The hairs on the back of my neck prickled. Nothing to do with magick: this was old-fashioned anticipation. Standing in that three foot deep, five foot wide entryway, I was the proverbial sitting duck.

I abandoned the pass, wheeled round and moved to the side. All I saw was commuters rushing towards the Northern Line, eyes on their phones or the ground in front of them. Except one. She was rushing towards *me*. This time the tingle was definitely magickal, and I could see her raising her left hand, ready to do something nasty. I had nothing. No defences and no options to counter-attack.

I could have stood there and taken it, but I'm not that sort of hero. I chose the biggest man moving in the corridor and dived at his legs. He crashed down on top of me, hitting a woman on the way. Two more human skittles were tumbling when a sonic boom rocked the concourse. A section of wall where I'd been standing was vaporised and pulverised. Sharp shards of brick flew into the air.

That guy was right in her line of fire. If I hadn't knocked him over, then he would have been killed, too.

All hell broke loose. Two very brave Transport Police officers ran towards us while everyone else ran away. The big guy on top of me looked to be in shock as he scrambled to his knees, then his feet, then he saw the police officers and legged it with the rest. I was lying on the ground scanning for the woman who'd tried to kill me. She'd gone. I looked at the doorway again. My Visitor pass had been released by the security plate. I'd just retrieved it and shoved it in my pocket when the Armed Response Team showed up.

The few of us left near the blast area were quickly corralled into a safe zone while the Armed Response guys set about closing the station. It can't have been ten minutes later when two familiar figures hurried down the steps from Threadneedle Street. Vicky was still one pace behind Li.

He showed some sort of ID to the senior police officer and started talking rapidly, while Vicky came over to my sad, scared little group and whispered to the body-armoured, helmeted, machine-gun toting constable who was keeping us safe/stopping us running away. She pointed to me, and the guy jerked his head. I was being extracted.

'We didn't get introduced properly,' I said. 'I'm Conrad Clarke. You could say I'm an aspirant to joining your mob.' I stuck out my hand. Vicky took it, and smiled.

'Yes. I asked Mrs Haynes about you. I'm Vicky Robson.'

I filed away Tennille's surname for future reference, and was about to ask something else when Li came across.

'Come on, Vicky. We haven't got long.'

I was trying not to take an instant dislike to Li. I introduced myself and offered a handshake, which he returned with minimal enthusiasm.

'Li Cheng, Royal Occulter. Wait there,' he said, pointing to a spot which had a view of where the blast had occurred.

Li marched down the concourse, followed by Vicky. He took off his jacket, shook out the creases and handed it to the young woman. She didn't object, and draped it carefully over her left arm, placing her right hand on Li's shoulder. He stood up straight and turned slightly. On his left hip was a dagger, previously hidden by the folds of his suit. He took it out and held it before him. Even at this distance, I could feel the magick building.

He concentrated on the dagger, making a square shape in the air. As it moved slowly around the four corners, I could feel the magick wash over me, prickling my scalp and making sweat run down my face. Everyone else in the station was oblivious.

The square was complete. Li had stains under his arms already, and then he started again. He'd already used more magick for this – more Lux, I suppose – than anything else I'd experienced. He used even more, and I felt another vibration, like a harmony. He was taking Lux from Vicky via the hand on his shoulder. By the end of the second movement, I could see her fingers digging into his flesh. That would be a bruise in the morning. He broke off at the end and they staggered into each other. The way she grinned at him was a mixture of personal and professional pride in whatever it was they'd done.

'I don't know about you, but I need a cup of tea,' said Vicky. She said it both to Li Cheng and to me. Li nodded in response. He was out of breath.

'I'll get them,' I said. 'Do you want to wait up top, in what passes for fresh air in London?'

He nodded again. The police cordon had extended outside the entrance to include the benches by the Duke of Wellington, who seemed unmoved by all the action around and beneath him. Hundreds of frustrated travellers were milling around, wondering what to do now that the station was closed. We got to sit in the eye of the storm.

When I returned with the teas, and several packets of sugar, I heard one of the Transport Police officers say, 'There's been a controlled explosion of a suspicious package. Northern Line is open via Monument. Central Line's open at St Paul's. This station won't reopen for a couple of hours while they make repairs.'

He said this with the sort of bored familiarity which told me that he believed it completely. I was beginning to understand why there was no reference to magick on the Internet, and what might be involved in the job of Royal Occulter. A crew of men in hard hats turned up and were shown through the cordon. I pointed to Li and Vicky and the officer let me through.

'Thanks for the tea,' said Vicky.

I took out my fags and offered them around. Li curled his lip at me, but Vicky hesitated, then succumbed when I took one for myself. Li moved further down the bench. I lit both cigarettes.

'How did you get here so quickly?' I asked.

Vicky blew the steam from her tea, leaving Li to answer. He pulled himself together. 'We felt it. I should think every Mage, Faerie, Gnome, Witch, Dwarf and giant mole in London felt it. Your new friend will have got a terrible shock.'

'Not my friend,' I replied. 'Moles don't do friendship. Too territorial.'

'We all felt it,' said Vicky, 'but I pinpointed it. Then we looked at the CCTV feed and I saw you there. Who attacked you?'

'Isn't she on the CCTV?'

Vicky shook her head. 'Watch this.' She took out a tablet computer. Not an iPad: something in a rugged rubber case. She unlocked the screen and hunted through the icons. When she'd found what she wanted, she passed it to me.

I had a good view of the back of my head. So did Vicky. She now knew all about my bald patch, which is worse at the moment because I need a haircut. I watched myself walk towards the opening for the security door, watched myself disappear for a second, then reappear and dive at the big guy.

Vicky pointed to the man I'd just tackled to the ground. 'Did he do it?'

'No. Rewind three seconds … then look at my eyes. I'm staring at the person who did it.'

We all looked down the screen. Where the attacker had stood was a hole, a gap in the crowd of people rushing for their trains.

'Shit,' said Li.

'Is that hard to do?' I asked. 'It's a neat trick. I wouldn't mind learning that myself.'

'You'll never do that,' said Li, without any malice. Another crushing blow to my magickal self-esteem. 'It's hard to keep up for long, especially with the number of cameras in a tube station. How did she know you'd be there? Did you tell anyone what time you were coming?'

'No. I think she must have put a spell on the security reader. She turned up seconds after it tried to eat my Visitor badge. In which case, she might have been lurking in the ticket hall, without that spell on her.'

'We don't call them spells. We call them Works, after the Great Work. Anything which alters an appearance is called a Glamour. Vicky, switch to the ticket hall.'

In the new image, there were several people standing round waiting. None of them looked like my attacker.

'Look, there,' said Vicky. 'That's Desirée.' She zoomed in to a young black woman with short, spiked hair. The ceiling camera gave a good look at her cleavage, which I shouldn't be seeing, because it was winter. No one wears a halter-top in this weather. We weren't the only ones looking. Most of the men, and a good few women, flicked their eyes at her.

'Are you sure?' said Li, frowning.

Vicky got out a phone, also in a rubberised mount which matched her tablet. She unlocked it by moving her hand over the screen, well away from the device.

'Was that a Work in progress?' I asked. Neither of them got the joke.

'No,' said Li. 'That's a Keyway.'

Vicky went on to Facebook, of all things. She showed us a picture of herself with the black woman. It was definitely her, the one in the ticket hall. I said so.

'No,' said Vicky. 'Desirée Haynes did not do this. She's too young to have the power, and she's got no Talent in Glamours. And she's Tennille's daughter. She doesn't do shit like that. This is someone taking the piss.'

In defending her friend, her Geordie accent had got stronger, and her cheeks had flushed red.

'What are you going to do about it?' I asked.

'Me?' said Li, genuinely surprised. 'Nothing. You're on your own, my friend. Do you know how many practising Mages there are, of all descriptions?'

'Obviously not.'

'About 2,000. You're not one of us, and this person clearly has a problem with you, and you alone. We have bigger fish to fry.'

'Sorry, Mr Clarke,' said Vicky.

'Call me Conrad. I won't take it personally.'

'Good,' said Li. He got up, looking for a rubbish bin. A police officer with a lot of silver on his epaulettes stopped him and said something.

'Excuse me asking,' said Vicky, 'you're not from Gloucestershire, are you?'

There's a time to lie and a time to tell the truth. This was a time for truth. For several reasons. 'I am. Why do you ask?'

'Oh. There was a Clarke who moved there in Queen Elizabeth's time. You're not descended from him, are you?'

'I have no idea. I doubt it. He must have been a bit special for you to mention him.'

'If you come across a couple of dozen magick books, the Keeper of the Queen's Esoteric Library would like them back. They're overdue.'

I laughed, and looked at Vicky a little more closely. She still looked a little wan, as if she spent far too much time indoors, and her body had little condition to it. She had a friendly, open smile which did a lot to make up for her rather long face. Long as in horsey.

'I quite like the idea of being descended from a book thief. It would fit with what my family got up to more recently.'

'Oh, no. He wasn't a thief. He just didn't bring them back. He was the first Keeper, so he had the right.'

'I'll keep my eyes open for them. Are you both in the Army?'

She smiled. 'Stupid, isn't it? I'm a captain, and Cheng's a major.'

I noted her use of his first name. 'And he's an Occulter. Are you his apprentice?'

'Sort of. He's very good at what he does. I've only been in the King's Watch for a few months and I haven't decided whether to do advanced Occulting or stick to Sorcery.'

'I can guess what Occulting is, having seen him at work. What do Sorcerers do?'

'We can see the Sympathetic Echo. Or hear it, or feel it. It was me who knew that the magick bomb had gone off in Bank Station.'

The policeman had finished with Li. I had to choose one more question before they buggered off. I could wait to learn what a Sorcerer is, and what they do with the Sympathetic Echo, so I opted for something more useful. 'That dagger your colleague used. I thought you had to have a sword.'

'Not any more. See?' She opened her coat. A very ornate, golden pickaxe hung on a long chain around her neck. 'My father was a pitman. A miner. The Watch Captains all have something physically lethal.'

'And the Constable?'

She stood up as Li came back over. 'Wait and see. It's worth the surprise. Nice to meet you, Conrad. And good luck.'

People keep wishing me good luck. I don't know whether to be cheered up by their good will or worried about my future. Both, probably.

They walked through the cordon and off towards the Tower. Neither of them had asked me what my attacker had looked like, because they assumed I'd been taken in by the Glamour. I wasn't, not even for a fraction of a second. I hadn't seen an image of Desirée Haynes, I'd seen a woman dressed for fell running in athletic leggings, rugged shoes and wearing a tight fitting waterproof. Her hair was in a long braid. Unlike Vicky, my enemy clearly worked out. She could have been any age from twenty-five to forty-five, white, with blue eyes. Show me an aerial photograph, and I won't forget the location. With faces, I'm not so good. That doesn't matter; I know that I'll recognise this woman again, wherever I see her, because I never forget an enemy.

They had left me inside the cordon. My attacker wouldn't be back until the police were gone, so I had a golden opportunity to get underground safely and see the Dwarves. No one stopped me when I went down the steps. When I got to the door, the guys in hard hats were starting to fix the hole in the wall where I'd nearly died. Cleaners had already removed the debris.

'Excuse me,' I said, waving the Visitor badge. 'I've come to check the switch gear down there. Make sure it's all functioning.'

They stood aside, assuming that the armed police had vetted me. My badge worked, and I shut the door firmly behind me to ensure some privacy. The Lord Mayor of Moles was coming down the corridor when I got to the bottom of the secret steps.

'What happened?' he asked after nosing me. One day I'll get used to a giant mole running his nose over my face. That day has not yet arrived.

'Someone wants to stop me seeing the Dwarves,' I replied. 'Or to stop me seeing you.'

He hissed, agitated. 'I did not sense the Spirit. I do not think he sent enemies after you.'

'Does this Spirit have a name?' I asked.

'He does, but I did not know your language when he left me. You have no use for his name in Moleish.'

'No. Talking of Moleish, have you been sending your brothers to dig up my lawn?'

The nose twitched. He was laughing. 'You know my territory. It seemed fair that I should know yours. You have free passage, so should my brothers.'

Great. I revised my plans for landscaping the gardens. Expanses of grass would not be a good idea. Shame. I was desperate to buy a sit-on lawnmower.

'Was the circular pattern a message?'

A twitch of the snout. 'No. It was not a circle. The holes are points of a shtar, with tunnels marking the lines, under the earth. It is the Moleish Shtar. Feel.'

He reared up and pointed with his paw to the chain of office I'd given him. The Essex County Swimming Award which I'd stuck on the bottom was gone. In its place was a gleaming gold circle, about the size of an Olympic medal. I could see it well enough, but he wanted me to feel it, so I did. The surface had a sharply raised design on it, a weird six-pointed star.

The points didn't come to an angle, like the Star of David, but ended in tiny circles of raised gold. Mini-mole hills. I could also feel the magick pulsing through the medal.

'Did the Dwarves make that?'

'Yes. And this,' he said, moving his snout to the other side of the tunnel.

I peered down. Fastened to the brick, about a foot off the floor, was a piece of trunking with mains electricity and what looked like a fibre optic cable running through it. This was now one very connected Mole.

'Have you reached an agreement with the Peculier Constable?' I said.

'Nearly. He drives a hard bargain.'

'She. Hannah is definitely a she.'

He hissed. I think that was incomprehension. He really is in for a shock when he comes into season. I thought about repeating Hannah's warning about sticking to his tunnels. No. I got the impression that the King's Watch was rather over-stretched. If Moley got too big for his tunnels, they'd warn him first. By then, I hoped to be part of the solution.

'I brought some more curried worms. Do you like them?'

He hissed in pleasure. 'The worms of Luksh have little taste. The worms you bring in offering are like … seasoning. If they are in the packets, please leave them.'

I put them down next to the wall. He flicked his snout over them, then left them for later.

'Thanks again, Your Worship,' I said. He did his U-turn and trundled off back to his nest.

The tunnel to the right wasn't completely open, and I wondered if Mole had problems with spoil from his digging. He'd cleared a four foot gap at the top, slightly larger on the left hand side, where the cables ran. I shone my big torch on the dirt. Mole's paw marks were mixed in with other spoor. I'd expected heavy boots from Dwarvish feet, but this was weird. If I'd had to guess what made those prints, I'd have said a three-toed Yeti had been down here. I squeezed through the gap, down the other side and walked slowly towards the vaults of the Bank of England.

There's a lot of gold in the Bank of England, and it's not just ours. Lots of countries use the Old Lady's vaults to keep their reserves out of the hands of rebels, crooks and revolutionaries. I don't blame them. The value of all that metal has a lot of 000s at the end, not something you'd normally keep in the middle of a metropolis. To protect this mind-numbingly large treasure, the bank was rebuilt between the two World Wars. On all sides but the front, it looks like a fortress, because it is. The same is true underground.

Over the last few days my sense of what was right in the world has taken a large step to the left. I had just watched a man years younger than me alter the memories of hundreds of people, including hard-bitten anti-terror officers. If I checked, I'm sure I'd find he'd altered all references on the Internet, too. If I discovered that the Bank had a dragon guarding the gold, I wouldn't be surprised, nor that they had subcontracted security to Dwarves.

Before I reached the Bank of England campus, the tunnel turned right and began a long descent, curving slightly round the raw concrete of the Bank vault. It was soon below them. At the end of the stairs was an ante-chamber, with a door to the left, under the vault, and another tunnel leading away to the South East. I held up the lantern, looked around me, and shivered.

This was not human handiwork: I could feel the faint echo of magick all around me, stronger at the door. The walls had been ornamented with a bewildering variety of icons, images and scripts, all in deep relief.

There were humans, many humans, some in robes, some in armour. A lot of them were women. Some of them were realistically naked. They were all walking or riding towards the door, like pilgrims. Or customers. I saw several Christian crosses and two Stars of David, but no crescent. The further you got from the door, the more up-to-date was the garb of the humans. Robes gave way to ruffs, to breeches, and most recently to robes again. Scattered throughout the designs were some mythical and not so mythical beasts. A cow. Several wild boar. At least three dragons that I could see, but they'd been carved high up the wall. I went to the far end, by the tunnel, and found a blank space. Right at the very end of the line was an image of Moley, pushing a six-pointed star with his nose.

There was another item in the ante-chamber, and it was most definitely a human artefact. Facing the bottom of the stairs was a small sign on a wooden stand. The wood had been painted in the same green as the secret door, and had probably been sitting there for sixty years. The sign itself was metal, enamelled, and had those wonderful curlicued arrows pointing left and right. Don't you just love British bureaucracy?

With a totally unhelpful generalisation, the right-pointing arrow, the one aimed at the tunnel, said, *Other Routes*. Great. I wandered up to the entrance and shone the torch down a brick-lined tunnel leading who-knows-where. I wasn't going to find out today. What I did notice was that the cables, which had followed the stairs all the way down, ran into this new tunnel rather than going through the wall into Dwarfland. Another thing about the tunnel is that it was dirty. The floor of the ante-chamber was spotless; the tunnel had a fine layer of dust and mud. And lots of footprints. Human footprints. I peered down and put my size thirteens next to the impressions. Most of the visitors this way were women, I think. Clearly

Mole did not have a monopoly on access to the Dwarves, so why had Hannah sent me through his territory?

The left-pointing arrow was marked *Hledjolf's Hall*. Underneath, in felt-tipped pen, someone had written *Ring Bell to Enter*.

I finally turned to face the doors. I've passed through lots of doors, large and small, ornate and functional, metal, wood, bamboo and plastic. Never, outside of a cinema, have I ever seen a door made of stone. It's just stupid. That's what these doors were made of.

The carving on them was plainer, more streamlined and in lower relief than the carving on the walls. The creatures pictured were presumably Dwarves, but they looked nothing like the ones in *The Lord of the Rings*. These Dwarves had three legs, that was clear, and if the carving was accurate, they appeared to have three arms as well. And no neck. If I had to put an image in your head, it would be R2D2 made flesh. Apart from being completely alien, every Dwarf looked alike. Perhaps it was all the same Dwarf, Hledjolf presumably. In every single scene, the little creature was making something, or holding something, or handing something over to an unknown recipient. My head was starting to hurt at this point, so I looked for the bell.

It took me a while to find it, because I was looking for a button to push. I had to scan the images of the Dwarf several times until I found one of them holding a large bell. I pressed it, and jumped back as something that sounded like Big Ben echoed behind the door. I adjusted my coat and waited nervously for someone to appear.

I'd jumped before, I nearly fell over when the little carving turned its head to look at me. Then it spoke. 'Extinguish your light. Stand well back from the doors.'

I turned off the lights, placing the lantern on the staircase. I kept the torch in my hand, because I was beginning to feel very vulnerable again.

The doors didn't swing open, they slid aside into the rock. The tunnel beyond the doors was higher and more arched than the human tunnels, and only dimly visible, illuminated by glowing crystals embedded in the rock. I'm not a geologist, but I'm fairly sure that London is built on clay, not sandstone.

About ten feet from the doorway was a Dwarf. In the dim light, this one looked different from the carvings. It was obviously bipedal and bibrachial (if that's the posh word for having two arms), though there was still no neck. It was four feet tall, if that. I could feel the magick from here, far more than I felt with the Lord Mayor of Moles.

'Who seeks admittance to Hledjolf's Hall?' it boomed. It was dark, yes, but I should have seen something move when it spoke. Moley breathes, and when he speaks his tongue, teeth and lips move like yours and mine. Mostly.

I put on my best parade ground voice. 'Conrad Clarke, aspirant to Merlyn's Tower.'

'In Hledjolf's Hall, all are equal. Come in peace.'

There was a pressure pushing me back when I tried to move forward. Not physical, more like a firm hand being pressed against your soul. If I hadn't guessed before, I now knew that this was the real point of no return. If I set one foot in Hledjolf's Hall, I was committing my future to the world of magick. The last time I'd felt like this was when I'd dispatched my first cargo of stolen banknotes from Afghanistan.

The Dwarf didn't speak until I'd stopped at a respectful distance. Even in the dim light I could see that Dwarves are not made of flesh in any meaningful sense: they're made of stone. Their eyes are not water-filled lenses, they are many-faceted jewels. On the carving, they had mouths. This one had a small round hole, and the voice which came out was smoothly modulated, masculine, and completely artificial. I wanted to run upstairs and give Moley a hug – he had more of nature about him than this ... thing.

The voice came again, with no warning. 'We were told by the creature that you would be coming. He said that you were a human of little Gift and less law.'

'I follow the law,' I said, nonplussed. 'Usually.'

'Lore. L-O-R-E. You know almost nothing of the magickal world.'

'I'm willing to learn, but everyone seems too busy to teach me.'

'They are. And you are too poor to pay for instruction. You must learn or die.'

That was the moment I realised just how alien these creatures are. From the Allfather down to Mole, everyone and every thing I'd met so far had some sense of humour. Dwarves do not. I'm not sure how I'll cope with that.

'We are Hledjolf,' said the Dwarf. 'Follow us and we will tell you of our Hall.'

As well as lacking a sense of humour, the Dwarf made no non-verbal communication. The eyes and mouth didn't move, and there was no gesturing. When the creature turned to move down the tunnel, I snuck a look at the hands. I won't call them fingers, because they aren't. At the end of the arms were five digits, made of something darker than the body. Silicon, perhaps? If anything, they looked more like five thumbs, because they were arranged in the shape of a pentagon.

The disembodied voice resumed its monologue. 'All of us in this Hall are Hledjolf. You may speak to one as to all.'

And that settled it in my mind: I assume they used the masculine voice to create authority, but these things were neither male nor female, because you need sex to have male and female. Not just that, they also seemed to have some sort of shared consciousness thing going on. I resolved, in my head, to use the indeterminate pronoun: *they*.

'Other Halls have other Dwarves,' they said. 'Some dig, some mine, some make. We make and we dig, but not in the ground.'

'Yes. I heard that you'd subcontracted the digging to the Lord Mayor of Moles.'

The Dwarf slowed down. 'Why did you give that creature a title?'

'Because he deserves it. He's not a creature, he's a giant mole.'

'You do not know with what you meddle. That is your burden.'

'Fine,' I said. 'If you don't dig tunnels, what are you digging?'

'Behold,' said Hledjolf.

A barely visible door in the tunnel swished open. Beyond it was a cavernous space full of very expensive looking scientific equipment. And three Dwarves, staring at arrays of computer monitors.

'We seek the nature of Lux,' said Hledjolf. 'This is the world's foremost laboratory in Quantum Magick.'

So. Dwarves have no sense of humour, but they do feel pride. How does that work? And more importantly … 'What is Quantum Magick, if you don't mind me asking?'

'Lux is a force of nature, somewhat akin to light, somewhat akin to electricity. It gives consciousness and free will to all creatures, and to us it gives life. Magick is the meeting of Lux and matter. Quantum Magick is the search for order in the world of Lux.'

I stared at the Dwarves staring at their monitors. In all of human history, no one has come close to understanding free will *or* consciousness. 'Good luck with that,' I said.

'Luck has nothing to do with Lux,' said Hledjolf, 'despite what the Higher Powers might say.' He pointed to the wall, and the doors closed.

When I'd watched Hannah blast me across the room, and when I'd watched Li Cheng alter the memories of all those people in the tube station, I had been watching a force that could definitely change reality. The Lord Mayor of Moles was a freak of nature; the Dwarves were beyond freakish and well into the realms of nightmare. Yet, I supposed that all I had seen *might* be explained by physics, if the laws of physics were radically incomplete. Quantum Magick, eh? Who'd have thought it.

'Come. Your time here is limited.'

The next room was more like it. I could have been back in the RAF, visiting a particularly busy and well run engineering workshop. If the light had been better, I would have soaked in all the milling, grinding, measuring and polishing that buzzed around us. Hledjolf led me past an identical looking Dwarf who was holding a diamond in their five digits and doing something to it with a glittering scalpel. I looked up to see where my Dwarf was going and stopped dead in my tracks.

The walls of these rooms were mostly unadorned. In this room there were some relief pictures, a sort of Dwarvish art which we didn't come close enough for me to see properly, and something else. Glowing with a vibrant purple intensity was this shape:

If you haven't seen it before, it's the Valknut. I've seen it in books and on the Internet, and I've got one on my back. It's how the Allfather lets people know who he is.

'What's that doing here?' I asked.

'You can see it?' Hledjolf said. Dwarves can be surprised. Good to know.

'Clearly.'

Hledjolf stopped. I'll say they were thinking, for want of a better explanation. Maybe they were talking to each other via WiFi.

'We found him,' said the Dwarf. 'After Ragnarok, his Imprint was broken and scattered, but the Imprint of a Higher Power is not an easy thing to destroy. We found him on the field of battle, and we put him back together.'

'I hope it wasn't easy.'

'It was not. When we finished our Work, his sign glowed brightly in here. He owes us a debt for bringing him back which he is still paying off. When the valknut goes dark, the debt will be paid.'

The Dwarf pointed a few feet further along the wall. In the gloom, I could just make out a circular door standing proud of the wall like the cork in a bottle of champagne. It was as richly ornamented as the main doors to the Hall. As yet I couldn't make out the details, but something about it shivered ever so slightly.

'Behold. Our Vault,' said Hledjolf. They pointed again, and the shivering stopped. That must have been a Glamour. Hledjolf thought I hadn't been able to see the Vault until they removed the Glamour. That was one piece of information I was going to keep to myself. Score one run for the tail-ender.

The Dwarf continued, 'The Vault is our strength, our life and our power. You should see what it is we guard, but come no closer.'

They moved up to the door and inserted their digits into several places. As my Hledjolf worked, two other Dwarves approached, taking their place behind mine. My Hledjolf stepped back, and the door swung open, like a proper door should. It was very, very thick.

I had to hold my hand up to shield my eyes. I'd been told to stay back because the Lux was so strong. I took two steps further back, because shielding my eyes had no effect: I could still sense the power with my eyes closed. The two Dwarves who'd approached when the Vault was opened went inside. My Dwarf stood still.

The others reappeared, carrying small bars of gold. I could tell that there was something very different about these bars. This, I knew without asking, was Alchemical Gold. No wonder they lived under the Bank of England. 'Come,' it said, closing the door and leading me further round the room, then through another door out of the workshop.

Because of the power of these creatures, your mental image might have made them grow into giants. They really are only four foot high, which makes you wonder why they dug such big tunnels and had such spacious rooms in the Hall. This new room was on a different scale, almost human in dimensions.

It was also human in terms of furnishings: a stone table with a stone bench before it, and cushions, real silk cushions. Was it empathy, or just good customer service? I shrugged to myself, then shrugged again in a French accent. No, the British version was more appropriate.

On the far side of the table was a mounting block, the sort you see in riding stables. Hledjolf climbed up and pointed to the bench. I sat down. On the table was a metal stylus with what looked like a diamond tip. A Dwarvish pen, I suppose.

'This is the book,' said Hledjolf, gesturing at the table.

It came alive. The smooth stone rippled and became a sea of writing, most of which I couldn't read. The magick they had used to reveal the Book was completely different to what I sensed with a Glamour. This was some other Work altogether.

'We dig. We make. And we trade,' said the Dwarf. 'It is how we build our hoard of Lux.'

'I can believe that,' I said. I was making conversation, even though it was completely pointless. The longer I spent in this creature's company, the more I wanted to make bad puns and act like an idiot, just to prove I was human.

'Most of you who aspire to the King's Watch come through the front door, from the Invisible College. The trades they make, the jobs they do, all are for less Lux than is on offer here.' The Dwarf pointed to a place in the stone book where the writing was not only in Roman letters, but English to boot.

I held up my hand. 'So what you're saying is that Li Cheng and Vicky Robson both sat at this table.'

'And Hannah Rothman, too. Like you, she came via Bank station. That was before the Mole.'

Which meant that Li and Vicky were part of some sort of magickal establishment, some old school tie network. No wonder that Hannah hadn't given up on me completely: she was an outsider, too, and one who'd risen to the top. If I ever get a foot in the door at Merlyn's Tower, I'm sure I'll find that the King's Watch is as riven with politics as every other human institution. I wonder if Hledjolf's Hall has its own version.

I pointed to the mission he'd shown me before. 'Why do I have to undertake a difficult mission? Why can't I have an easy one, like Li Cheng?'

'Watch Captains must always climb the steeper path. Yours is the steepest of all because you have so little Gift. If you want any probability of survival, you need a powerful weapon to make up for your lack of Art.'

'You know that the Allfather put me up to this, don't you?'

The Dwarf nodded. For the first time, the creature nodded to me. When it did so, the head seemed to tilt on bearings.

'Did the Allfather send anyone before this mission came up?'

'No. This is the highest paying mission to appear for some time.'

I rubbed my chin.

I don't know why, but the Dwarf decided to add some information, *gratis*. 'This mission was first advertised in September, and it was open to female humans only. We believe that three died trying to get here. It was opened up to males as well as females on the first of December.'

'That's interesting. How long has the Lord Mayor of Moles been around?'

'He first broke out of his nest and into the tunnels last spring.'

A coincidence? Possibly. I nodded to the Dwarf to show my thanks and said, 'What's the mission?'

'A coven of Witches has lost a member. They wish to find her.'

I had some idea of how dangerous the magickal world could be. 'What if she's already dead?'

'Forgive us. In Dwarvish, we use the same words for *find what is stolen* and *take revenge on the thief*. If the Witch is dead, you must avenge her.'

I leaned over to try to read the Book.

'Do not waste your time,' said Hledjolf. 'It is only a contract. You will be given all the details when you visit the Coven. There is also a confidentiality clause. Do you accept?'

'How restrictive is the confidentiality clause?'

'The Coven must remain secret. In these cases, you have to accept a small Work. It will warn you before you breach the clause, but it is not invasive.'

I picked up the stylus. 'Where do I sign?'

The book flowed and reformed in front of me. A blank section appeared near my right hand. The text above it read *So shall it be unto Death*. I'd guessed that part already. The diamond tip of the stylus wrote as smoothly on the stone as a Mont Blanc pen on parchment. As I wrote, I felt the valknut on my back tingle. No going back now.

'Could we borrow your mobile phone?' said Hledjolf.

I passed it over. They stuck one of their digits into the USB socket, and went stock still. The screen of my phone lit up for a second, then went dark again. I was rather unhappy about that.

'Who said you could hack my phone? That wasn't in the deal.'

'Our apologies. We have not altered it in any way, merely added our contact details and a message giving you directions. What you do in the sunlight is as invisible to us as what we do in the dark is to you.'

I wasn't sure about that, but I wasn't in a position to argue. Seeing the phone did, however, jog my memory. 'I believe that you made a trade with Mole recently.'

'We have made several trades with that creature.'

'You took four phones from him.'

'We did.'

'I'm interested in one of them. It belonged to a man, and I'm guessing that it didn't have any social media apps on it.'

'We know the one you mean. You seek to identify its owner.'

'Did you?'

There was a pause. I'm not sure which emotion it represented, but I'm guessing annoyance or shame. Or both.

'We can see a long way into the communications network, but that was of no use. We do not know who that man's master was.'

'How about a deal? I'll take the phone off your hands, and I'll give my word that I'll let you know what I find out.'

Another pause. Did I see a glint in the crystal lenses that passed for eyes? I think there was definitely some sort of conversation going on.

'If you return from your first mission, and we have no news, then we might trade. You must go now.'

We were soon on our way back to where I'd first come in. The tradesman's entrance, I was going to call it, because that's what I am. Yes, I'm richer than most people, and yes I had the benefit of a private education, but I'm still a tradesman, hired to do other people's dirty work.

On the way out, Hledjolf said nothing, and I was too busy thinking over what I'd learnt and what I'd gotten myself into. When the doors were opened, and I saw the ante-chamber again, I had one last question.

'Where does that tunnel lead? The one that's marked *Other Routes*?'

'It is part of what we call the Old Network. Some humans call it by other names. You would become lost very quickly, and you are not ready to meet the Fleet Witches.'

The Dwarves were wrong about me getting lost, but I'll take their word about the Fleet Witches. One day, I'll come back to this ante-chamber and walk down that tunnel just to prove I can. So there.

I tried not to let all that show on my face, because even if Dwarves don't have the full range of human emotions, they clearly recognise them. I turned to Hledjolf and swallowed hard.

'Thank you,' I said. 'A pleasure doing business.' Then I held out my hand, to see what the creature did.

Blow me. The digits were rearranged into a line, and shook hands with me. Like a natural. I stepped in to the ante-chamber and the doors slid shut behind me.

7 — *Sisters, Sisters*

There was enough light in the ante-chamber to see outlines and shapes. When I'd first approached it, my torch and lantern had overwhelmed the Dwarvish illumination. Not wishing to spoil the moment, I left them switched off and took out my phone. I now had three magickal entries in my contacts list: Allfather, Lord Mayor of Moles and Hledjolf. There was a message from the Dwarf:

Contact the Lunar Sisters of Wray. You will find them at 54.094610, -2.589438.

That would be somewhere in North Lancashire, I think, and on almost the same longitude as HMP Cairndale. How do I know? Because one idle day last month I plotted hiring a chopper to break Mina out of prison and fly off into the sunset. I even plotted a flight path to the Isle of Man. I switched on my torch, and my foot was on the first step back to Moley's domain when I felt a little pulse of magick. It was behind me, low down and to my left.

I turned round and saw nothing. I crossed the ante-chamber and shone my torch on the carvings. A new image had appeared, just behind the carving of the Lord Mayor of Moles. It was me, marching into Hledjolf's Hall. The Dwarvish sculptor had missed something out, something which stoked my vanity enormously: he'd been too short to see my bald patch. Whatever happened to me in the future, there would always be a carving of me down here with a full head of hair.

The Lord Mayor himself didn't show his snout when I returned to the surface, and the work crew had repaired the wall of the tube station concourse. It had even been re-opened to passengers. With a shrug, I re-joined the rat race and grabbed some lunch. I spent the afternoon with a junior clerk at my solicitor's, drafting a new version of my Last Will and Testament. Mina would not be broke if something happened to me.

By then, the offices were starting to empty all around me. On a whim, I wandered up to Praed's Bank and lit a cigarette. At ten past five, Alain appeared, looking very chic in the new suit I'd paid for. He even looked quite pleased to see me.

'How's the placement going?' I asked.

'Very well, I think. This week is induction, so I 'ave met a lot of new people.'

'Fancy a coffee? Or a drink?'

'A drink sounds good, but not near here.'

'I'm not that disreputable, Alain.'

He shrugged. I do envy that. We walked slowly down St Swithin's Lane while he described some of his new co-workers. 'You haven't got a girlfriend at the moment, have you?' I said.

'Is it so obvious?'

'Yes. Let's try in here.'

He looked up at the sign on the wall. 'The Churchill Arms. That makes a change. Winston Churchill came to the rescue of France.'

I pointed to the picture nearby. 'Wrong Churchill. This bar is named after John Churchill, first Duke of Blenheim. As in the battle of Blenheim.'

'Never 'eard of it.'

We snagged a table ahead of the rush, and I chose a bottle of red from near his home town. He nodded approvingly at the label.

'You look tired, Conrad,' he said. I was exhausted, and I could see that the adrenalin was draining out of Alain's system now that he'd left the office.

'I am,' I said.

He smiled at me, in a totally human way, and I nearly kissed him. Spending time with Dwarves is not good for the soul. Or the Imprint, or whatever.

We raised our glasses. Alain took a long draught and sat back.

'There was a great bother at work today,' he said, 'when they closed the Bank Station. Was that something to do with you?'

Perhaps meeting Alain hadn't been such a good idea. On the other hand, it would be good practice for keeping the two worlds apart.

'Yes,' I said. 'But I was working for the good guys. I helped stop it.'

'I didn't think you would plant a bomb, Conrad, and if you 'ad, you would not be walking around 'ere in the open. But you were there last week.'

'I know. I was installing additional surveillance equipment. Acting on intelligence received.'

'That is all good, but why was I there? Your security services do not need me.'

This is what happens when you employ bright people. They ask awkward questions. Damnit.

'Do you want the truth?'

'Is it dangerous for me?'

'No. Not for you. Look, Alain, I've applied for a job. A very difficult and dangerous job. There was no real bomb at the Tube today, because it was part of a selection process. I was told to monitor Bank Station in whatever way I saw fit, using only my own resources. I had to show that I could hire people and keep it secret.'

Alain was troubled. 'Should you 'ave told me that?'

'It's allowed. I promise you this: if I pass the test, I won't recruit you for anything without telling you what's going on. At least enough for you to make what they call an informed decision. Deal?'

'Deal.'

We clinked glasses to seal it. I'd just made him a promise. I am now acutely conscious that if I make a promise, to anyone, I have to keep it. This was going to be a difficult path to tread.

'I'm allowed to cheat in this test,' I said, with a change of tone.

'That does not surprise me.'

'I found out the name of one of the other people involved. I want to track her down and talk to her. Well, I want you to track her down.'

'You want me to track down a spy? That sounds dangerous.'

'She's not a spy. She works in support. Not dangerous at all, because she's not trying to hide.'

'Then find her yourself.'

I waggled my phone at him. The one with no Internet, apps or video function. 'While you were learning about social media in school, I was flying Wokka Wokkas in Afghanistan and getting shot at. We play to our strengths.'

"*Comprends pas.* You fly a Wookie? Like *Star Wars*?'

'No. A *Wokka Wokka* is a Chinook helicopter. The really big ones. That's beside the point. Will you find this person for me?'

"Ow much?'

'How much do you get paid per hour at the bank?'

He frowned. Very deeply. 'We get 1.5 times your Minimum Wage. In France, this would not be allowed.'

'And in France, you wouldn't have a job, would you?'

He shrugged. I sighed.

'This is easy stuff, Alain. I'll pay you twenty pounds per hour, minimum two hours.'

He held out his hand. We shook. I gave him forty pounds. 'Cigarette?'

'*Oui.*'

We took our glasses outside, just as my phone burst into one of its very limited range of ringtones. Bollywood music filled the street, the sound of Mina.

'Girlfriend,' I said, pointing to the phone. Alain tried to give me some space, but there wasn't much room in the smoking zone. I took a deep breath. 'Hello? Is that you, Mina?'

'Conrad! Thank God. I didn't know if I'd got the number right. Why did you have to put it in code?'

'To give you something to do. It's so good to hear your voice, love.'

'And yours. I got your letter. Obviously. I mean, wow, Conrad. You wrote so much…' She stopped to take a breath. I could hear that she was nearly in tears. So was I. 'I'm fine,' she continued. 'What are you doing? Remember…'

'…I can't lie. I don't want to. I'm out for a drink with a French colleague. I'd rather be out with you, but that can wait.'

I heard a catch in her throat. 'Is your colleague gorgeous and sexy and very chic?'

'I'll ask.'

'No…'

I turned to Alain. 'Are you gorgeous and sexy?' From the phone, I could hear Mina's continued embarrassment.

'*Mais, oui*,' said Alain.

'Yes,' I said to Mina.

'That was a man's voice!' she said. I could almost see her standing with her hand on her hip, wagging her finger at me.

'Of course,' I replied. 'You didn't ask…'

'I'm sorry. I know I've got to trust you, Conrad, but it's not easy. Every day one of the girls finds out that their man's gone off with their best friend, or their sister. Or their mother. That's really common. And so wrong.'

'It won't be long. Four months.'

She sighed. 'I know. Everything just drags in here. That's the worst part. Even worse than the food. That's disgusting. Unless you like endless piles of carbohydrate.'

'Can't be worse than the RAF. I survived nearly twenty years of that.'

'Damn. I've only got a half a minute left.'

'Listen, I've got a job up your way soon. What do you want me to bring?'

'Warm clothes. Lots of warm clothes. And books. I love you, Conrad.'

'I love you, too.'

The screen went dark. I didn't know whether to feel happy or sad.

'She is far away?' said Alain, gently.

'Very far. I'll tell you about her one day. Let's get this job sorted.'

We returned to the bar and I took out my little notebook. I need one because I can't add to-do lists to my phone like everyone else. On a blank page, I wrote,

Vicky Robson, born Newcastle upon Tyne. Mid to early twenties. White. On Facebook. Friends with Desirée Haynes, same age, black, born London. Probably.

'Call me or email me,' I said, handing over the note. We finished our wine and left.

Before my visit to Hledjolf's Hall, I'd been planning to re-occupy the spare room in Clarke's Mess. Now that I knew my mission was up north, I relented. Only another two nights on the bed-settee. I could live with that.

One of the tenants was going out, and he never makes his bed. After the day I'd had, and half a bottle of wine, I waited until he'd gone and crashed out in his room for a couple of hours. There is more than one sort of hot-bedding in the RAF.

Next stop, Wray. I entered the co-ordinates for the Lunar Sisters into Google Earth and wasn't surprised to see an empty field in the middle of nowhere. They must have a good Occulter, but I was right about the general location – it was about twenty minutes' drive from HMP Cairndale, just over the watershed into the Cowan Valley. I spent a desultory twenty minutes looking for other references to the Lunar Sisters, but if you can manipulate satellite images, fooling the rest of the Internet is a doddle. I turned up nothing.

Alain called me at half past nine and told me to check my email. I brought up his message. 'Is that the woman?' he asked.

He'd sent me several pictures of Vicky, mostly selfies, some with Desirée. The snap she'd shown to Li Cheng and I was not amongst them.

'Should your girlfriend be jealous?' he asked.

Oh dear. I was going to have a very distressing conversation with Vicky, and the sooner the better.

'Conrad? Are you there?'

'Sorry, Alain. Thanks, and no, Mina doesn't need to be jealous. I, on the other hand, am not going to introduce you two for some time. Look, could you keep an eye on their feeds, or whatever, and let me know if Vicky goes out somewhere. The very second. I want to catch her away from work.'

'No problem. You 'ave twenty pounds of my time left.'

'Oh, and another thing. Amélie works in that upmarket boutique on Regent Street, doesn't she?'

'Yes. Why?'

'They don't open until ten thirty. Tell her to meet me outside Primark, Oxford Street, at half past nine.'

'I can do that. What do you want with 'er? I don't want anyone else to get 'urt.'

'Only some shopping.' I took the plunge. 'It's Mina. She's in prison. She needs clothes, and if I send anything more expensive than Primark, it causes trouble. I'll tell you about it later.'

'OK. I'll be in touch.'

Prison is a bad experience. I've had some bad experiences, and pretending that they haven't happened is not an option. If Mina ever met my parents – or Alain – it was best they knew the truth in advance. You might say it's not my decision; that's a risk I'll have to take.

I also sent Alain a link to the French Wikipedia entry for *La Bataille de Höchstädt*, their name for John Churchill's triumph at Blenheim.

Alain text back: Amélie would see me tomorrow. He ignored the reference to Blenheim.

He could have warned me that Amélie's English isn't wonderful. It took nearly ten minutes, and two cigarettes, before I got through the message that Mina was shorter than Amélie, the same size width-ways, needed warm clothes and that she was of Indian extraction. In the end, we resorted to a translation app. Finally, the light dawned.

'*Bon!* Follow me,' said Amélie, sweeping into the store and handing me a large basket. She was ruthless, determined, and finished in twenty minutes. There was far more colour in the basket than I would have chosen, but what do I know? I gave Amélie some money for herself and headed for the cash desk.

I spent the rest of the day sorting out cars, returning the hired Hyundai to a branch in Luton and retrieving my Land Rover Defender, along with the AK47 from the woods.

At lunchtime, Alain called. He sounded quite excited. 'Your lady friends are very well connected, Conrad.'

That made me slightly uneasy. 'Oh? What makes you say that?'

'Tonight, the girls will be in Club Justine, in Mayfair. Vicky says that she 'as an invitation to the birthday party of a footballer. You've probably never 'eard of 'im.'

'Brilliant. I'll catch her there. Did they say what time?'

He laughed. '*Mon ami*, you 'ave more chance of getting a Légion d'honneur from the French president than you do of getting into that club. It is way out of your league, as you say.'

'We'll see about that. Many thanks.'

Two minutes on the laptop told me he was right. I drummed my fingers on the table and looked out of the window for inspiration. I checked Club Justine's location, and realised that I knew someone who might well have entry to such a place.

'What on earth do you want to go there for?' said Rachael, two minutes later. At least she'd taken my call.

'I want to crash the party, of course. And I want to see someone away from work. Their work.'

'It's not my natural habitat, but I have been. I think I could get us on the list. It's very expensive.'

'Then it would be cheaper just to get me on the list. No need to drag yourself out on my account.'

She laughed. 'If you're going, I'm going. I'm not going to miss this.'

I couldn't argue with that. 'I'm not stopping all night. Once I've made contact, you'll be on your own. Quite literally, I should think.'

'You'd be surprised. What are you going to wear?'

'Clothes.'

'Ha ha. You won't get in wearing your normal wardrobe. Have you got that evening suit in London?'

'Yes.'

'Good. It's your only hope.'

Many years ago, I invested in a Saville Row hand tailored dinner suit. It came in very handy on many occasions with the RAF. It's one of the few suits I've ever owned which fitted properly. When I said to Hannah that I couldn't afford a new uniform, I wasn't joking. That had to be custom made, too.

This is going to be embarrassing. I have to state, as a matter of fact, that my baby sister looked very good when I picked her up. I won't go into details, because it will only inflate her ego further. We were on the list. We got in. I spent fifty quid on a cocktail for Raitch and a mocktail for me. I hated the place.

'Why are we here?' she asked, slurping most of her drink.

I had to lean right in to be heard over the noise. I won't distinguish it with the description *music*. Do I sound like an old fogey? Do I care?

'I need to find someone. Look out for two young women, one black, one white.'

She pointed to the door. 'Not those two, surely?'

Rachael had just spotted two supermodels sashaying into the club. I'd looked up and seen Vicky and Desirée, and that was the problem. I stared hard at the magickal pair, trying to see them as others saw them. It was hard work, but getting easier: I could now use my Sight to flick between a Glamour and the underlying reality.

In reality, Vicky had made an effort to look her best. She'd got a nice dress, new shoes and she'd spent a long time on her hair and makeup. All of this contributed to the Glamour, in its way. In everyone else's eyes, her dress was tighter, she was thinner, her legs were perfectly shaped in near transparent nylon, and her heels were two inches taller. Her hair glowed and her skin was a flawless bronze.

Desirée had done the same, in a way. In almost every measure of beauty, judged by women, Desirée was better looking than Vicky, and her Glamour was less extreme. Except for one thing. She'd lightened her skin shade by two tones, and made her nose more pointed. I didn't know who to feel sorriest for.

'Bloody hell, Conrad. If you're interested in one of those two, you're playing well out of your league.'

'You're not the first person to tell me that today.'

'Does Mina know about this?'

'Knock it off, Raitch. This is business. Tell me, do you recognise any bits of their outfits?'

'I see a Gucci dress, Balenciaga shoes, and the one on the right, she's got a di Sanuto Exclusive.'

'What's that?'

'Her bag. Wow. I've only seen two of those before, in real life.'

Oh, Rachael. How I wish I could tell you the truth.

Vicky and Desirée moved through the club with assured grace. The one thing their Glamour hadn't been able secure for them was a reserved table, but judging from the looks they were getting, it wouldn't be long before they were invited beyond the rope into the birthday party. I had to make my move before then. I was working out how to split them up when they did it for me: Vicky found a seat and Desirée headed for the bar.

I pointed to Vicky. 'Go over and keep her occupied. Just for a second.'

Once upon a time, Rachael was a shy girl. Not any more. She hooted with laughter and headed for Vicky. I intercepted Desirée just ahead of an overweight, overprivileged oligarch's son. 'Is it Miss Haynes?' I asked in my best Wimbledon voice (it's what we call the accent that most of the Air Commodores put on).

A look of caution came over Desirée's face. 'Who wants to know?'

'Conrad Clarke. I met your mother the other day. Please give her my regards when you're next in touch. I love what you've done with the dress. Was it from Topshop originally?'

The caution turned to naked fear. I was right: Desirée had more to lose than Vicky. 'Come with me,' I said.

I headed towards the table where my sister was fawning over the young sorcerer. As soon as Vicky spotted me, she leapt up, barging Rachael out of the way and coming up to us.

'What the fuck are you doing here?' she demanded. You can take the girl out of Newcastle… Rachael looked very bemused.

'We need a word, Vicky. Where does one go for a smoke in this place.'

She grabbed my arm and marched me into a hidden corner. She pushed through a door and I found myself in a dinky little outdoor area, complete with canopy and patio heater. Very select. Vicky dragged me into a quiet corner.

'How did you find us?' she hissed.

'If I'm still alive, I'm going to have words with the Constable about use of social media. I'm guessing that what you've done with the Glamour won't go down well either.'

She looked genuinely distressed, and very young. 'They don't care what I get up to, so long as it's not illegal. It's Desirée. If the College find out, she'll be in serious trouble. Like really serious.'

'I don't answer to Hannah, or the College. Yet. I won't say anything about tonight if you give me some help.'

She nodded.

'Good. Go back in and separate Desirée from my sister, then pack her off in a taxi. Oh, and bring me back a bottle of water.'

She shuffled on her heels. 'We don't bring any money with us. It's part of the game.'

This was a game I'm glad I'll never play. I handed her some money without further comment and made myself comfortable. Vicky stood a little taller and put her Glamour back on. She must have been at the bar when I got a text from Rachael: *You are so going to tell me what's going on.* There was only one thing to say in return: *I could tell you, but I'd have to kill you...*

Vicky returned, deflated, and carrying two bottles of water. She put a five pound note and some change on the table. 'Give us a fag,' she said. I lit two and passed one over. 'I don't know what I can do, Conrad, I really don't. You could be up against anything, and you can't tell me, can you?'

Out of perversity, I tried to tell her about my mission in Wray. As soon as I opened my mouth to speak, the valknut on my back made its presence felt. It burned like molten gold, then stopped when I changed my intention. 'Why do you do it, Vicky?'

I know I sound like a teacher, saying that, but I was trying not to sound like her dad.

'Do you know how much a captain gets paid?'

'Yes. About ten grand less than a Squadron Leader. It's still a bloody good wage for someone your age. How old are you, anyway?'

'Twenty three.'

Blimey. Nearly a child, barely a woman in some ways. 'How many kids from your school are on that wage, or anything like it? Even if they'd joined the real army, they'd still be second lieutenants.'

She waved her cigarette around. 'It's easy for the Watch Captains. They get overseas allowance automatically. And they get the plunder. My flat's costing me a fortune. All I was doing was having a bit of fun.'

There was an issue here, but I don't know if it's an issue for the Constable or for Vicky's therapist, if she has one. Tennille said that a lot more women were coming into the system. I'm willing to bet that most of the top brass in magick are male, and even older than me. Not that I'm old. I decided to park the whole question of Glamour for another day. Conscious of the rune on my back, I tried something vaguer than *Lunar Sisters*. 'I've got my mission,' I said. 'I just need to know a hell of a lot more about magick, that's all.'

Vicky looked as if she wanted to help. She really did. She also had no clue where to start.

'Look, Vicky, is my Gift really so small? Is there nothing I can do, magick wise? I'm beginning to feel like a small boy in the grown-up changing rooms round here.'

'Howay, man, that's not a good image to put in me head.' She shuddered, then shook herself back together. 'Have you found yourself doing *anything* different since you were enhanced?'

I decided to be honest. 'I can see through Glamours. Not just yours, even the Dwarven ones. Don't tell anyone.'

She nodded in approval. 'There's hope for you yet. Give us your lighter.'

I handed over the fake Zippo. She looked at the lurid image of Ganesha with distaste and pulled the lighter apart, then passed the innards back to me. 'Here, I don't want to ruin me nails. Take out the flint and spring for us.'

I did as she asked, passing the now useless mechanism back to her. She reassembled the lighter, and lit it. There was just a flicker of magick when she made the spark with no flint.

'How did…?'

'Watch carefully. I'm gonna do it again. A few times.'

I watched. She rolled the wheel with her finger, and a little burst of light came from where the flint should have been. It worked. I was amazed. The second and third time, I tried to see what she was doing by using my Sight. I got a feeling of heat, great heat. And pressure.

She passed the lighter to me. 'This is your first Work. Where I studied magick, we called it Quantum Magick.'

'I heard about that yesterday. Hledjolf told me the basics.'

She nodded enthusiastically. 'That's right,' she said. 'What I'm doing is using Lux to compress a small amount of air. Really compress it. It heats up to hundreds of degrees Celsius when you do that. Then I let it go in the direction of the wick. That ignites the vapour. Simple.'

'Right.'

'Honest.'

She watched me stare at the lighter, and she watched nothing happen. She took it back.

'You need to use your thumb. You have to be really, really good at Works before you can do them without a hand gesture, or a wand, or whatever. It's how the brain works: you channel the Lux through your arm. Have another look.'

She made the flame again, and this time I sensed the tiny pulse of magick leave her finger. She passed the lighter back to me. This was the moment I was going to prove them all wrong. This was the moment when I proved that Conrad Clarke was going to be a power in the world of magick.

I focused on the lighter using my Sight. My thumb became a press, squeezing down the air and forcing it towards the petrol vapour. I felt the magick flow through my arm into my finger. It felt like I'd just done a one-handed pull-up, and then my lighter farted.

There's no other word for the noise: it let out a limp fart. Vicky had the good grace not to patronise me by taking it seriously, and laughed like a Geordie drain.

'That's so funny, Conrad. I've never seen that before.'

'I'm glad I've brightened your evening. What went wrong?'

She calmed down. 'Actually, nothing. You just need to try harder. A lot harder. And try to work with a smaller volume: you only need a tiny amount of heat to light the vapour.'

I can do harder. I tried again, and this time the effort was like doing a one-handed pull-up whilst strapped to a horse. When the flame ignited, I had sweat pouring off my forehead and ruining my dress shirt. The first thing I did was unfasten my bow tie.

'Cheers,' said Vicky, raising her water bottle. 'You've now mastered Magick 101. With that, you can do all sorts of things. You know that woman who tried to kill you yesterday? That was exactly the same Work.'

'But on a bigger scale, I imagine.'

Actually, I couldn't imagine. I could see that they were the same in theory – my assailant had used compressed air to mimic the effects of a bomb blast, localised to a tiny vector. Hannah had done the same in her office. I could not imagine having the power or skill to attempt anything similar.

'Does it get easier with practice?'

'A bit. And before you ask, no one knows how or why.'

'While I rest my arm, can I ask you a question? I really understand if you can't answer.'

She nodded.

'How did the Constable get her injuries?'

Vicky used the smokers' trick of tapping ash to give herself some thinking time. She looked me in the eye when she answered. 'I really don't know all the details. It happened before I joined the King's Watch. I do know that she lost her husband because of it, and that she destroyed a Revenant. She was promoted to Deputy after that.'

I left it there. Vicky snagged another cigarette from the packet and held it for me to light. I gritted my teeth and tried to reduce the volume of air even further. It worked, and it took less effort than last time, but I was starting from a point of near exhaustion.

'I'll finish this, then I'll go,' said Vicky. 'Do you want to see what the next level is all about?'

'Go on. Depress me even further.'

She dipped into her bag and took out a very slim silver lighter. 'I don't bring my own fags,' she said, 'but I always bring my own lighter. Have a look.'

I fiddled with the lighter. As far as I could tell, the electronic ignition had been disabled, and instead of gas, it was filled with some liquid. I shook a drop on to my hand. 'What's this?'

'Water. Lick it if you don't believe me.'

'I think we've gone beyond the conjuring jokes. I can see your power, Vicky.'

She accepted my remarks as an acknowledgement of reality rather than a compliment. She reminded me of a lot of the young female officers in the RAF – accomplished professionals in a dangerous world, but naïve in so many ways. This often led to problems, or, for some of the older men, opportunities. I had made, and kept, a vow not to sleep with any woman below Flight Lieutenant.

Vicky took her lighter and lit it as if the little device were full of gas. Now I really was impressed.

'Mages have always been able to do that,' said Vicky. 'It was only in the eighteenth century that they worked out what they were doing, and only recently that we've truly understood what the Work does.' She lit the lighter again. 'What I'm doing is loosening the covalent bond in the water molecules. That gives a stream of hydrogen and oxygen atoms. As they rise up, I just light them again.'

My mind boggled, and grasped the only thing it could focus on. 'Isn't that rather inefficient?'

She gave me a strange look. 'Obviously. It's only an exercise, Conrad. If I really found myself without a light, I'd just do this.' She picked up another cigarette, sucked on it, and the end glowed. 'See?'

This gave her two fags. She passed the new one to me, and I could taste her lipstick. It was time to go home. Thankfully, Rachael had already disappeared. I convinced Vicky to give me her phone number on the understanding that I wouldn't use it. No, I don't understand the logic either, and I saved my last question until we were waiting for her taxi.

I pointed to her bag, the one thing that had remained the same when I saw through her Glamour. 'My sister told me about the bag. How did you come by that if you're so poor?'

She looked away before replying. 'Officers of the King's Watch can't accept cash payments for outside jobs. I did a Search for someone. They gave me the bag.'

I didn't push. Whatever she was hiding could stay her own business for now.

Before going to bed, I got out my notebook and jotted down a list of things I'd come across and which I still knew next to nothing about. Or completely nothing. It was quite a long list:

- The Invisible College
- Sorcerors and their Searches
- Higher Powers
- Demi-Powers
- Spirits
- Dragonlings
- Revenants
- Chymists
- The Lunar Sisters

I left early on Friday morning for Clerkswell, and spent the afternoon talking things through with the builder. We began by standing on the edge of the lawn, admiring the perfect symmetry of the six molehills. I knew what had caused them, and I knew that he could see them as plainly as me. I asked him what he thought it might be.

'Victorian drainage,' he said confidently. 'Your Victorians were great underground engineers. I'm sure they put radial drainage under the grass. The moles are just following the pattern.'

I wondered, after that, how many other manifestations of magick were casually brushed under the carpet. Or buried under the grass.

The builder didn't want to start on the roof until the spring, and I didn't want him to until I had more of an idea of where I'd be living. The old stables were different. He could start work on them in a week. We agreed a price and shook hands. The hardest part was telling Dad that he had seven days to decide what to do with the remains of his rubbish – sorry, the last of his stock. He said he'd get an old friend to deal with it. At the end of the conversation, he thanked me.

'What for, Dad?'

'For making me cut the tie. I'll feel a lot better when that lot's gone. I can concentrate on building up the business over here.'

That's the Clarke spirit all over: it's never too late for new beginnings.

'But don't tell your mother,' he added. I said goodbye, promising to keep it our secret.

On Friday evening, I got two calls. One was from Rachael.

'I'm not going to give up, Conrad. Please give me *some* idea of what you were doing in that club with those two gorgeous creatures.'

'A favour for an old friend. He's in Afghanistan, and he's not happy about the company his daughter is keeping. He's divorced. My mission was to tell her some home truths.'

She sighed contentedly. 'That's a lovely lie, Conrad. I feel so much better now.'

'Rachael! How could you say such a thing about your brother?'

'Because it's true. See you later.'

The second call was from Alain.

'Why did you not tell me 'oo is your sister?' he said, in a very accusing tone.

'Eh? How do you know about Rachael?'

'Because I looked at photos from Club Justine last night. I saw you with that girl, Vicky. In another picture, someone 'ad tagged you with Rachael Clarke. Why did you not tell me you know 'er.'

'Because she's my little sister. Why should you be interested in my little sister?'

'*Merde*. For such a dangerous man, Conrad, you know very little. Your sister works for one of the richest asset management firms in London. I would give anything to 'ave 'ad my placement there instead of Praed's Bank. In fact, I can change after six months…'

'If you knew my sister, you wouldn't be so quick to work for her. And if you want me to put in a good word, you're going to have to do me a massive, massive favour. One day.'

'If you could get me into her business, I would be your bitch for a month.'

That was the most alarming thing I'd heard in weeks. Even more alarming than meeting a talking giant mole. 'We'll see,' was all I could manage over the phone.

The weekend was spent checking out second hand cars in Cheltenham. I found a low mileage Volvo XC70, as used by traffic police all over Britain. It didn't quite have the all-terrain capability of the Defender, but it wouldn't destroy my fillings every time I went over fifty – the drive down on Friday had not been a pleasant experience. I also spent time practising my little Work.

I got slightly better at focusing, and I came to the conclusion that I was actually draining something from my arm muscles. I'd seen Vicky's arms quite clearly in that dress – they had less muscle on them than the average chicken drumstick. That's not an insult, just a statement of fact. Clearly things were different for her.

On Sunday morning, I did thirty press-ups. The same muscles which had contracted when I heaved myself off the ground were used when I sparked my lighter. I made a note in my magickal journal, and tried to light a fag without a flame.

This meant using my lungs to generate the magick. The first time I tried, the whole thing burst into flames and singed my eyebrows. I got through four packets before I had any element of control.

I didn't go straight to Wray on Monday. I was saving that for the following morning, when I could make an early start. After slogging up the M6, I dropped in on some people whose lives I'd saved when an associate of mine had set their farmhouse on fire while they were asleep. He was the guy I shot on Cowan Sands.

I found the Kirkham boys in the barn, looking at a cow. They have a prize dairy herd and spend a lot of time staring at various parts of bovine anatomy. This one was clearly in calf. The Kirkham boys are a double act – father and son, Joseph and Joe. In their flat caps, only the more severe slope of Joseph's shoulders allowed me to tell them apart at a distance.

'Conrad!' exclaimed Joe when he saw me. He gave me a vigorous handshake. 'We were just talking about you,' he said, pointing to the cow.

'I'm not sure that's entirely flattering,' I replied. 'How are the kids? And Kelly's arm?'

When I did my heroic rescue, Joe's wife had broken her wrist climbing out of the upstairs window.

'She's doin' OK, considering,' replied Joe. 'Mind you, Dad's having to help out with the cooking, which isn't always a good thing. House is coming on.'

All three of us turned to look across the farmyard at the ruined hulk of their home. I hadn't been back since the night it all happened, and I was relieved to see that the fire brigade had managed to stop the fire spreading to the roof. All the windows were now boarded up, and several builders' vans were parked in the lane leading up to the house. I could hear radios tuned to different stations blasting out from inside.

'It's funny,' said Joe. 'Plasterers always listen to hip-hop and joiners like cheesy pop.' He felt absurdly grateful to me; I felt equally guilty for what had happened. If I'd have found things any worse, I'd promised myself that I would make up the financial shortfall. It didn't seem necessary, as Joseph explained.

'You know we're living in the cottage,' he said. It was part of the farm and I'd stayed in it myself for a month. 'Well, because that's registered as a rental business, the insurers are paying the going rate. We're making money. Not only that, some fella from the Ministry came along and said they'd pay us a grant if we kept quiet about what were going on in yon shed.'

You can trust farmers to fall on their feet. What was going on in the shed had been very illegal – wholesale money laundering. I'd been doing that, too.

'That bonus you gave the lad,' continued Joseph. 'We were just discussing what to do with it.' (When I shot Will Offlea, I'd swiped twenty five grand from his backpack and handed it over to them.)

107

Joseph pointed back to the cow. 'If the old girl doesn't produce a heifer, we were thinking of raising our own bull. She's from the best stock. If you've got the cash, you can clean up big time. It's a risk, of course...'

'But one worth taking,' I said. 'I'm up north on a job. Strictly legal, this time. I'd love to pop back and see what happens.'

'That would be grand,' said Joseph. 'We might have something for you, as well.'

On that tantalising note, I left them and drove a short way north to the Fylde Equine Research Centre, home to Olivia Bentley (née Jennings). At some point in the near future, Olivia and the rest of the Jennings clan would be sitting at the inquest into Sir Stephen's death. They would recognise my voice when I gave evidence from behind the screen: 'Squadron Leader J' would be telling a pack of lies about what had gone on. It was part of the price for my freedom: I had to be part of the cover-up. I wanted to square things with Olivia before that happened. But not today. I set off for Hartsford Hall.

Joseph and Joe Kirkham are distantly related to the Earls of Morecambe Bay. Their great-something grandfather was a Kirkham-Malbranche, younger son of the Earl and founder of Fylde Racecourse. They dropped the Malbranche bit when they became farmers. The current Earl spends most of his time in London, and the ancestral home is a country house hotel with Michelin starred restaurant. Very nice it is too. Being January, I got a good rate for three nights. Regardless of what happened tomorrow, I had to stay until Wednesday because that was when visiting happens at the prison.

I didn't eat in the restaurant on Monday night. There are limits. I drove down to Cairndale, a small market / railway / university town between Lancaster and Kendal with several good Indian Restaurants.

I did enjoy the Hartsford Breakfast on Tuesday, though. Most hotels don't serve cooked breakfasts warm enough, and you find yourself rushing to eat it while the food is still hot. Not at Hartsford Hall. The plate was almost glowing, and every component had been carefully chosen. I made a mental apology to the Moorgate café and tucked in.

To get to Wray, I went through Kirkby Lonsdale and took the road down the Lune valley. Just after the turning, I slowed right down because I was laughing so much. There is a hamlet there called *Burrow with Burrow*, and a place called *Burrow Hall*. I wonder if they have problems with moles.

Wray itself is a lovely little Lancashire village, complete with pub etc, and stands on the river Roeburn. If this job took a while, I fancied staying here. To get to the Lunar Sisters, you take a tiny road out the back of Wray which leads nowhere, and takes a long time to get there. The only traffic is farm-related.

The road out of Wray runs along a ridge, with dairy farms sloping down to either side, some sheep... I'm losing you, aren't I? I'd worked out that the latitude and longitude which the Dwarves had given me pointed to a location 1.7m along the road, on the right, or south west side of the carriageway. I slowed down as I approached the target. A post and wire fence ran unbroken into the distance. I slowed to crawling pace and stared hard at the flock of sheep grazing up to the fence. Nothing.

I picked up speed and started to look for a turning place. I drove back past the sheep, closer this time because they were on my side... I slammed on the brakes. As soon as I'd approached the target, I'd started staring *at the wrong side of the road*. The sheep were on the northern side, so close you could see their ear-tags. I put the car in gear, ready to drive away, then put on the handbrake.

This was more than just a Glamour. There was a compulsion here which stopped me looking at where the target was located. I checked for traffic (I don't know why – there hadn't been so much as a quadbike since I'd left Wray), and closed my eyes, putting my hands in my lap and relaxing. I imagined flying over the Roeburn valley, following the road, and looking... left.

I opened my eyes. There. A gap in the fence, just wide enough for a small lorry, and a tarmac road leading down. I put the car in gear and swung round to make the descent.

Just down the hill from the road, the track widened into a turning circle with no exit. Convenient if you've taken the wrong route. I was swinging the car round to drive back up to the road when it hit me again: *No one builds a turning circle in a field*. With some difficulty, I reversed part of the way back up the hill and drove down again, imagining my Volvo was a chopper. I risked closing my eyes and opening them at the right moment. There again – a cattle grid and another track leading further down the hillside. I drove straight at the cattle grid and machine gun fire echoed around me.

I did what I always did on a mission. I gritted my teeth and flew into the danger. There were women down there relying on me...

When I got over the cattle grid, the gunfire died away, and I could stop to get my breath back. I turned off the engine and opened the window. Nothing but birdsong and the breeze. I was shaking like a leaf.

This was powerful stuff. The Ward on that gate had reached inside my head, found my biggest fear and delivered it in stereo. It wasn't just a sense of impending doom, it was big-screen HD sound effects, and delivered instantly. How was that possible? And that was an automated Ward, not the deliberate probings of a powerful magician. Perhaps Hannah was right, and that this was a suicide mission.

I drove round a corner, down a dip, and found myself in front of a big stone wall. The track had given way to gravel, and there was a neat little area for me to park, next to a blue Renault. There were big gates in the wall, and they'd made no effort to hide them with a Glamour. I got out of the car and lit a cigarette.

Through the gates, I could see a drive which curved to the left and was soon obscured by mature trees. The wall disappeared left and right, unbroken except for a small door, about twenty yards away. A cottage, or lodge, had been built up to the main wall, and that little door clearly led inside. It was free of glass, and made of stout wood. No point in having a wall if you put a shoddy door in the middle of it.

I could see a small, gleaming brass plate next to the gates. I carefully stubbed out my fag, dropped the butt in my ashtray and sauntered over to the gates. The brass plate announced that this was the Convent of the Holy Mother. The gates were padlocked. I was trying to see further into the property when a voice from along the wall disturbed me.

'Can I help you?'

A middle-aged woman wearing an apron over a sweater and jeans was standing in the doorway to the lodge.

'I was rather hoping that I could help you,' I said, walking towards her. She had an outdoorsy look, little makeup and her greying hair was cut short. When I got a little closer, she put her hand on the door, ready to jump back inside. I stopped walking and smiled at her. 'I'm looking for the Lunar Sisters,' I said.

Her left hand flew up to her chest in shock, and she gripped a pendant hanging round her neck. I braced myself for another assault: this world of magick is worse than the Wild West.

'Who sent you?' she said.

'The Dwarves,' I answered simply. It either meant something or it didn't.

'Wait there.'

She disappeared through the door. I used the time to examine the wall more closely, running my fingers over the surface and trying to sense magick. It was there alright: deep within the stones I heard singing. A woman singing. A women's choir answering in the chorus. I couldn't make out the words.

The woman reappeared from the door, now minus apron. 'Come in. The Mother will see you.'

It's not every day you get an offer like that.

8 — *Hospitality*

The little door in the big wall led to a passageway which ran right through the lodge and opened on to a garden beyond. Further stout doors along the passage offered security and privacy to whoever lives here. I was shown through an open door to the left and into a sitting room.

'Tea or coffee?'

'I'll have whatever the Mother is having.'

The woman retreated to the passage, leaving the door open behind her to get some fresh air inside.

The sitting room was a temple. A temple to chintz. There had been a room like this at Elvenham House when I was growing up, and Mother – *my* mother – had gotten rid of it a long time ago. The soft furnishings in here dated from the same period, judging by the degree of fading on the back of an armchair which faced the window. Everything was spotless, and it looked like it was used only once a month. If that. I was torn between having a good look at the garden and examining the pictures. I opted for the pictures, because not all my time in Dad's shop was wasted: I could see that the artwork was all original.

Two photographs were paired together, both showing a building nestling in folds of wooded countryside. On the left was a monochrome print, almost sepia in its browns, and with the completely washed out sky you get from Victorian negatives. The one on the right was more recent – it was dated two years ago, and the artist had helpfully added *Lunar Hall* to the caption. Sharp, saturated greens from the foliage contrasted with a honeyed, sunset glow on the building.

Lunar Hall is much bigger than Elvenham House. I could detect a core of thick walls, probably hundreds of years old, with side extensions in similar stone but with different windows. The photographs were taken looking uphill, and I'm guessing that a lot of the paintings were made from the same spot, but with the artist facing downhill, looking across the valley.

There were oils and watercolours, pencil drawings and one engraving. The styles ranged from cubist to realist. I think. I'm not that much of an expert, nor could I tell you whether they were any good. All featured a wood – sometimes with women walking towards it, sometimes with a single woman, usually with no figures at all. On the wall opposite the door was a set of four oils by the same hand. I didn't need the labels to tell me that there was one for each season.

The detailed changes to nature had been meticulously recorded by the artist. Dying snowdrops and proud daffodils stalked the fringes of spring;

the superabundance of berries and damp grass could have been Keats's *To Autumn* rendered in paint. Such detail had come at a price – the perspective was all wrong. I'm guessing that someone had filled four sketchbooks with studies, then rammed them into a broad-brush background wherever they would fit. Or maybe it was deliberate. As I said, I'm not much of an expert on art, but I can tell that you that I wouldn't have used those paintings to navigate by.

'Do you like them?'

I didn't jump out of my skin because I'd sensed a new presence. I hadn't heard anything, I'd sensed her coming into the room, and I was sensing her trying to scope me out with her Sight.

'I'll save you the trouble of assessing me,' I said. 'I can make a spark with my lighter. See?' I flicked the wheel and lit the flame. 'But that's it. That is the limit of my magick. Sorry if I've disappointed you.'

She stopped using her Sight to evaluate me, and we both looked each other up and down. I hope she saw me as the prosperous countryman I sometimes am; I saw her as a nun. A green nun, with sweeping robes in pale green and a darker green cloak with hood. I put her age at about sixty, and her hair had once been blond, now a most attractive silver, swept back from her face, tied in a loose braid and piled in the hood of her cloak. She wore even less makeup than the woman with the apron, but she did have intricate dangly earrings, and I could see other glints of gold on her wrists and around her neck.

I stepped forwards and held out my hand. I wasn't sure whether she would touch a mere man like me, but she returned the handshake with warm, professional grip, before withdrawing her hand to the sleeve of her cloak.

'Conrad Clarke, former squadron leader, No 7 Squadron, RAF. At your service, ma'am.'

She looked a little alarmed at the introduction, not because it was intimidating, but because it meant she was expected to do the same.

'I am the Second Sister. People call me Mother, not ma'am.'

There was no offer of a given name. I could wait. The other woman reappeared, carefully negotiating a heavy tray through the narrow doorway. While she set it down, the Mother pointed back to the Four Seasons pictures.

'It's a tradition,' she said. 'We all have to respond to the Grove in different seasons during our novitiate here. Some write poetry, some compose music. Those are my paintings.'

I peered at them again, and said, 'You have a very observant eye. I can tell each species of tree, and even the different varieties of apple.'

'You're a flatterer, Mr Clarke. What you're trying to say is that the Grove is too big for the skyline. You wouldn't be the first.'

I pointed to the photographs, and then to the window. 'Would the Hall be through the trees, and the Grove downhill, closer to the river?'

'Very astute. This is the closest you'll get to it, I'm afraid. No man has set foot in our Locus Lucis since it was planted. Nearly five hundred years.'

Locus Lucis? Place of Light? No: Place of Lux.

The other woman had finished laying the cups and saucers. She pushed down the plunger on the cafetière and left us to it, closing the door behind her. The Mother sighed and shook her head.

'You're going to stop being polite, now, aren't you?' I said.

'Yes, I bloody well am. You are not what I was hoping for, Mr Clarke. You can sit down, though. I take it there's something wrong with your left leg.'

I eased myself into the floral settee and lifted my trouser leg. She grunted at the scars and sat in the matching armchair. Her cloak and gown flowed smoothly around her, and I upped my estimation of the fabric: it looked like wool but acted like silk. She set about pouring coffee; I declined milk and sugar, and took a sip. Delicious.

She saw my face. 'Decent coffee is one of my few indulgences.'

'Thank you. Do I get to meet the First Sister?' I asked.

'No. The Second Sister lives in the gatehouse. It's symbolic – I deal with the outside world as well as looking after the estate. The First Sister lives separately and has no contact with the outside world at all.'

'I take it that the other lady, the one who wore the apron, must have a very low number.'

The Mother didn't like that. 'Susan is not a Sister. She is a member of the congregation who chooses to act as my housekeeper. We all serve the Great Goddess here.'

'Aah,' I said, as if that explained everything. She saw straight through me.

'You're not just underpowered, you're ignorant.'

'You sound like my own mother, only ruder. Men have feelings, too, you know. I did manage to get here.'

'With a Dwarven Keyway.'

'A what?'

She put down her coffee and took out an iPhone from her cloak. 'Hledjolf has billed us for giving you a Keyway to pass through the Wards and Glamours. See?'

She thrust the phone in front of my face. I saw an email confirming that *A Human male has taken the contract. 12.5% of commission has been charged as a non-refundable deposit, plus a fee for ensuring his ability to access your location.*

'No they haven't,' I said. 'The Dwarf has charged you for ensuring I can get here. What they actually did was give me the geo-location and left me to fend for myself.'

'How did you get through, then? You might have unravelled the Glamour, but those Wards have never been breached by a man before.'

'I just gritted my teeth and put my foot down. Your Ward made me think I was under enemy fire; I just imagined a bunch of squaddies under siege. You do what you have to do to get the men out.'

'I see. That shows determination, Mr Clarke, but I'm not sure that it will be enough. If you don't mind me asking, how did you find yourself in Hledjolf's Hall, and why on earth are you doing this?'

'Keeping up my side of the bargain. If I want to join the King's Watch, the Allfather said…'

She jumped up, pushing back the heavy chair. 'May the Goddess preserve us. How could you come here? How *dare* you come here?'

I could feel the magick flaring around her. She was winding herself up for something, and do you know what? I couldn't give a flying fuck. If she wants to blast me through the wall and back to Wray, bring it on. People need to learn to love me for myself.

The Mother touched a rope round her waist, and the heavy cloak slipped off. She began to raise her hands, and I placed the cup on the table. No sense in destroying the china.

'Is it my Patron you object to, or my prospective employer?'

'It is not given for us to understand the Higher Powers, but a *Witchfinder?* You insult the Goddess just by being here.'

'I thought that's what you wanted. Someone to find a Witch.'

That was a mistake. She made a sign with her fist, pointing her first and fourth fingers at me. She started to say something in a very strange language, which quickly grew in pitch until my ears started to throb with agony. I could have taken being blasted; this was entirely too painful. I sank forwards, pressing my hands to my ears and trying to press back with my head. It was the most painful thing that has ever happened to me, and it was getting worse.

I threw up my hands. 'Forgive me! I would no more disrespect the Goddess than my own mother!'

I didn't know if it was the Mother's conscience which saved me, or what happened next. The door crashed open, and Susan collapsed unconscious into the room, blood flowing from her ears and her nose. Either way, the noise stopped. I flopped back on to the settee; the Mother rushed to help Susan.

In the aftermath, I thought I'd gone deaf for a moment, then I heard the Mother speaking into her phone. All I caught was, '… to the Lodge. Immediately.'

I tried to calm my breathing, and heard Susan whimper as she regained consciousness. The Mother helped Susan to her feet, the poor woman still clutching her head as she was led out of the sitting room, across the passage and into the other side of the Lodge. I clambered off the settee and went outside for a fag. My hand was shaking as I tried to do the Work, and I had nothing left. There was no pain in my arm, but I knew that my reserves of Lux had been temporarily exhausted. How had that happened? I dug out my emergency lighter and drew in the smoke.

I looked around the garden. It was small, neat and contained far too much colour for January, given the harsh winter we were suffering. It looked like the Mother's fingers were as green as her dress, either that or she had another servant who looked after it for her. Remembering the detail in her pictures, I was probably being unfair. The Mother looked like a woman who knew her plants.

My domestic reverie was interrupted by hasty footsteps on the path. Another sister appeared from the trees and hot-footed it through the garden, lifting her robe high to give her freedom of movement. This one wore a blue gown with white sleeves; she'd been in too much of a hurry to put her cloak on. She had the same lined face as the Mother, wore her hair in the same loose braid, and had the same youthful figure. Life was kind to the Lunar Sisters.

A minute later, the Mother appeared from the passage, slipping on her cloak and fastening the cord around her.

'How's your hearing?' she asked. She looked ever so slightly guilty. Just a little bit.

'It seems fine. I didn't suffer as much as Susan. Is she going to be all right?'

The Mother looked away, taking a sudden interest in one of the small shrubs. She bent down and peered closely at the buds. She pulled up a pendant or amulet from her gown and held it in her left hand. She muttered something to the plant, then pricked off a small stem with her fingers. She stood up with a grace I could only dream of.

'I saw you admiring the garden,' she said. 'If coffee is an indulgence, my garden is a compulsion. Take this.' She offered me the small stem. 'If you pop it in some compost on the window sill, it should take. You do *have* a garden?'

'I do. It's been neglected rather badly.' I accepted the small twig. 'What is it?'

'*Viburnum Opulus*, also known as crampbark. It's been used for centuries to relieve menstrual cramps.'

'Oh.'

She gave me a smile. A rather sad one, that had something to do with her past rather than this morning's encounter. 'This is our own variety. It's slightly magickal all on its own, and if cultivated by a woman, more so. By the time it's fully grown, you might need it for your leg. You might be married, as well.'

'How do you know I'm not?'

'Because I can't imagine anyone with domestic responsibilities doing what you're doing.'

'Thanks for the vote of confidence.' I put the crampbark cutting carefully in my cleanest pocket. 'Is this by way of an apology?'

'Yes and no. It's a personal apology, not an official one.' She began a slow tour of the borders, bending and checking, occasionally dipping her fingers in the soil. 'I've been Mother for three years. When the sisters chose, four of them had reservations about my impetuosity. Perhaps they were right.

'We are much closer to the Goddess here than most, a lot closer than you are to your Patron. When I used the power of sound against you, I was wrong. You are not yet a Witchfinder, and you have done us no harm. The harm I intended for you was reflected back on me via the damage to Susan.'

At some point soon, the issue of Higher Powers would need a great deal of clarification. The Allfather would not have interfered with me if I had tried to kill someone. This I know, yet the Mother was utterly convinced that her Goddess (name unspecified) had played a part in what had happened inside. I decided to push her sceptical button.

'I could have bounced it back on her. After you stopped, I felt myself very low on Lux, if that's the right term.'

In response, she shook her head. 'Your natural instincts absorbed some of the energy. Quite a bit, actually. Enough for Susan to be badly hurt.'

I wasn't going to leave it there. 'You talked about Wards,' I said. 'How do you lot – Mages, Witches, Chymists or whatever you're called – how do you lot stop yourselves getting your heads blown off. And what would happen if I tried to shoot one of you?'

'Now that is a good question. The answer is an Ancile.' She pronounced it *ansile*. 'It's a shielding Charm, one of the oldest Charms in magick. It was updated during the Renaissance to work against bullets.'

'How does it work?'

'By deflecting the energy. Whatever force is used against you, the Ancile turns it aside. Like all Charms, it needs Lux to work. Only a supremely powerful Mage or Witch could survive a bomb blast, for example.'

'What if someone shoots you in the back, from long range?'

'If you look at an Ancile, it has a triangle with an eye in the centre. The eye is always watchful.'

I stopped walking. This was absolutely terrible news. I had felt vulnerable before; now I felt like a blindfold naked man in the gladiatorial arena: no weapons, no armour, no vision. 'Where do I get one?'

Her smile was sad, almost affectionate. 'We have no use for such things. Watch Captains usually have one enchanted into their Badge of Office.'

Footsteps from the passageway heralded the reappearance of the blue sister, wearing a rather tart expression.

'Susan is healed,' she said to the Mother. 'Physically, at least. You have work to do of your own.'

The Mother looked from the blue sister to me, then down the passage. 'Of course,' she said to her colleague. 'I will go straight away. I'm sure you'll be glad to get back to the Hall.'

I smiled at the blue sister. She was younger than the Mother, though with these women it was hard to be sure. Either she dyed her hair or there was some Work afoot: it was jet black. She gave me a searching look before moving off down the path. I was fairly sure that she was one of the four who had spoken against the Mother in the last election.

The Mother excused herself for a second and returned with a blue cardboard folder. 'I might be a while with Susan. Perhaps you should take this, read it over lunch in Wray, and either come back this afternoon or call me. My details are inside.'

I took the folder and nodded my acknowledgement. The Mother escorted me down the passage and unlocked the door to the outside world.

9 — *Momentum*

It was much colder outside the wall. I fastened my coat closer around me and hunched my shoulders as I crunched across the gravel. Back in the Volvo, I turned on the engine and turned up the heater before opening the blue folder. The first document had a business card clipped to it. I removed the paper-clip and stared at the card. On the left was a swirling green, semi-abstract line drawing of a mother cradling a child. On the right it said, *Mother Julia*, and had a mobile number. It was the bit across the top that puzzled me: *Convent of the Holy Mother*, just what it said on the plaque by the gates. Another mystery. I quickly saved her contact details in my phone and looked at the first of only three A4 sheets of paper.

It was a screenshot from Facebook – the home page of *StonerAbbi*. There was a profile picture of a young woman, no, a girl. She can't have been more than eighteen. She was seated on some stone steps, outside, and wearing casual clothes. The most striking thing was the enormous spliff in her left hand. She was taking a toke on it, and the joint obscured most of her face. All that I could really tell was that she had long brown hair and brown eyes.

The screenshot also showed that StonerAbbi shared nothing with people who weren't her Friends, not even to say which school she'd been to. The only other piece of information was a date generated automatically at the bottom of the page, a date two and a half years ago.

I turned to the second page and found a few lines of type which told me that Abigail Virginia Sayer would be twenty-one in a couple of weeks, that her blood group was O-, and that she did not suffer from allergies.

The third sheet contained her academic qualifications. Abigail's GCSE results were stellar, all A*s and As; the girl had nine more of them than I do (I got an A* in maths and an A in English, if you're interested). In stark contrast, her A levels were crap. Sorry, that's the only word for them. She had bombed at English Literature, Biology and History. All three of my grades were better than hers, which doesn't say an awful lot.

I looked at the back of all three pages: blank. How on earth does the Mother expect me to find someone with only this to go on? I turned to face the Lodge and announced, 'You're taking the piss, Julia. Again.'

I didn't feel particularly sorry for Susan. Yes, she'd been injured, but Mother Julia had tried to maim me – or worse. Susan should choose her employers more carefully. Even so, Mother Julia had some fences to mend and wouldn't be answering the door any time soon. She'd need to talk to the 1st or 3rd Sister as well, whichever one it is holds the balance of power inside their walled garden. It was time for a light lunch.

January sunlight can be strong, but this wasn't: it was hangover sunshine, half-hearted and only technically daylight. It was good enough to see by, and that's all you need when you're driving.

I knew that there were a couple of surprises on the road back, as in sharpish bends on a hill. The second one came when the wire fence had given way to drystone walls, so I was going a bit slower, and stopped thinking about duplicitous Sisters to keep an eye on the road, luckily for the mad fell runner coming towards me.

Fell runner. Woman. Bank Station. It was her, my enemy.

She stopped running and braced herself with her back to the wall. If this had happened yesterday, I'd have done an emergency stop. Not today. Right, Ms Ponytail, let's see if you have enough Lux to kill me *and* absorb the momentum of 1.8 tonnes of Volvo doing 40 mph. I put my foot down.

She raised her hand, stopped, and opened her mouth. Closer. Going to smash.

She pointed right, blasted the drystone wall to fuck and dived through the gap. I had just enough time to turn and slam on the brakes, but not enough time to avoid the wall completely. The car bumped and slammed off the verge before coming to rest with a sigh. I yanked the handbrake and dived out, pulling the lever which opens the tailgate.

On the way round, I peered over the wall and saw that she had rolled down a bank and was still pulling herself together. It was time for another experiment.

I pulled up the carpet in the cargo area and shoved off the cover for the spare wheel. There was no spare wheel, because I'd put my AK47 in there. I prefer pistols, for all sorts of reasons, but beggars can't be choosers. I grabbed the rifle and two magazines, slipped one in the gun, unfolded the stock, and went to stand in the gap she'd blown in the wall. I laid the Kalashnikov on the grass first.

My enemy had recovered, and was walking up the hill. When she saw me, she broke into a jog, determined to get to me before I could disappear. In her head, my only possible reason for still being here was that my car was out of action. She knew I had no magick with which to retaliate.

I dived behind the wall and took up a defensive position. She had just used a *lot* of energy to blast that wall. How much did she have left? I let her take the initiative, because that's what you do when you're defending. She paused to look, using her Sight, and sensed me behind the wall. With renewed focus, she walked slowly up the wet hillside until she thought she had me in her range; she was certainly well within mine. When her body language said she was slowing down, I raised the AK47 and fired.

Jeremy Clarkson is right. In continuous fire, a Kalashnikov is a weapon of Totally Random Destruction. It's completely useless. I fired a single shot at her chest, the bullet was diverted, and she did what any normal person would do when shot at on an exposed hillside: she dived for cover.

The grass tussock covered her backside, but nothing else. I had a clear shot at her head and upper chest, so I fired again. And again.

After the third shot, she rose to her knees and raised her left hand. I ducked.

I heard a howling wind pass over and one of the stones moved. I thanked the farmer for doing a good job with his wall, and the EU for subsidising him to do it. I looked up, and I could see her laboured breathing was getting worse. Whatever Work she was doing didn't work properly if she wasn't upright. She stood, and got two more shots for her trouble.

I could see her trembling when she started to advance. Everything she'd done, everything she'd planned told me that she was not ex-military. Whatever was driving her was much stronger than discipline and training, but it was running out. I could see that in the naked fear on her face.

She advanced five steps, and got seven more bullets. I'd known since our first encounter that she was left-handed, and her right hand was now clutching something on her chest. I took half a second to look properly, and I saw smoke rising from her running top. She stopped, raised her left hand and did her worst. I ducked.

The top layer of slanted stones blew off the wall, one of them hitting me on the arm. Was that a feint? If I showed my head, would it get blown apart? The fear I'd seen convinced me that this had been her last, best shot, so I looked up. She was running drunkenly down the fell, gripping her right hand in her left.

Would I shoot someone in the back when they were running for their life? Absolutely. I've done it before. Her Ancile – if that's what it was – absorbed the first two shots. The third shot pitched her forwards, but it was too late. She rolled into a dip, and then she was lost amongst the trees. I paused to pick up my shell casings, then went to examine the car.

The first thing I did was pat it on the bonnet and offer a prayer of thanks. Not the silent prayer of thanks you read about in stories, but an out-loud fervent hymn to Odin the Allfather. I don't think it's a coincidence that XC70s are made in Sweden.

The nearside wing was a little dented. So far, so farmyard; it was the front tyre which caused the problem. It was completely flat, and as you know, I don't have a spare.

I didn't want to get stung for a new wall, so I apologised to the car, did a three point turn in the gap and drove half a mile back up the hill to a flat spot. I grabbed a few bits, hid the AK47 under my coat and started marching towards the turning to Lunar Hall.

I waited until I was outside the gates before I stopped to have a fag. For one thing, it was sheltered there. For another, it was quite a long way. It had only been an hour since Mother Julia had sent me packing, so I gave her another twenty minutes to make her peace with Susan and consult her colleagues. I'm guessing that the latter would take longer than the former.

I had one big question to think about, and so many small ones that I couldn't count them without getting out my notebook, and it was too cold for that. The big question was not *Who is trying to kill me*, but *What are they trying to stop me doing?*

Ms Ponytail had first targeted me *before* I'd met Hledjolf but *after* I'd struck my bargain with the Lord Mayor of Moles, so it isn't about me as such, it's about the Lunar Sisters. Why hadn't she just offered me a bribe? It's what I would have done.

Sitting shivering by the gates wasn't going to answer my questions, and I knew enough to make my next step, so I got up. My next step was rather slow, because my leg had seized up. I hopped about, and did a circuit of the turning area to get it going, then limped up to the Lodge door. I unshipped the AK47, removed the magazine and hammered loudly on the door with the stock (after emptying the chamber of the live round).

I paused for five seconds, then started hammering again. The Sisters had made a mistake when they planned this part of their estate: the door opened outward. Poor Susan got a terrible shock when she tried to sneak a peek, and I pulled the door out of her hand. She nearly fainted when she saw the gun.

'Where is she? We need to talk.'

The housekeeper took a second to swallow hard, and managed to rally. 'The Mother is in Chapter.' She even managed a smile. 'I don't suppose you're going to wait outside, are you?'

I put the gun slowly on the ground; it had served its purpose for now. 'Sorry, no. Could you run down to the Grove, or text her, whichever's quicker. This won't wait.'

'They're in the Hall. The Grove is for celebration or contemplation, not discussion and decision. I'll text her.'

She took out her phone and sent a message much faster than I could have done. It took the Mother less than thirty seconds to respond. 'She's on her way,' said Susan. She stepped back to show me to the sitting room.

'I'll wait here, thanks. I don't suppose there's any chance of lunch?'

'Of course. I was preparing it for Mother anyway. It's only soup.'

'Just right for today. I'll let you get on.'

She needed no further prompting to disappear into the private quarters of the Lodge. While I was waiting, I put the full magazine back in to the AK47 and held it in the safe position, pointing down. It took the Mother only slightly longer to get here than the blue sister had done after Susan's injury.

She stopped in the archway when she saw my silhouette against the open door, then straightened her shoulders and came forwards. 'Why have you brought that weapon here, Mr Clarke? This is a place of peace.'

'No it isn't,' I said bluntly. 'You hired me on a contract with a vengeance clause. You may have subcontracted the dirty work, but your hands aren't clean.'

She blushed red, the first time I'd seen her at a moral disadvantage. Even the unintended assault on Susan hadn't fazed her as much.

I pressed home the advantage. 'Not only that, someone tried to kill me on the road to Wray. I wasn't going to leave this in the car, was I?'

'What? Have you...?'

'She got away. Unfortunately. Look, Julia, our relationship needs to change. You need to help me, starting now.' I raised the barrel of the gun to point it at the ceiling. 'What would happen if you tried to use your sonic blast?'

'What do you mean? Are you all right?'

'Perfectly. I asked you a question.'

She shrugged, in a helpless English sort of way. 'You'd die, I suppose.'

'No. I'd scream, and drop the gun. AK47s have a notorious hair trigger. When the gun hit the floor, it would go on full auto. In three seconds, you'd have thirty 7mm bullets whizzing randomly round the passage and ricocheting off the walls.'

She looked back over her shoulder at the end of the passage and the security of her garden. Without thinking, she took a step towards it.

I brought her back to the point. 'This situation is nearly out of control, Julia. You invite me into your home, attack me, then palm me off with the rubbish in that folder. I don't know what games you and your sisters are playing down there, but when my life's at stake, the games stop.'

She blinked. 'Would you murder me here?'

'Yes. It would void the contract, and I'd find another way to pay off the Dwarf. Problem solved.'

Her shoulders were shaking and her lip was quivering. She had frozen completely. Good.

I lowered the gun and ejected the magazine. I placed the gun on the floor. 'But I'd rather not. Nor will I force you to make a promise under duress. That woman who tried to kill me will be long gone by now, but she'll be back. Either you promise to give me *all* your help, or I'll take the chance to walk out and get myself a magickal lawyer. It's up to you.'

She took a deep breath. There were no histrionics or seizing of sacred books, she simply nodded and said, 'By the Great Goddess, I promise. So mote it be.'

'Good.'

'Shall we take a walk before lunch? Work off some of the adrenalin?'

'Good idea. Get Susan first.'

She frowned, but opened a side door and called out. Susan, pinny restored, appeared in the doorway. Her eyes flicked around until they'd spotted the gun on the floor, then she stepped forwards. I could see an extensive farmhouse kitchen behind her.

'Susan,' I said. 'Could you sort a couple of things?'

Susan looked at the Mother, who said, 'Hold lunch for a while, and could you ask the Seventh Sister to join us? Mr Clarke and I need to talk; perhaps you could look into these matters for him while we do so.'

Susan turned to me with a smile. I'm guessing she hadn't heard our showdown in the passageway.

'I'm sorry to impose on you,' I said, 'but someone's just tried to kill me. In the process of saving my life, part of a wall got blown away. Could you ring the farmer and say that the Convent will pay for the damage? I assume the Convent is your cover name.'

Susan looked bewildered.

'Do it,' said Mother Julia. 'I just hope no sheep got out.'

'I checked,' I said. 'There were none in the field. I did grow up in the country. When you've done that, ring Lancaster and get a garage to come out urgently.' I passed her the contents of my pocket. 'Here's the size and make of tyre needed, the locking wheelnut and the car keys. When it's fixed, bring it down here, if you wouldn't mind. I'm not walking up that hill.'

It was the Mother who spoke first, 'But you expect Susan to do it.'

'I'm sure there's a bike somewhere around. It's a Volvo. Shove the bike in the back when you're done. Or one of the others can drop you off.'

Susan's hand, the one holding the bundle of bits, was shaking. 'I'll get straight on it,' she said.

The Mother led me through her garden, told me I could smoke if I stood downwind of her, and guided me along a path which branched away to the north. From the amount of fallen leaves still lying, it was not a well-trodden route.

We walked in silence for a while. I'd done my thinking; now it was her turn.

'Believe it or not, men are allowed in the Hall,' she said. 'Under certain circumstances. This is not one of them. I'm taking you to a place where you can see the big picture. It's where I should have sat to do my sketching.

Tradition says that you sit by the monument to compose your response to the Grove. Sometimes tradition can be a straightjacket. Here we are.'

We left the trees and made a short climb until the boundary wall curved in to meet us and the path ended at a bench next to its foot. We turned round to admire the view.

The trees we'd come through were little more than a screen to hide the Hall from the gates and the higher road. Beyond them was the Hall itself, and I could immediately see why the two photographs had been taken from the other side. From here, the original farmhouse could barely be recognised amongst all the additions, and the walls were disfigured by service pipes, chimneys and the clutter of real life, which had been invisible in the pictures.

From our vantage point I couldn't see much of what was immediately beyond the Hall. I got an impression of lawns and a formal garden ending with a sculpture surrounded by benches. Beyond the sculpture was the Grove, a stand of ancient woodland which had probably been growing in the Roeburn Valley since the glaciers retreated. Even up here I could feel the tingle of magick. I stood on the bench and I could just see the outline of a clearing. I stood down and knocked the muck off the bench.

The Mother tilted her head to one side. 'What did you see, Mr Clarke?'

'That there's a clearing about twenty metres into the wood, and that it's about sixty metres in diameter. I couldn't see what's in it.'

'You do have a talent for seeing through things.'

I pointed to the sculpture and said, 'Is that the monument?'

'Yes. A monument to the lost sisters of Pendle.'

'Anything to do with the Pendle Witch trials?' I asked.

'Yes. What do you know of them?'

'I've heard of them.'

'After the Reformation, there was no official body in England which concerned itself with magick. You'll find out all the details at some point, but neither you nor I would be sitting here without James the First and his fear of witches.'

'I've heard of that, too,' I chipped in. 'Something to do with being a gay man and having issues with female sexuality.'

Mother Julia smiled at me as you would a colleague. Things were looking up. 'You might say that,' she said, 'I couldn't possibly comment, being a mere woman. James appointed the first Peculier Constable to "keepe the Kings Peace". James wanted to call him the Witchfinder General, and that's pretty much what the first Constable did, with the help of his Watch Captains. Especially the Watch Captain of Lancashire.' She paused. This was a familiar tale, but one that clearly didn't get any easier with the telling.

'The Watch Captain identified a coven based in the Ribble Valley and he pushed the local magistrate to arraign them for witchcraft in 1612.' She closed her eyes. 'Eleven people – nine women and two men – were put on trial. Ten were found guilty and hanged.' She re-opened her eyes and stared at me. 'Nothing can put right that wrong, but that doesn't mean that the wrong cannot be acknowledged and atoned for. Every Constable since then has maintained that justice was done. It is not a happy legacy.'

I pointed to where she kept her phone. 'I'm amazed at how connected the magickal world is, and I'm sure you've got a wider network. You must know that the Constable is a woman, and I know for a fact she's appointing women to good jobs there. Perhaps things might change.'

'Perhaps. Things are changing in many places.'

I thought about the River Roeburn. 'If the road from Wray led anywhere, it would lead to the Ribble Valley, wouldn't it?'

'Very astute of you. It used to be the main road. Two sisters escaped the Watch Captain, and both of them had a strong Gift. The Goddess led them over the Trough of Bowland, and they found shelter at a farm here. When the tenant farmer died, the Earl of Morecambe Bay gave it to them as a sanctuary for aged and fallen women. He also agreed to close the road to Whalley.'

I could see all that happening in my mind's eye. It fitted neatly with what I'd learnt about the world of magick. It left me with a question. It left me with hundreds, but I chose this one. 'How do people find you?'

'For a while, the Goddess guided them to us. Women with the Gift were guided here for sanctuary. When we established contact with the other Circles of the Goddess, we became known for taking in those who would benefit most from a secluded and separate life.' She turned to face me. 'I don't know about you, but I'm rather hungry.'

'Me too.'

We started to walk back, and she continued her story. 'Men have always resented the fact that a Gift cannot be passed down the male line. Most naturally Gifted children are female. They have faced a lot of prejudice. What do you think happens to our children?'

She said it as if speaking collectively: *some* Sisters had children, but not *her*. 'The Constable told me not to talk about Muggles. I suppose there's no Hogwarts, either.'

She laughed. 'And if there were, it would be a terrible place. No, there are a number of very good private schools which accept children with Gifts, and staff who train them to make the most of that Gift. I spent twenty years doing so, down the road in Stonyhurst.'

'Oh.'

'Oh indeed, Mr Clarke. Girls whose Gift is rejected by their family find a haven here, and we pay their fees at Stonyhurst. Most of them come to

Lunar Hall for a year after leaving school; some of them stay on and become a full Sister. I was one of those.'

Aah. Now we were getting down to brass tacks. I let the Mother take her time.

'Abigail was born here, and lived amongst us until she started walking. Lunar Hall is no place for children, so they moved into the village and she went to the village school. When she was at Stonyhurst, her gift manifested itself. She did a year here, and became a Novice. The Thirteenth Witch. After another year, she decided to go travelling. It's quite common and we actually encourage it, but she needs to return before her twenty-first birthday. You know that's in thirteen days, and she hasn't been in touch.'

'You think she's still alive?' I said.

By way of an answer, she dropped her hood and loosened her cloak. She put her hands in the top of her gown and carefully lifted out a necklace. On a gold chain were several pendants, charms and what looked like small medals. All of the ornaments were very fine, light and designed to lie flat against the skin. She lifted the intricate fretwork pendant which hung at the bottom.

'This amulet binds me to the Grove, and the Grove to me. Abigail has one, too. If she had died, we would know.'

'Can you not perform some Work to track her?'

She let the necklace rest on her chest. 'Only graduates of the Invisible College call them Works, after the Great Work of Alchemy. We call them Charms.' She held up a small medallion. 'All of these are Artefacts. An Artificer can create a physical object which, as we say, works like a Charm. This one is a Persona – a mask. All Mages have one, or something similar, because it makes us invisible to Sorcerers. The art of occlusion, magickal hiding, is quite difficult. All I can say is that wherever Abigail is, she's using a very strong Persona to occlude herself.'

'Or someone is using it on her.'

'Quite.'

I gestured at the other Artefacts. 'What do these do?'

She returned the necklace to its place under her gown. 'I'll forgive you for asking. It's considered very rude to ask that question. Even ruder than asking a woman's age or sexual orientation, and as you haven't asked about those, I'll assume you were ignorant of the rule.'

Ignorant. Having a small Gift. Lacking in lore. If I didn't have such a thick skin, I could very quickly get an inferiority complex around here.

On an impulse, she withdrew the necklace again and fiddled with one of the attachments. 'Here,' she said, offering it to me. 'It's the Persona.'

'Will it work for me?'

'Yes. Some artefacts are tied to an individual; this one is not.'

'Have I got enough Lux to make it work?'

'Yes. It's not a cloak of invisibility. It smudges your Imprint from a distance, so you look like everyone else. If you broke into a Mage's house, he'd know he had a burglar, but he wouldn't know it was *you* until he saw your face.'

I accepted the Artefact, and felt it tingle against my skin. It was made of gold, thin and stamped with the mask of tragedy on one side and comedy on the other. Even with my eyesight, I couldn't make out the writing.

'You need to have it next to your skin,' said Julia. 'I'll give you a chain after lunch.'

'Thank you,' I replied. 'Thank you very much. You've just eliminated a huge risk factor. Did you ask the Seventh Sister to lunch for a specific reason?'

'Yes. She looks after our novices. I knew Abigail as a student at Stonyhurst; Sister Theresa knew her as a young woman here.'

'I thought as much. Before we get back, perhaps you can tell me why you were so disappointed in me this morning.'

'I was more unhappy with the Dwarf, and I'm afraid you got the backlash. We really were hoping for someone else to take the contract.'

'Someone without a Y chromosome, I presume.'

'That, yes, and someone without any connections to the Watch.'

'And you've got me instead. Indulge me, Julia, and describe your ideal contractor, if you wouldn't mind.'

She blew out her cheeks. 'I mentioned Sorcery before. Some things you seem to know, some you don't, so don't take it the wrong way if I ask this question: do you know what a Sorcerer does?'

'I've met one, but I don't know what they do exactly. I can take an educated guess, but I'd rather have that part of my ignorance eradicated.'

'All of nature is connected in the Sympathetic Echo,' she began.

I was determined to show I'd been doing some thinking, so I said, 'That's some sort of quantum entanglement, isn't it?'

She pursed her lips. 'Chymists do not have a monopoly of truth. There are other theories which are not so reductive. If we can leave Quantum Magick aside for now, we'll concentrate on Sorcery. Some people with a Gift can use a Focus to uncover things. If they pursue this talent, they are known as Sorcerers. If a Sorcerer had enough of a clue about who you were, they could track you from a long distance. It's possible that the woman who attacked you this morning is a Sorcerer, but it's more likely she is working with one.'

'I see. What does this have to do with Hledjolf's choice of contractor?'

'We went to Glastonbury – that's where the Daughters of the Goddess are based, the most senior group of sisters in Britain. We asked their Sorcerer for help and got nowhere. Our only option was to go to Hledjolf and offer a substantial reward in the hope of attracting a better Sorcerer –

one with other skills to offer. The matter is rather urgent, and the job is not attractive for most Mages. Hledjolf said that we had to pay twice what we thought reasonable and offer the Dwarves double the normal commission. They said that if we did, they would find someone.'

'Aah. I think it makes sense now.'

'In what way?' she asked. It was the first time I'd had anything like a constructive idea to offer.

'The Allfather is in debt to Hledjolf,' I explained, 'and Hledjolf can call in that debt by getting Odin to find volunteers. Like me. The Dwarves gets their deposit on commission regardless, and I don't think they expect me to succeed – I don't think they expect *anyone* to succeed.'

Mother Julia made a real effort to sound supportive. 'Then let's prove them wrong.' I admired the thought, if not the execution. We were back at the Lodge.

The kitchen wasn't as airy as Elvenham House, nor did it have any more "heart" to it. My mother is as much of a home-maker as any of the Sisters. What it did have was decades of continuous loving care from people with nothing else to do. Having mentally scored a point for Mrs Mary Clarke, I settled back to enjoy lunch.

Susan was about to serve when there was a knock on the door and the Seventh Sister joined us. Sister Theresa wore black, all black, and her robes were closer to being a nun's habit than either of the other Sisters I'd met. She even kept both hands up her sleeves. She looked a lot older than Julia.

I remained standing and waited for the introductions, which duly arrived. I offered to shake hands and was rudely rebuffed. The last person to refuse to shake hands with me was a Taliban ambassador. I wondered if the Afghan and Sister Theresa had more than rudeness in common.

I got a partial answer before we sat down, when Theresa manoeuvred herself between Susan and Julia. On a nod from Julia, the women joined hands, inviting me into the circle. I took Julia and Susan's hands, and it was Susan who spoke next, not one of the full-time Sisters.

'*Lord and Lady,*
Sun and Moon,
Accept our thanks for the sacrifice of Mother Earth,
And help us return it threefold with grace.
So Mote it Be.'

We all repeated the last line and tucked in. The leek soup and home-baked bread were both excellent. The saying of Grace was Susan's last spoken contribution to the meal.

The silence was heaviest between Julia and Theresa. The Mother was deferring to her older colleague, waiting for her to move the conversation beyond platitudes, but Theresa was stubbornly silent. I sighed inwardly.

'I'll start, ladies,' I said. Theresa flinched at the word *ladies*. Oh joy. 'What happens to Abigail on her twenty-first birthday if she hasn't clocked in by then?'

'Abbi,' said Sister Theresa. 'She prefers Abbi to Abigail.' Her voice was as firm as her gaze, and neither was welcoming.

'It's not just what happens to Abbi,' said Julia, 'it's what happens to us. If she isn't part of the circle, we are all drained. She can leave, and we can replace her, but so long as she is bound to the Grove, it will hurt us as much as it hurts her, and there are twelve of us to share the burden.'

'Thank you,' I said, nodding sagely. 'Let's move on to the obvious question: family. What about Abigail's – sorry, *Abbi's* – parents?'

'Her mother is no longer with us,' said Theresa.

'Her father?'

'She doesn't have a father.'

'Everyone has a father. Unless you're telling me that there's a Charm to replace fatherhood.'

Julia looked embarrassed. 'We have an arrangement with other Circles, the ones which admit men. It used to be done anonymously, wearing masks. Now it's done via sperm donation.'

That was a dead end and a half. I turned to Julia. 'What about her friends from school?'

Julia looked troubled. She stirred her soup and put down the spoon. 'I left Stonyhurst five years ago to return to the Coven. Abbi was just starting to appreciate how different her Gift made her. These things go in cycles, Mr Clarke. There happened to be no other students with a Gift near her age. All the other Gifted students were younger.'

I tried to be sympathetic. 'I think something similar happened to my sister. She was a very gifted mathematician. Teenage girls don't like to be different.'

'No, they don't,' agreed Julia. 'From what I understand, she changed her friendship group completely after I left.'

'Hence StonerAbbi and the A level results.'

'Man-made qualifications,' sniffed Theresa. It sounded like the ultimate insult in her book. Her book was not one I felt in a hurry to read.

Julia flicked her eyes to Theresa, then back to me. 'Yes, well, most of that set dispersed. Some knuckled down at university, some went travelling, some went down to Cornwall to live off their trust funds. Because I knew them, and their parents, I was able to get in touch. None of them have heard from Abbi since she came here as a Novice.'

'I'll need a list of names and details,' I said.

'Of course.' She turned to Theresa and put her hands on the farmhouse table. 'Sister, could you tell Mr Clarke about Abbi's time here, and who she was close to?'

'I can tell him that it was a bad idea to bring her here, and it wasn't my idea, either.'

Julia cracked. 'And I could tell him that it was your idea to pretend that the twenty-first century never happened, and that she left here with little more than the shirt on her back.'

Theresa placed her spoon carefully in the bowl. 'Thank you for the food, Susan. It was a blessing upon us.' Then she stood up.

Julia had nailed her colours to my mast and it was time to show some solidarity.

'Sit down, Lady Macbeth,' I said to Theresa. 'It's too late to wash your hands now.'

Sister Theresa rocked back, too stunned to respond.

'Don't,' said Julia. She didn't say it to me, she said it to Theresa. 'Mr Clarke has earned his place at this table, and Abbi's life may depend on him. Violence has been used against him, which can only mean that violence will be used against Abigail unless Mr Clarke finds her first.'

Since entering the kitchen, Sister Theresa had neither shown nor used any magick, now she did both, opening her arms and making a rainbow between her hands; it was as scary as it was impressive.

'What have you got in your pocket, Frodo?' she said to me. Now that wasn't what I was expecting. I was about to say *Nothing, I'm just pleased to see you*, when she forestalled me. 'It's a cutting, isn't it? A cutting from the Mother's garden. Show me.'

I carefully fished the little twig out of my pocket and held it forwards in the cup of my hand. The rainbow expanded and left her hands to fulfil its destiny. If you've never seen a whole rainbow from the air, you've missed one of nature's greatest sights.

The ring of seven colours floated across the table and closed around my hand like a bracelet. I flinched as it approached my skin, only just holding my nerve. The magick passed through my flesh and soaked into the crampbark cutting, which grew three inches and sprouted roots and more buds.

Susan made a whimpering noise, Mother Julia sucked air through her teeth and Sister Theresa held the floor.

'That school of yours is more prison than sanctuary,' she announced, 'and how can you expect a girl who is born to magick to make a choice when she has no knowledge of the options? I told her to go on a pilgrimage, and that's where she went.'

Mother Julia recovered first. 'Where did you send her?'

'Oxford. I told her where her aunt lives. You should tell Mr Clarke to start there, and you can give him these, too.'

From who-knows-where, a tiny stack of postcards had appeared on the table. Sister Theresa put her hands back in her sleeves and saved her parting shot for Julia. 'Mother, I need hardly remind you that Chapter was adjourned, not closed. I shall see you in the Hall.'

Julia wasn't completely done over. 'And I need hardly remind you of my obligations as host, obligations which I neglected earlier, and which nearly cost us dearly. I shall return to Chapter when our guest has left.'

Sister Theresa nodded to the Mother and to Susan, then left the room.

'And breathe...' said Julia.

I breathed.

Susan spoke in a very small voice, 'I've never seen that done outside the Grove.'

Julia brushed some breadcrumbs off the table. 'Neither have I, and I doubt that I ever will again.'

The moment was shattered by a ping from Susan's apron. She checked her phone and announced, 'The YouAuto truck has arrived at your car. I could do with a walk after lunch.' She dumped her apron on the table. 'I'll clear up later.'

I thought about joining her: the atmosphere in here was more than a touch strained. Instead, I pointed to the postcards. 'May I?'

Mother Julia slid them across to me, and without thinking, we moved closer to examine them together. She started by turning them message-side up.

'Is this what you meant by *leaving the twenty-first century behind*?' I said, pointing to the messages. 'I haven't seen an actual postcard in years, never mind four of them.'

'Amongst other things. Before she left Lunar Hall, Abigail, sorry *Abbi*, deleted all her social media profiles, closed her email accounts and got herself a dumb phone. That's why the only picture I could find was the one in the school records, from when she was disciplined for posting that image.'

I leaned in to read the cards, starting with the address: *Sister Theresa, Convent of the Holy Mother, PO Box 247, Wray, Lancs.* So that's how they got their mail. I bet the post is delivered to someone like Susan and brought up here.

When it came to the messages, Abbi's handwriting was atrocious. It took us ten minutes to decipher the text between us, and at the end we'd learnt nothing except that Abbi had indeed visited her aunt. The rest of the messages said absolutely nothing at great length, unless these snippets were a coded message: *Found the most amazing wild hemlock near the Cherwell* and *Have you thought of yew?* I suggested as much to Julia.

'I doubt it's a code. Abbi's particular Talent is very similar to my own: she's a herbalist and naturalist.'

'As is Sister Theresa, I presume.'

Julia shook her head. 'No, and that was the point of her little demonstration. That Charm is called Iris's Rainbow, and it took me years to get the hang of it. I wouldn't dream of attempting it indoors, which shows you just how powerful a Witch Theresa is. She's a Memorialist: she uses magick to …' she trailed off, unsure how to explain things to me, and her gaze settled on the empty chair where Theresa had sat. 'I left Stonyhurst to take over Theresa's job as Novice trainer, you know.'

'Was she reluctant to step down?' I asked gently.

'Far from it – it was her who asked me to return to the Coven. I worked with her for a year, and then my predecessor as Mother passed over very suddenly. To my surprise, I was chosen to become the new Mother. Theresa was not amused at all.'

'How many candidates were there in the election?'

'We don't have elections. We sit in Chapter, and all have a say in turn, starting with the Thirteenth Sister. After all have spoken, the First Sister chooses the Mother.'

I didn't want to delve too deeply into Coven politics unless I absolutely had to. 'Do you think any of this has a bearing on Abbi's disappearance?' I asked.

Mother Julia shook her head.

'Then perhaps the pictures are a clue,' I said, turning over the postcards and using the postmarks to put them in chronological order.

The four pictures made no obvious sense. The first card showed a promotional image for Tabard Gin.

'Aah, that explains it,' said Julia. She pointed to the gin, flipped the card and pointed to a line we hadn't been able to decipher. 'I think that says, *Distilling some wicked botanicals.* Believe it or not, Theresa is a connoisseur of artisan gin.'

'I don't believe it.'

'Well, she is. She passed on her tastes to Abbi, partly to stop her trying to grow ever more potent varieties of cannabis. She'd turned part of the grounds at Stonyhurst into a Pot Plot, you know.'

'An enterprising girl. So what's all this about?'

'It's a joke. She's been looking for wild magick, and suggesting to Theresa that she could use the herbs to make gin. It's a joke because they're all poisonous.'

We looked at the sequence of images again. The Tabard gin was followed by an image of two bucket helmeted knights on a horse: a statue from the Templar church in London. I opened my mouth to say something about the Holy Grail.

'Don't,' said Julia. 'Dan Brown has nothing to offer this party. Moving on…'

The third image was a Norfolk windmill. Julia shrugged. The fourth postcard wasn't actually a postcard, it was an Internet image printed on postcard-sized stiff paper: Camp Alpine Training Center, New Jersey.

'It's definitely a clue,' I said.

'How come?'

'She got a postcard from Norfolk, but posted it in … Sussex. She sent the London card from back in Oxford, and she went to a lot of trouble to show us this image of New Jersey. It means something.'

We re-read the fourth card. 'Look,' I said. 'The writing slopes awkwardly in the last four lines, and the syntax is all over the place, even by her standards. I think she wrote the first word of each line, then made up a message to fit: *Next, card, the, end*. The fifth card should be the end of a sequence.'

'I think you're right,' said Julia. We stared at the images again. After two minutes, she sat back. 'There's something we're not seeing, isn't there? I wonder if Theresa has any ideas.'

'If she does, she's not going to tell us, is she? No, we need an expert. You're not the only mother in my life.'

She blushed, a little. 'Do you have an ex-wife, perhaps? With children?'

'No. I do have a real live mother, though, and she was a cryptographer for GCHQ. I'll talk to her tonight, and if you could email pictures of the front and back…'

'Take them.'

'No thanks, Julia. I don't want to be carrying these around.'

I stood up, leaving the cards on the table, and put my coat on. 'If you could do me a favour tomorrow morning, I'd be very grateful.'

'Yes?'

'Get hold of the aunt's contact details and have your sketch pad at the ready.'

She stood up and smiled. 'I won't ask what for. Give me a second to get you that chain.'

I collected my AK47, and Julia returned with a beautiful gold chain on which she threaded the Persona. She offered to hang it round my neck, and I let her.

'Go with the Goddess, Mr Clarke.'

'Thank you, Julia, and it's Conrad.'

10 — *Too Many Mothers*

It was a tough choice, but I didn't have an option. After leaving the Sisters, I had called Joe Kirkham and asked him to empty my room at Hartsford Hall. I might have the Persona to shield me now, but if the enemy had tracked me last night, they'd know where I was staying, and they knew my car. The one risk factor I was determined to eliminate was any danger to Mina.

I could see patterns in my enemy's plans: yes, they were resolute, brave and determined, and yes, they had a lot of magickal power. What they didn't have was access to the apparatus of state surveillance; in that respect we were equal. Nor did they really have an idea of tactics.

For example, when Ms Ponytail tried to kill me on the road, she made a stupid mistake. In her position, I would have hidden behind the wall and blasted the oncoming car. The real me, the one behind the wheel, wouldn't have stood a chance. I had a feeling that they wouldn't be so naïve again.

That was why I was determined to stay below the radar until after I'd been to the prison. Mina not only has no magick, she is a sitting duck behind the razor wire. If the enemy were able to use her as leverage, my quest would be dead in the water. So would I.

Against that weak spot in my position, I had a rope which I was clinging to. Ms Ponytail and her associates were trying to stop me. If Abbi Sayer were completely hidden, if she were tied up in a basement, then all they had to do was sit tight. But they hadn't. They'd shown their hand. *This means I've got a chance. This means she can be found.* Good.

I had asked Joe to meet me at a small B&B near Cairndale town. He handed over the cases, and I gave him twenty quid to cover his time and petrol. He didn't bother asking what I was up to. When I was looking for my wallet, I found the now sprouting crampbark cutting.

'Here,' I said. 'Give this to Natasha.'

Natasha is Joe's step-daughter. She's about five.

'What is it?' said Joe, turning the cutting over in his hand.

'A magick plant, of course. Tell her to pot it, look after it with love and keep it safe. I'll collect it in the spring.'

'A magic plant?'

'Magick with a "k". Yes. Don't worry, it's not a coca bush, or any other form of illegal narcotic. They don't grow well in England.' I had no idea about that, but I didn't want Kelly to get worried. 'It was a gift, that's all. I haven't got the time to look after it right now.'

Joe slipped the cutting into a carrier bag and left me to it.

I emailed the images of the postcards to my mother, and had the usual strange conversation.

'Is this a competition, dear? If it is, I want a share of the prize.'

'No, Mum, it's real life. Just imagine the cards have been intercepted by Five and they want ideas about the sequence.'

'I am retired, you know.'

'I know. That's why you've got time to think about it.'

'Not tonight, dear, it's the semi-final.'

'Well, good luck, Mum. When you're basking in your triumph tomorrow, I'm sure the answer will pop into your head.'

'What if I lose?'

'Then it will take your mind off the pain.'

I don't know who I feel sorriest for. I've had to live with my mother's odd view of things for my whole life; my dad's only had to put up with it since he married her. To be fair, he does see more of her than I do, and she hadn't finished yet.

'Rachael said something about you, a night club and two young women. She said that you took one outside who was young enough to be your daughter, and that you were looking very paternally disapproving. Did something happen when you were at officer training?'

I stared at the phone. Rachael had outdone herself this time. Right. Two can play at that game.

'Mum, you know me better than that. I took Vicky outside to leave the field clear for Rachael to pursue the other one.' I sighed theatrically. 'She never told me how she got on.'

'Conrad! Are you serious?' She paused. 'I'll tell you what. I'll solve your puzzle if you tell me what really happened.'

'Nice try, Mum. You'll crack the puzzle, and then you won't be able to resist picking up the phone to show me you've still got it.'

'You know me too well, Conrad. Better than your father.'

'Oh, no, Mum. Dad knows you perfectly, but he can get away with pretending not to.'

'Hmm. I'd better go.'

I also got a call from Alain. Very unexpected.

''Ow is your sister?' he began.

'A pain in the arse, as usual. Do your sisters wind up your mother like mine does?'

'Hnnh,' said Alain. I pictured him shrugging. 'Listen, Conrad, something weird 'as 'appened.'

Alarm bells started ringing. Alain wasn't a true weak link, not like Mina, but I wanted to keep him out of harm's way if possible. 'Go on.'

'Those 'ot girls you were with at the club. You remember them?'

'Yes. Please don't tell me you've been stalking them. They're both way out of your league.'

'I wish I could stalk them. They 'ave both gone *poof*. Vanished completely from the Internet.'

'What about the images you sent me?'

'What about them? They are all I 'ave left.'

Interesting. Very interesting. I suspected that Vicky had done her own Occulting, and that she wasn't as good at it as Li Cheng.

'Thanks for telling me, Alain. Which one do you fancy most.'

'It is so 'ard to choose, but I think Desirée is an angel. I don't do angels, so I will go for the other one.'

'If I see her again, I'll give her your number.'

'Do not torture me, Conrad. I 'ave 'ad no luck on Tinder since Christmas. Well, not much.'

Oh, the young. Such a different world. We said our goodbyes and both went to our single beds. Actually, I suspect Alain would be going out, but you get the idea.

If I were on TripAdvisor, I would have given the bed 2* and the breakfast 4*. Battered though it was, the Volvo's seats were more comfortable than the soggy mess I'd slept on last night.

I got a text from Mother Julia asking me to drop in for coffee at ten o'clock. Susan was having a day off (I don't blame her), and had been replaced by a woman whose name I forget and with whom I exchanged not a word all day. She made nice coffee, though.

'How did the Chapter meeting end up?' I asked Julia. We were back round the kitchen table, alone. Much nicer than the sitting room.

'I'm still allowed to speak to you. Just.'

'Let me guess: Sister Theresa voted against you.'

'You must have pricked her conscience, Conrad, because she kept her peace. I told you – we don't have elections or votes. Four spoke against me talking to you; four spoke in favour. The First Sister concluded that there was no mood to change. If Theresa hadn't kept her peace, I think I might have been gagged.'

'She's still not telling us everything.'

'No. I'll try to build bridges, and keep her informed. She may change her mind. Right, I've got those details you asked for.'

'Just one question. Is the aunt part of your world? Does she have a Gift?'

'A very, very small one. Enough to win the flower and produce show every year. She does know about magick, though not enough to have a detailed conversation about it with Abbi.'

'Oh good – someone less talented than me.' Julia managed a smile at that. 'What does she do? For a living?'

'I have no idea. I didn't know Abbi's mother very well, and her aunt even less so.'

'What was her mother's name?'

'Deborah Sayer. Debs.'

I looked at the printout, and the aunt acquired a name, too: Miranda Sayer. I took a moment to use the Lodge's WiFi to email Alain, asking him to put a trace on Miranda Sayer. Yes, the Lodge does have WiFi, but not the Hall, apparently.

'I've got my sketch pad,' said Julia. 'I'm guessing you don't want me to draw you a crampbark plant.'

'No. I want you to do me two portraits. One of Abigail, and one of the woman who attacked me yesterday.'

Julia gave me a grin. 'I'm ahead of you there,' she said, and slid out a pencil drawing of Abbi. 'I did it last night.'

I looked at the picture. Julia was clearly out of practice, and better at plants than people, but it was unmistakably the same girl as the one in the spliff-toting photograph. 'Thank you. That could be very useful.'

'I've never sketched to a verbal description before,' said Julia dubiously. 'I'm not sure if I can.'

She could, and she did. I left the Lodge with a credible likeness of my enemy, all the better for being vague in a couple of areas: it wouldn't make any witnesses rule people out. I also left with Mother Julia's personal blessing and a spring in my step.

Hannah Rothman, Tennille Haynes, and even Vicky Robson had wished me luck, but they didn't really care whether or not I succeeded. Mother Julia was positively rooting for me. No matter how battle-scarred you get, it makes a huge difference to morale when you know you've got someone fighting your corner.

The other person fighting my corner is Mina, or she would be if she knew what I was doing. The last time I saw her, I'd been able to snag a private room for the visit. Unfortunately, MI5 were video-taping the whole thing, so we couldn't get too passionate, and besides, I had a broken collarbone. That's a real passion-killer, but we did get beyond the *minimal physical contact at the start of the visit*, which is all you're allowed in the regular visitors hall.

Waiting patiently for the prison officers to search the clothes Amélie had chosen, I couldn't wait for the brief kiss, which you're allowed, if you keep your hands visible. When it finally came, it was delicious, a strawberry kiss from the cheap lipstick she was wearing. I made a mental note to bring her something more sophisticated on my next visit.

'You look so beautiful...' was all I managed before she burst into tears. Not being able to comfort her was the worst part. After a couple of minutes, she told me to go and get some teas. Prisoners are not allowed to leave their seats for ninety minutes, and they have to sit in the red chairs, not the blue ones.

I joined the queue, and tried to identify which occupants of the red seats had featured in the letters which Mina had sent me. When I got back to our little table, I got her to tell me. It brought her out of herself as she whispered a running commentary on Davina, Chantelle, Sarah, and the others; it also meant we didn't have to talk about me. Another delay came from her examination of the Primark bags (she was impressed).

It couldn't last for ever. 'I've only just realised,' she said. 'Your shoulder. You said it would be a month at least.'

'Doctors. What do they know? How's your teeth?'

'Good, I'm afraid.' She pouted. 'No excuse to visit Luke the hot dentist any more. If you're not ill, you must be up to something, Conrad.'

'Must I?'

'Yes. And it's dangerous. I can see that in your eyes.'

I sat back. 'Yes, it's dangerous. A vulnerable young woman has gone missing, and I only really started this morning. I can't tell you who I'm working for.'

She nodded. 'Will it always be like this?'

'I hope not. I don't know how, but we'll make it work. It's different in here.'

'Why is it?'

'You can't run off and leave me. I'm not going to leave you at home worrying about me because, if I were you, I'd bugger off.'

She looked a little offended at first, then she laughed. 'Okay. If you can't tell me what you're doing, tell me about home. Tell me what it's like, oh, and you promised to tell me where you got all your money from.'

'You know that.'

'No I don't. You can't have made *that* much money from Operation Blue Sky and all the rest.'

So, I told her about Elvenham House, and my family, and she told me more about hers. Her mother moved to Mumbai after her father died in prison, and when Mina was arrested, her mother had severed contact completely. She did cheer up when she announced that her surviving brother had written from America.

I managed to spin that out until we got the two minute warning. 'I'll tell you about my ill-gotten gains next time.'

'I'll look forward to that.' She took a deep breath. 'And I'll also look forward to hearing about why those clothes you brought me smell of another woman's perfume.'

'Well, she's chic, French and gorgeous…'

'Conrad!'

'… But not as gorgeous as you. I'll explain it all in a letter. Promise.'

I heard her voice as I retreated from the visitors hall: 'You're not coming back until you have, and that's *my* promise...'

I had twelve days to find Abbi Sayer before there were serious repercussions in Lunar Hall. One way or another, I don't think I'll be back to HMP Cairndale until all of this is sorted out.

My enemy clearly knew who I was. The new Persona would shield me when I was moving about, but it wouldn't be difficult for them to track me down at Elvenham House. Even though my next port of call in Oxford was only a short hop from Clerkswell, I opted to stay in a hotel.

The new term at the University didn't begin until Monday, so there were rooms to be had in the city, and spare tables in the restaurants. There's an excellent Indian on the Banbury Road which does a chicken tikka to die for, and is happy to serve single diners if they're not too busy. If you're wondering whether my partiality for Indian food is because of Mina, no it isn't. Food is a very touchy subject with her.

After dinner, I stretched my legs by walking into town and getting a drink in one of the smoker-friendly pubs down there. It didn't have the view over the Cherwell that Inspectors Morse & Lewis used to get when they fancied a pint, and that wouldn't have been much good anyway because it was dark. I turned my phone back on, and the first person to get in touch was Mother. My mother.

'How did you get on with the bridge tournament?' I asked straight away. Mother does like you to take her interests seriously.

'It was close, but we won. The final's in ten days' time. Have you heard from Rachael again?'

Oh dear. It looked like Mother was determined...

'Tell me, dear,' she continued, 'are you sure you don't know what she wants from ... relationships?'

'Of course I know what she wants, but what she wants and what she needs are two different things.'

She sniffed. 'I'm not sure I like the sound of that. It sounds like the sort of thing your father would say.'

'Well, there you go, Mum.'

There was a long enough silence for the virtual line to go quiet.

'I won't push you any more, then. I won't forget it, either,' she said, in her best WI voice.

'No, Mum, I'm sure you won't.'

'Right, dear, about those postcards.'

Good. We're finally getting somewhere. 'Have you had any ideas?' I asked.

'I told you that you should have done English for A level, not maths, didn't I?'

'Yes. And you continued telling me that right up to the moment I got a grade D. That was twenty years ago, Mum. I've moved on.'

'Well, that's as maybe. If you'd done English, you might have recognised the sequence.'

Good. At least there *is* an answer, even if I have to eat a portion of humble pie before I get it.

There was a slight pause. I think Mum was putting the cards out in front of herself. When she spoke again, there was a slight change – her teacher voice, with a touch more of the East Midlands vowels coming out.

'The first card was a giveaway. It wasn't the gin itself, it was the brand: Tabard. Then the last card, that one of the lodge in America. I had to look that one up, but I'd already worked out the answer. The fourth card is a picture of Reeve Lodge. Which work of English literature starts at the Tabard and proceeds via a knight, a miller and a reeve?'

'I have no idea, mother. Is it Shakespeare?' I was fairly sure that it wasn't Shakespeare, but you have to give her something to shoot down.

'Don't be silly: it's Chaucer. The Canterbury Tales.'

'Oh. Are you sure?'

'It's the only thing that makes sense. The pilgrims meet at the Tabard Inn, in Southwark, and the Tales are in order: Knight's Tale, Miller's Tale, Reeve's Tale…'

'That's brilliant, Mum. Well done. What's next?'

'The Summoner's Tale. Does it mean anything to you?'

Summoner? I had a bad feeling about that. 'No, Mum, it doesn't, but I know a woman who does. Thanks. Love to Dad.'

I messaged Mother Julia, asking her to call me at her earliest convenience in the morning, and got myself another pint just before Alain checked in.

'The woman you ask me about, Miranda Sayer. She is a technician at the Life Science Research Centre. She 'as a son, James, and she is divorced. I think she is about forty-four years old. You owe me thirty pounds.'

'Noted. You sound busy.'

'I 'ave a date, but she is a lawyer. Pff.'

I couldn't agree more, and I left Alain to his romantic pursuits and went back to the hotel. It was getting colder by the minute, so I warmed myself up by doing some calculations in the snug warmth of the room.

If this whole business about Quantum Magick has any consistency, then my gut instinct about the energy in a speeding Volvo compared to a gun would be correct. I worked out that my XC70 at 40mph has 150 times as much energy as a single AK47 bullet. No wonder Ms Ponytail blasted the wall to get out of the way. I did a few more sums and went to sleep.

Mother Julia waited to call me until after I'd sampled the hotel breakfast (3*) and after I'd made a disturbing discovery: my trousers were getting smaller. I put this down to one of two possibilities – either Ms Ponytail had cursed my wardrobe and made it shrink, or I'd been overindulging lately. That's the problem with Bed & Breakfast, unfortunately. You pay for it, and it's there, so you might as well eat it. I suspected that the state of my arteries wasn't being helped, either.

'I'm going to see Miranda Sayer today,' I said to Julia. 'I'm sure you got in touch with her when Abbi fell off the radar. What did she say?'

'That's part of the problem, I'm afraid. She said that Abbi came to see her in the summer, but she wouldn't say any more. She was quite dismissive, actually.'

'You didn't send anyone to see her, or go yourself?'

'Chapter decided that we should hire someone. Did your mother have any luck figuring out what the postcards meant?'

'Yes and no. Do you mind me asking what you taught at Stonyhurst? Officially, of course. I'm sure that *Director of Magickal Studies* doesn't appear on their list of staff.'

'Biology. Why do you ask?'

'I didn't want to embarrass you by saying that the answer is a literary one. I take it you're not familiar with *The Canterbury Tales*.'

Julia sounded genuinely nonplussed. 'No. I've heard of the Miller's Tale, of course… Oh. Windmill. Miller.'

'Yes,' I said, then I went through my mother's reasoning, giving the old girl full credit for her insights, then paused.

'What's the next tale?' said Julia.

'I've heard of Artificers, Sorcerers and Memorialists in connection with magick,' I said. 'And I assume your some sort of Herbalist.'

'Guilty.'

'Then what about a Summoner…?'

There was a sharp intake of breath. And a long silence.

'Julia? Are you still there?'

'Thank you, Conrad. I shall have to talk to Chapter. Immediately. I'm afraid I can't say any more until then. Good luck.'

'Should I keep going?' I asked, but the screen had already gone dark.

The village of Raybridge, north east of Oxford, is very pretty. I don't think it's as nice as Clerkswell, but I am biased about my place of birth. Raybridge has a similar mix of Cotswold stone, modern infills and the compulsory block of social housing. It also has two pubs. Competition is a good thing, but neither of them can offer Inkwell Bitter. A good job, really, because it was only ten o'clock in the morning.

Miranda Sayer lives in one of the village's older properties, according to Alain's research, and according to Google Streetview, it's tiny. If it were any bigger, I doubt she'd be able to afford it on a technician's salary. Even so, it must be worth a fortune because Raybridge has a railway station, and access to Oxford is considered very desirable according to my research. You can learn a lot about a place by what estate agents do – and don't – say.

I left the car at the station and walked, because a pedestrian passing through always attracts less attention in a village than a car. I should know – I grew up in one. This visit was for reconnaissance purposes because mother and son would be out, and although I'm an optimist, I doubted that Abbi would happen to be outside cleaning the windows. I used up my slice of luck a long time ago.

The route from the station led me past the church, and on an impulse I paid it a visit. This was the first time I'd been in a church since my pact with the Allfather, and I wondered if I'd get struck by a bolt of lightning (from either party). I didn't get the chance to find out today because I had to stop in the churchyard to take a call.

My phone said *Julia*, but a new voice greeted me.

'Mr Clarke, I am Dawn, Fifth of the Lunar Sisters and the Coven's Occulter.'

'And you do some fine work, if I may say so. I had a hell of a job finding Lunar Hall.'

Her response was beyond acid. 'Mr Clarke, the fact that a man with so little Gift as you was able to find us tells me that I was *not* doing a good job.'

This was clearly one of Mother Julia's enemies, and the fact that she was using Julia's phone to call me did not bode well. I opted out of further banter and politely asked how I could help.

'The First Sister has asked me to inform you that Lunar Hall is going to make a temporary Separation while we resolve our issues. I assume you don't know what that means.'

'You assume correctly. Why can't Julia tell me herself?'

'It is as the First Sister wishes,' said Dawn, as if that explained everything. She took a breath and continued, 'The Hall will not be accessible for a while. We are Separating ourselves completely from the mundane world. I have been asked by the Mother to reassure you that your contractual status will be resolved amicably in due course. I...'

'...What about Abigail? She's in danger. You could start by...'

'Abigail Sayer is one of the issues we need to resolve. Goodbye, Mr Clarke,' said Dawn, and ended the call.

There was no one about in the churchyard, so I retreated to a bench and considered my options. Dawn clearly expected me to stand down and let them get on with it. Whatever I'd told them this morning had tipped some balance within the Chapter, such that the First Sister now considered that the whole Coven was in danger, and that this danger outweighed the risk to Abigail. The girl hadn't been a threat on her own, and I presumed that there were always Summoners (whatever they might be) lurking in the undergrowth, so it was the *combination* which posed a threat.

From what I'd discovered about Abbi, she may have been disgruntled, but she wasn't one to turn nasty. Potheads rarely are. This meant that the Summoner might have been looking for her – and it didn't take my imagination long to come up with a fairly grim reason for wanting a naive young witch.

Was the threat to Lunar Hall physical, or was it something else? The sisters were very guarded about their existence and what they got up to, so it was possible that the threat was to their reputation in some way. Mother Julia is not Abbi's mother, but she's taking her responsibilities *in loco parentis* very seriously. I think she would have objected strongly to the Separation, and for some reason they didn't trust her to make the phone call. Every instinct about human nature told me that the Coven as a group were covering their arses and hanging young Miss Sayer out to dry. Or worse.

Could I stand back and leave the Lunar Sisters to their fate? Yes. Easily.

Could I stand back and have Abbi on my conscience? Mmm. No. The hunt continues.

There wasn't going to be any help from the Lunar Sisters, so that left me with one card to play. The worst thing I could do now was blunder into Miranda Sayer's life and have the door slammed in my face. Some people I've met would simply use force to find out what they wanted to know, but that's not my style.

I once flew a Special Ops mission in Iraq which went deep into Sunni territory, the same area which gave birth to ISIS. We arrived at our rendezvous, and the sergeant in charge of the special forces team asked – politely – if I'd buy food and drink from one of the farms while his men got on with their thing. Unless you need to keep the engines running, you don't sit in a chopper on the ground. Too much of a target.

My co-pilot that day was young recruit, and the first woman I'd flown with in a combat zone. We knew the farmhouse was safe because the Iraqi army was on guard outside, but they didn't want to let us in. I was trying to work through the language barrier when my co-pilot shouted to me.

'Sir! Take a look at this,' she said, peering through the shattered shutters of a window.

I took a look and saw a woman tied to a chair being harangued by Iraqi soldiers. Why they were doing it, and how we got her out, doesn't matter. The point is that I had to fly home solo, because my co-pilot was in the back comforting the woman, who was too scared to get into a plane full of men on her own.

Miranda Sayer has even less Gift than I do, so intimidating her into co-operation would not be difficult, except for the part where she never sleeps in the dark again, and has so many nightmares that she takes her own life.

If I had incontrovertible evidence that she was planning to harm Abbi, I might exert pressure. I once broke someone's kneecap to make them talk, but he deserved it. Until then, I needed to win Miranda over, and the best way to do that is with an ally.

I sprang up, as best I could after freezing my arse off on the bench, and went to test the lightning-bolt theory by going into the church. Nothing happened. I doubt that the Allfather cared, and I suspect that both St Thomas (patron saint of Raybridge Church) and his boss considered me too unimportant to be worth damaging this beautiful old building. Even so, I apologised to the saint before getting on with business.

I got out my camera and took pictures of every rota, competition and list of committee members that I could find. One of the good things about churches is that you can hear it when someone is coming. Today, the villagers of Raybridge left me alone.

The village is not large, so it didn't take me long to walk around the whole thing. I paused occasionally to note the name of a house, or examine a particularly fine example of vernacular architecture. One of these was Yew cottage, home of the Oxford branch of the Sayer family, and before you ask, no, Abbi was not cleaning the windows.

Yew Cottage had been upgraded recently. There was a conspicuous alarm box on the front, ruining the effect of the thatched roof and no doubt getting up the nose of the Tidy Village Committee (Chair: J Evans). The alarm box was so big that it had room to announce a 24 Hour Response Service and featured a CCTV lens in the bottom. I peered over the fence and saw that the original wooden panelled door had been drilled to accommodate a multi-lever lock. I didn't bother looking under one of the many flower pots for a key.

During my tour of Raybridge, I said Good Morning to three dog-walkers, two of whom struck up a conversation. For a cover story, I flashed a printout from the estate agent and said that I was thinking of moving here. The good thing about village life is that people are generally trusting; the bad thing is that they only trust their own. I'm ashamed to say that if I'd been black, I doubt that I'd have had the same reception.

The beer in both pubs was acceptable, as was the food in the Coach and Horses. I'll start a proper diet when this thing is over. After lunch, it was back to the hotel because I needed to pull all my intelligence together and add to it with information from the Internet. By the time I went out for dinner, I had a shortlist of three: the Chair of the parish council, the President of the WI and the secretary of the Raybridge Flower and Produce Show.

I finally chose the third because a) she lived near Miranda and would have to know her, b) she was referred to positively in several places and c) she constantly came second to Miranda in the show that she organised. Devious? Moi?

Another piece of information from the church notices was that flowers at St Thomas's are done on Friday mornings, and that was where I found Mrs Rhoda James, wrapped up warm and stripping the twigs off some branches.

'This is very eco-friendly,' I said, pointing to the distinct lack of actual *flowers* in the display.

'Quite right, too,' said Rhoda. 'Hothouse flowers would be a waste of energy and money.' She surveyed the architectural foliage and added, 'I do have some irises and a few snowdrops, but I'll pick them on Sunday.'

She tilted her head to one side and said, 'You're after something, aren't you?'

'If you're Rhoda James, then yes I am.'

'That's me.'

I introduced myself, including my former rank. 'If I help you clear up, can we have a chat somewhere private afterwards?'

'Those vases need a good wash and there's no hot water. You can get chilblains instead of me.'

I washed up, helped out, was introduced to the vicar and found myself carrying a very heavy bag when we left the church. I saw her eyes flick to the war memorial as we passed.

'Any of your family on there?'

'Yes. There are Robinsons honoured from both wars, including my grandfather.'

I was made to take my boots off outside Holly Cottage, and toasted my feet on the gas fire while I waited for Rhoda to emerge from the kitchen. She took a long time because she diverted upstairs to get changed and do her makeup. I was almost asleep when she carried the tray in, and I discovered that the bedroom hadn't been her only diversion.

'I looked you up, Conrad,' she said. 'You've got a DFC.'

'Yes, and I don't blame you for looking me up.'

'Good. You'd be surprised at some of the people we get hanging around the village.'

'And that brings me neatly to my business.'

'Fire away,' said Rhoda.

I stirred my tea, resisted the sultana flapjacks (third place in traybakes), and plunged straight in.

'I'm here on behalf of … a friend. He's worried about his daughter.'

'Oh. Does this friend have a name?'

'Yes. We'll call him Mr Bunbury, but it doesn't matter because his daughter took her mother's name.'

She smiled round the flapjack. 'I like that. "Mr Bunbury". You think I know "his" daughter?'

I took out Mother Julia's drawing and handed it over. 'Abbi Sayer,' I said.

She studied the drawing, though I could tell that she recognised her straight away. 'Why is Mr Bunbury worried about his daughter?' she asked.

She knew what I wanted, and I knew that she knew. I also knew that I'd butted up against the limit of gossip. She would need a good reason to go any further.

'Radicalisation,' I said.

Rhoda looked nonplussed. 'Miranda's not a Muslim,' she said. 'Vegetarian, yes, but not a Muslim. She rather likes a drink, actually.'

'Islam doesn't have a monopoly of radicalism,' I responded. 'There are many sorts of fanatic, and my friend doesn't want Abbi to end up with a criminal record for something stupid, or worse still, to throw her life away.'

Before Rhoda could object, I drew out the second drawing, the one of Ms Ponytail. 'This is the woman we're worried about. Have you seen her?'

'Yes, they were all here just after Christmas, a couple of weeks ago.'

'All?'

'Abbi, her mother and Keira,' she said, pointing to the drawing of Miss Ponytail when she said *Keira*.

I nearly dropped my cup when I heard her say *mother*. Julia had told me that Abbi's mother was dead. Thankfully Rhoda missed my surprise because she was still staring at the drawing of Keira. She tapped it with her finger. 'I'm not surprised about this one. The first time Debs visited, she sat in the car, and she's never out and about when they stay. I only know her name because Abbi told me. Who is she?'

I took the drawings back and folded them into my pocket. 'Rhoda, I need your help. This is all very unofficial, I'm afraid. I'm not a member of MI5 or anything, I really am trying to help out a friend.'

Rhoda stared at me. 'Are you Abbi's father?'

'No. He's a long way from England serving Queen and country, and he asked me to track down Abbi and talk to her.'

'What about Debs? Why don't you go through her?'

'It was a messy divorce,' I lied. 'She won't talk to any of Abbi's father's friends. With Miranda, I can at least get a hearing, with your help. Then I can see where to go next.'

Rhoda finished her tea and came to a decision. 'I'll come to the door with you and make sure that Miranda doesn't slam it in your face. After that, you're on your own.'

'Thank you. You don't know what this might mean.'

'No, and I don't want to. Virtue is its own reward in these cases. Would you like another cup? I know that Miranda finishes early on Friday, but not for a few hours. I'm afraid I'm due out later, otherwise you could dig the garden while you wait.'

'I'll take the tea, but pass on the garden. My leg's not up to it, I'm afraid. I've booked into a local stables to go riding. Since I left the RAF, I've not been looking after myself.'

'Have some flapjack. You'll need the energy.'

11— *Handbags at Dusk*

The Phoenix Stables of Raybridge provided me with a sturdy mount and a guide to the local bridleways. I headed north, out of perversity, because that would take me close to St Andrew's Hall, where Sir Stephen Jennings had lived. I looked down on the house from the ridge and wondered whether his widow was running the show, or whether his son had left the army to take over. I had unfinished business with his daughter Olivia, it's true, but I felt nothing when I looked down on the house.

Clouds were rolling in from the west signalling a change in the weather as I returned my ride to the stables. When I dismounted and asked if there was somewhere to change, I could barely walk. The exercise must have done me some good.

The few streetlights in Raybridge had already come on when I collected Rhoda and we sheltered under my umbrella as we made our way up the lane to Yew Cottage. She pointed to the rain. 'No chance of getting out in the garden tomorrow with this weather. Are you all right, Conrad?'

'No, but it's my own fault. I'll let you do the talking.'

Rhoda strode up to Miranda's front door and rang the bell. As we walked up the path, a high capacity security light had come on, and I saw the curtain twitch before the door was opened.

'Come in out of the rain,' said Miranda Sayer brightly, addressing Rhoda rather than me.

I followed Rhoda inside and ducked my head to avoid the beams. We were straight into the cottage's living room, so I had to dump the brolly by the door and hope the water didn't run across the flags into the nice rug. I turned around just as Rhoda was pointing to me.

'This is Conrad Clarke. He's ex-RAF, and I've checked him out. He is who he says he is.'

'Really?' said Miranda, her hackles rising at the very sight of me.

Rhoda pressed on. 'He's here on behalf of Abbi's father, and I hoped you could spare him some time to talk. That's all he wants.'

'No he doesn't,' spat Miranda, 'and he's not here on behalf of Abbi's father, because she doesn't have one. Who sent you Mr Clarke? I bet it was those bitches from Lunar Hall.'

Rhoda had gone red with embarrassment, and her look would have killed me if she had any Gift.

'It doesn't matter who sent me,' I said with as much resolution as I could muster. 'Abbi is still in danger.'

'Who from?' said Miranda. 'From her mother, perhaps? The mother who I thought was *dead*? The mother who those bitches forced into giving up her daughter so they could indoctrinate her? And who they forced into cutting herself off from her sister?'

Rhoda was edging towards the door. I would have joined her if I could.

I stood as tall as I could under the beams. 'I give you my word, both of you, that I had absolutely no idea that your sister was still alive. None.'

'So?' said Miranda. 'That just proves you're as much of their plaything as everyone else.'

'Who are we talking about?' said Rhoda, unable to get past me to the door.

Before Miranda could come up with her own non-magickal explanation, I butted in. 'The Convent of the Holy Mother. In Lancashire.'

'Convent of slags and bloodsuckers,' said Miranda, but she didn't deny the basic truth. The mention of a Convent stopped Rhoda in her tracks and she raised an eyebrow.

Miranda started jabbing her finger at me. 'Are you on a percentage, Mr Clarke? How much are you getting for this?' She turned to face Rhoda. 'The Convent want Abbi to join them on her twenty-first birthday, when she gets access to her inheritance. They want her to hand it over when she takes her vows.'

What a horrible possibility. Had the Lunar Sisters played me like a fool? They might not want Abbi's money, but they could want her Lux. Or something worse. I felt my hand shake in my pocket, and I gripped my lighter, not because it has Ganesha on the front, but because of the engraving of a little fish on the back. In Hindi, *Mina* means 'little fish'. I always gripped it for luck when I was in a tight spot.

There was a hard chair near the door. I took it and sat on it, because my back and leg were killing me, and the low ceiling made it impossible to stand. I had one thing to say to Miranda:

'What about Keira?'

Rhoda is a shrewd judge of people. She noticed that Miranda didn't respond straight away, and she noticed the change in her tone.

'Keira was a friend to my sister when no one else was around,' said Miranda. 'She's been a good friend for a long time.'

Now that I wasn't blocking the door, Rhoda positioned herself for a getaway. 'I think you two have got some things to work out,' she said. 'Will you be OK on your own, Miranda? Is James here?'

'I'll be fine,' said Miranda. 'James is at a friend's.'

Rhoda let herself out without looking at me. We waited until she was out of earshot.

'Have you even got any magick?' said Miranda. 'Because I can't sense any. At first I thought you were completely ignorant.'

'Of course I've got magick,' I snapped back. 'What made you change your mind about me?'

'Keira. The Lunar Sisters know nothing about her, so you must have done some digging on your own. I'm only talking to you because of Rhoda: if anything happens to me, she's got your number. I want to find out how much you know.'

'Miranda, I really think Abbi is in danger, but before I tell you why, what's all this business about your sister being dead?'

Miranda breathed out slowly. The anger was fizzing off her. 'When Abbi was thirteen, I got a call from the Mother Superior. She said that Debs had died suddenly, and could I come up straight away to break the news to Abbi.' She shuddered at the memory. 'I won't go into the details, but we had everything: post-mortem, death certificate, funeral. I even went through probate and settled her estate as executor.'

'You had a death certificate?'

She stared at me. 'Oh, yes, Mr Clarke, and Abbi and I went to see her in the hospital morgue. Not only did I think she was dead, so did the paramedics, the hospital and presumably the pathologist.'

I could – just about – see Hannah organising this with the power of HM's Secret Service behind her, but the Lunar Sisters?

'I see,' I said, very much in the dark. 'So, how…?'

Miranda's shoulders slumped. 'Abbi stayed here during that summer. It was rather crowded, and my marriage was breaking down. After that, she drifted away. The school looked after her during term, and she was taken under the wing of the Coven when her gift developed. She came for a week the year after, and then nothing until last summer.'

I shivered. The door may have been given new locks, but it wasn't very well fitting. 'Do you mind if I move closer to the fire?'

She waved for me to move, then when I was comfortable(ish), she continued, 'When Abbi came last year, she said that she wanted to go through her mother's things, that she wanted to see if she, too, had a talent for Summoning.'

I had no idea what this meant at the moment, but I didn't want to interrupt.

'You probably know I'm no great Witch?' she said. I nodded. 'Debs' Artefacts weren't any use to me, nor were her books. I sold them on through the network, but I did take a list. I talked it over with Abbi, and she set off on her travels. To cut a long story short, she found that one of the Artefacts was bound to her Imprint, and that it could only be unlocked by discharging it over Debs's grave.'

'I'm surprised it was still around, that it hadn't been melted down or something.'

She shook her head. 'Some dealers will hang on to them while the beneficiary is alive, in the hope that they'll get redeemed. Sort of like a magickal pawn shop.'

A horrible thought struck me. 'It wasn't anything to do with the Dwarves, was it?'

'By the Goddess, no. I wouldn't dare. It was a Mage in Bloomsbury, actually.'

'Not Sussex?' She shook her head. 'If you don't mind me asking, where did Abbi get the Lux from to pay him off? It seems to be some sort of currency, and in case you hadn't guessed, I'm really, really new at all this.'

'I noticed. I don't know where she got it – if I had to guess, I'd say someone in the Coven lent it to her.'

Sister Theresa, I thought. 'Go on.'

'Abbi discharged the Charm, and she knew, she *knew* straight away that her mother was still alive. They were reunited within days, and they came here shortly afterwards.' She gave a bitter laugh. 'It's a good job I don't talk about family much. I was able to pretend to the village that the woman we'd buried was Abbi's adoptive mother, and that this new person was her birth mother. If Abbi wasn't over eighteen, some of my nosier neighbours would have been on to social services.'

I spread my arms in a complete confusion. 'How...?'

'I don't know. Debs won't tell me the ins and outs, the "how". You'll have to ask the Sisters. I do know the "why". She wanted to pursue her talent for Summoning, and they told her she had to give everything up. They made her.'

It sounded to me like Deborah Sayer had chosen this for herself, and my scepticism was clearly visible.

'She knew she'd made a mistake the day after the funeral, but there's no going back. All she could legally do was leave that Charm for Abbi to discover.'

She sat up straighter. 'So now you know. The Lunar Sisters made Debs give up her daughter, and they want to tie Abbi in to the Circle. And they've sent you to try and find her. Well, tough, Mr Clarke, I'm not going to help you. You seem like a decent man: perhaps now you know the truth, you'll do the decent thing and walk away.'

I doubted very much that I'd heard the whole truth. I looked around the room, pretending to think things over, and took in the dresser jammed against the tiny dining table. I could see a picture on the dresser which included all four women. There was something about Keira in it...

I turned my attention back to Miranda. 'Why doesn't Abbi just leave the Sisters?'

She shook her head. 'Why should she? She's only just discovered that her mother's alive, and she needs a lot longer to sort out her future. I bet they told you that Abbi would start getting weaker, didn't they?'

I nodded to show that that was the line I'd been spun.

'Well, she doesn't have to. Debs has shown her how to draw Lux from the Grove. She'll quit when she's ready, and they can go play with themselves until then.'

'What about Keira?'

'What about her?'

'Are you sure she's someone who has Abbi's best interests at heart?'

'She has my sister's best interests at heart, and what Debs loves, Keira loves.'

'Are they lovers?'

'No. They're friends. Why do men always think that women friends are lesbians?'

I tried to disarm her with a smile. Nothing doing. I could have told her that Keira had tried to kill me twice, but she wasn't going to believe me, or if she did, it would be "self-defence" on Keira's part.

'Look, Mr Clarke,' she said, 'I'll tell you how good Keira is – she sold her prized possession to help Abbi pay off some of her debts.'

Suddenly I had to look at that picture. I prayed for a downstairs toilet.

'Can I use your bathroom before I go? You can follow me to make sure I'm not up to no good.'

'I will,' she said, rising from the couch and pointing to the door beyond the dining table. 'Through there, through the kitchen.'

I didn't have to put on the limp, and it gave me a good excuse to shuffle sideways past the dresser and take a good look at the picture with Keira in it. Julia must have some sort of Talent for psychic drawing, because her sketch was probably a better likeness than the photograph, though what the sketch didn't show was Keira's prize possession hanging from her arm. I had confirmation, and I knew where I was going next. I was also absolutely bloody furious. Miranda did follow me to the bathroom, and she did make me leave the door ajar. At least she could only see my back.

When we'd returned to the main room, I leaned against the staircase. 'Thank you for talking to me, Miranda. You're right: I wasn't told anything like the whole story by the Sisters, and I need to think this over. If I give you my word not to look for Abbi until Monday, will you promise not to tell her I've been here?'

She fell for it. 'Reluctantly, but yes, I'll hold my peace until Sunday night. Debs doesn't need to be afraid unnecessarily.'

We shook hands on the deal, and I took myself and my brolly out into the rain. I had promised not to look for Abbi, and I'd keep that promise.

The deal had said nothing about looking for Keira, and I now had a fairly good idea how to find her.

It was a long, wet, painful walk to the station. I collapsed in to my Volvo and turned on the engine. While I waited for it to warm my bones and demist the windscreen, I lit a fag. There was so much guilt, so much secrecy and so many unanswered questions floating about that any survivors from this affair were going to need their own Truth and Reconciliation commission. That was not my problem, though. My problem was to ensure there were as many survivors as possible. Well, at least three survivors: me, Abbi, and someone to pay my bill.

The screen cleared, and warm air started to percolate through the cabin. Volvos are good like that. I closed the window and sent a text to Vicky Robson: *Call me. Immediately. Conrad.* After pressing Send, I turned right out of the car park and headed for the M40. I was on my way to London.

Vicky called about half an hour later, and being young and female, she started by apologising for the delay in getting back to me.

'Doesn't matter,' I said. 'We need to meet. Where are you?'

'I've just got home, and I was gan' out tonight. Can't it wait?'

'No. Pack a bag and put something comfortable on.'

'Howay, man, we're not even supposed to talk to each other. What's gan' on?'

'Not over the phone, Victoria.'

'*Victoria?* You sound like me mam.'

'You really, really need to see me, Vicky. Text me your address, and I'll be there in an hour. If what you've done is kosher, then I'll drive away.'

'What *I've* done?'

I could hear the hesitation in her voice. She'd be there, wherever "there" was.

'Fine,' she said. 'I'll text you.'

She did, and "there" turned out to be Camden. If she was renting round here, no wonder she was short of money. I circled round for a bit and found a Macdonald's with almost legal parking. I text her back and told her to meet me. I was starving.

I was just finishing my Big Mac and large fries when she bustled in, dressed for Saturday morning, not Friday night. She slid into the booth without saying anything; with that look on her face, she didn't need to. I wiped my hands and passed her Julia's drawing of Ms Ponytail, aka Keira.

Vicky went even paler, and swallowed heavily. She shoved the drawing back across the table, as if trying to disown her actions. 'How did you get that?' she whispered.

I folded the drawing and tapped on it with my finger. 'After our encounter at Club Justine, I did some research. Di Sanuto Exclusives are unique, and this woman used to have one. She doesn't any more, and you do.'

Her mouth twitched in a smile. 'You're telling me that you found us out 'cos of a handbag?'

'Yes. This woman was responsible for that attack at the tube station. She's tried to kill me again since then, and I believe she's involved in the abduction of a young Witch. Why she's been abducted, I don't know, but Ms Ponytail here is up to her neck in it.'

'I had no idea, Conrad, honest I didn't. Oh my life, this is terrible.' She stared at the folded paper. 'What are you gonna do? Are you gonna tell the Constable?'

'No, because it's more important to find the girl. If you help me out, I'll make sure Hannah stays off your case. If you get my back, I'll get yours.'

She nodded.

'Good. What did she call herself, and what did you do for her?'

'She called herself Jane Doe; I didn't ask why.' Vicky looked around the busy room. 'Can we go somewhere else?'

I got us two coffees and we adjourned to my car. Vicky grabbed a cigarette and stared out of the window.

'She brought me an Imprint map. It's a sort of magickal DNA printout, and it's as unique as real DNA. Does that make sense?' I nodded my understanding. 'Well, your Imprint actually includes your actual DNA, in a weird sort of quantum way. I don't understand that part 'cos it's all maths, but I can use Sorcery to track back. Jane Doe wanted me to get the Imprint of this girl's father.'

Oh. This did not sound good. 'You're sure it was a girl?'

'Why, aye, man. I know my Imprints. I was able to give her the Imprint map of the father, and I picked up his trace in Sussex.'

That made sense. Sort-of. But why did Miranda Sayer know nothing of this? I turned to Vicky. 'When?'

'Last August.'

How on earth did that work? According to Miranda, Abigail was still looking for her mother at that point – which means that Keira must have seen and spoken to Abbi *before* this business with the Charm on the grave was carried out. That was one detail I couldn't afford to worry about.

Talking of worry, Vicky now seemed on the verge of complete panic. 'For fuck's sake, Conrad, tell us what's going on.'

I tossed her a packet of fags from my stash and told her. It took nearly an hour, and we had to move the car because I saw a parking enforcement van approach. We ended up in the residents parking outside her flat as I was finishing my story.

Vicky had asked a lot of questions along the way, and I was quite disturbed at the tenor of them. From what she was asking, she had as little clue about what was going on as I did. When I mentioned the non-arriving fifth postcard, she sat up in her seat and twisted her hands in her lap.

'A Summoner? Are you sure?'

'Miranda Sayer confirmed it. Since we last met, Vicky, I've learnt about Sorcerers and Artificers, but what's a Summoner.'

She waved her arm vaguely towards the sky. 'The world is full of Spirits. Greater Powers, Angels, Daemons, Ghosts. Loads of them. Most of the time, we can't see them because they exist as, like, pure Lux. At the Invisible College we all do really basic Necromancy, which is how you talk to Spirits. It takes a lot of time, and a lot of Lux, unless you've got a real Talent. I haven't.'

'So a Necromancer could talk to the Allfather?'

'Aye. If he was nearby. Lux is energy, it's just as real as light and electricity. Just because you're made of Lux, it doesn't mean you don't have an actual presence somewhere. It's a big subject.'

I sighed, inwardly and outwardly. Every time I thought I'd got a view of the world of magick, another vista opened up. 'Give me the headlines on Summoners.'

'Simple. A Summoner can bring a Spirit to a place, lock it down and bind it to the material world.'

'Wow.'

'Wow indeed. It goes without saying that it takes industrial quantities of Lux to bind anything more than a very simple Spirit. It's also very, very dangerous, and it's strictly forbidden for members of the Invisible College. If you're outside the College, the rules are so tight, it's almost impossible to do it legally.'

We both went quiet, ruminating on what the implications of this might be.

Vicky spoke first. 'How am I gonna help? If the Sorceress at Glastonbury can't find them, how do you think I'll be able to manage?'

I turned in my seat and edged a little closer. 'Because you're young and, can I say "canny"?'

'If you must. Flattery won't help me find them.'

'No, but I'm willing to bet you wouldn't have agreed to that job for Keira if she didn't have full provenance for that di Sanuto bag.'

She gave me a blank look. 'Aye, I did. I even authenticated the paperwork meself.'

'Go back inside, get the paperwork, and all your magickal bits, and an overnight bag. Oh, and change into something suitable for outdoor work.'

'You're jokin', aren't you? I'm 100% city girl, me.'

'Do your best.'

'Where are we going?' said Vicky, as I drove us slowly round north London.

'To meet my own Sorcerer,' I replied. While Vicky had been getting her gear together, I'd called ahead and told Alain not to go out yet. I was looking forward to this.

We dumped the car and Vicky followed reluctantly up the steps to that little part of Hammersmith which is forever Bordeaux. Alain came to the door, and under the lamp I delivered the line I'd been working on all the way down from Oxfordshire.

'*Bonjour*, Alain. Do you remember that girl from the nightclub? I'd like you to meet the real Vicky Robson. The one in those pictures was her older, more attractive sister.'

I paid the price immediately, when Vicky kicked my bad leg. It was worth it, though.

We sat down in the living room. Vicky and Alain were both staring at me in a very hostile way. Oh, well. I thought they looked like a nice couple.

'Alain, we need to find this woman,' I said, showing the drawing. 'Vicky has got some details.'

Vicky showed Alain the di Sanuto paperwork, and he asked a few questions. I thought we were heading for a dead end until he saw something on Vicky's rugged tablet (which he disdained).

'*Bon*,' said Alain. 'This 'ere is the account number your woman used to pay Victoria's expenses. The sort code is from Praed's Bank. We will have her real name and address on file, but even for you, Conrad I cannot get the information without authorisation.' He looked at Vicky. 'If what you 'ave said about your new job is true, surely Victoria can get it for you.'

'What lies have you told him?' said Vicky, outraged on Alain's behalf. 'You shouldn't get … civilians involved.'

'It was part of the test,' I replied. 'Don't you remember? I had to recruit my own staff because your boss wouldn't help me.'

She looked at her trainers and said nothing.

I pushed on. 'When I passed the first stage, Alain, I was given a mission. A real mission, with a real young girl in danger. I need to find this woman, but I'm not on the payroll yet.' I turned to Vicky. 'When your lot need to find people, or need the police to get involved, who do you contact.'

'I don't know,' she said, twisting her hands. 'I'm not authorised to use our contact at Scotland Yard.'

It was time, as my poker playing friends would say, to go all in.

'Alain,' I said, 'if you find that address now, I'll get the authorisation. I promise you that you won't get in any trouble.' I said that to Alain, but I was looking at Vicky. Alain looked at her, too. Mutely, she nodded her head.

'OK,' said Alain. 'But you know what the price is? I want an interview with your sister.'

'Done,' I said. If Rachael and I fell out, the price I'd have to pay to get Alain an interview might be astronomical. I'd pay it, though, if I had to.

'We can do nothing tonight,' said Alain. 'Even my manager could do nothing. I will go into the office tomorrow and text you. You will 'ave the name and address at five past nine.'

Alain and I shook hands, and we left him to enjoy his Friday night. Vicky looked more miserable than a trainee pilot who's just been told they've failed their medical.

'How am I gonna get authorisation for that, Conrad?' she moaned. 'I'm gonna get the sack for this.'

'Come on, Vicky. Let's get a drink. There's a decent pub round the corner.'

'Dressed like this? And with you? You're joking, aren't you?'

'Pretend I'm your ruggedly handsome uncle.'

She hooted with laughter and shrugged. Just like Alain. I led her to the pub and bought her a large mojito. I stuck to scotch.

'Cheers,' I said. 'This is what we're going to do. You're going to get in touch with Desirée, and tell her to get on to her mother. Mrs Haynes is going to get protection for Alain on Monday morning, for her daughter's sake, not yours. I'll sort it out with Tennille when the dust has settled.'

'Can I go home tonight?'

'No. Too risky now that you're with me. We'll find a Premier Inn somewhere.'

'Get us another mojito, Uncle Conrad.'

'Only after you've spoken to Desirée.'

She shook her head. 'Not from here. I'll call from the hotel.'

'Just one more, then.'

When I got the drinks, Vicky refused point blank to talk magick. I couldn't blame her, really, though it would have been nice to know more about the sort of Spirits that Debs Sayer might be Summoning. She wouldn't talk about magick and I wouldn't talk about my sister, so what we talked about was Afghanistan – not my role in combat, but what the people there are actually like, especially the women. Underneath, Vicky is a great kid. I'd be proud to have her as my niece.

12 — *Families need Fathers. Apparently.*

Being in England must be rubbing off on Alain. He sent the text, as promised, at five past nine. Very efficient. By ten past nine, we were in the car and heading for the leafy suburbs of Guildford, arriving at ten o'clock. I had my first disappointment of the day at five past when I asked Vicky about her Ancile.

'I haven't got one.'

'Shit. Why not?'

'Because I'm not a Watch Captain. Even Cheng hasn't got one.'

'Damn. Hang on, we're nearly there, and I can't afford for her to see the car.'

I parked down the street from Keira's address — a very well-heeled Victorian terrace, close to shops and amenities. Whatever line of work she was involved with, it certainly paid well. No wonder she'd owned a di Sanuto.

'You're good at Glamours,' I said. 'I've got the evidence for that. Can you put one on me? Enough to fool her into answering the door?'

Vicky looked dubious. 'I can try. What are you going to do?'

By way of an answer, I got out of the car and went round to the boot. Vicky followed. I checked that no one could see, and lifted the cover on the spare wheel.

'Howay, man,' said Vicky when she spotted the AK47. 'You cannat be serious.'

'Deadly serious. Can you make me look like a woman, and that gun look like a bunch of flowers?'

She stared up at me. 'The flowers, yes, a woman, no. Have you got a hat?'

I rummaged in the boot and offered her a choice of beanie or baseball. She put the baseball cap on my head and told me to fasten my coat.

'I'm gonna turn you into Interflora. You'll look like a delivery driver to the Great British Public, but I've no idea what Keira will think. Or Deborah, or Abbi, if they're there.'

'Do it.'

'Bend down and close your eyes. Pick up the gun and stand still.'

I did as I was told, and felt the discharge of Lux trickle over me.

'You're good at seeing through things, aren't you?' said Vicky.

'Yes,' I said, eyes still closed.

'Then hold the flowers down by your side, and don't, whatever you do, look at them. And try to *think* like a delivery driver.'

'Right.'

I wrapped my hand round the gun. Every instinct told me that walking down a suburban street with a weapon was a bad idea, but I tilted my head back and opened my eyes.

'You're mad,' said Vicky.

'Thanks. Just what I wanted to hear. Wait for me in the car.'

I walked down the street, staring at the house numbers until I reached number 73. Trying to ignore the pain in my leg, I jumped up the steps, rang the bell and hammered on the door like all the best delivery guys do. Then I rang the bell again for good measure.

Anciles only work against missiles (arrow, spear, bullet…), and only if they're launched outside the wearer's personal space, hence the Glamour. I needed to get up close and personal with Keira before she could get the drop on me.

It was Keira who answered the door, and the Glamour lasted long enough for me to barge the door open with my shoulder and sweep up the gun at her left hand. She staggered back and moved her arm out of the way. It gave me a fraction of a second to use my momentum.

I dropped the gun (it wasn't loaded), and made a grab for her arm as I barrelled into her body. We collapsed in a heap, and I made my first mistake. I pinned her left arm to the ground with my right, and made a grab for her necklace with my left. When my hand closed on the gold chain, it wrapped itself around my fingers and started to burn and cut.

In half a second, I could feel my fingers about to be severed, red hot pain searing through them. I tried to disentangle the knot and half rose from squashing my opponent. As soon as I did, she kneed me in the balls.

Blood was dripping from my hand, the wire was tightening and my knees came up automatically as the agony in my groin exploded. I don't know if it was reflex or grim death which kept my hold on her left hand. Either way, it stopped her long enough for a blast of air to hit us both from behind, flattening me on top of Keira again.

Absorbing the blast relaxed the chain's grip on my left hand enough for me to pull it out, but it also gave Keira enough room to raise her right hand and punch me in the face. I only turned my nose away from the blow at the last second, and heard a crack when her fist connected.

I finally let go of her left hand and curled up in a ball, protecting my face. I could feel the wetness of blood from the wound in my hand. Instead of Keira finishing me off, it was another blast from behind that sent us both spinning down the hall. I hit my head on the stairs, and everything went black.

A bucket of water hit me in the face.

'Conrad! Wake up, man!' shouted Vicky. 'The house is on fire!'

I rolled onto my left side and put my hand on the floor. Thundering hell, that hurt. I tried to focus on my hand. The water had turned red from the blood, and I couldn't open my fist, but that wasn't the worry. The important bits of your hand are actually on the back – that's where the tendons are. No tendons, no fingers. I still had tendons. I could also smell smoke.

I pushed myself up on one hand and used the newel post to make it to an upright position. 'Where is she?'

'Gone. When I blew you apart, she knocked me down, but she didn't finish us off. She picked up a bag and ran out the back door. I heard a car start, then I realised she'd set fire to the kitchen. I just closed the door and left it.'

A totally random thought struck me. 'Where did the water come from?'

Vicky pointed to a cut glass vase on a console table. 'Looks like Keira really did have some flowers delivered.'

I realised that I was standing in a sea of tulips. Hey ho, I was alive and not maimed. Onwards.

Apart from the kitchen, two other doors led off the hall. 'You take that one,' I said, pointing to the rear.

We opened our doors and found ourselves staring at each other from different points of a knocked-through room. The rear of the space was a library cum office, the front was a comfortable, if rather chintzy living room. What is it with Witches and chintz? Whatever.

'Grab anything you can before the fire alarm goes off,' I said, gesturing at the library.

I limped over to a coffee table and saw a load of papers spread out. I swept them up with one hand and glanced around. Keira was too young to have photo frames, but she did have a collage of images next to the window. I started peeling the pictures off the wall, trying not to get blood on them.

'This isn't her occult library,' said Vicky. 'It's just mundane stuff. I'll check upstairs.'

The heat alarm in the kitchen started wailing. 'Time to go, Vicky. Can you take the Kalashnikov and put a Glamour on?'

'What's a Klash-thingy?'

'The gun. Quickly.'

She picked up the weapon from the hall, grabbed a carbon fibre walking pole from the coat stand and thrust it at me.

'You pensioner, me nurse. Don't hurry.'

'Ha Ha.'

We hobbled down the steps. Well, I hobbled, she supported my arm. Out of the corner of my eye, I could see that her coat had become a blue nurse's uniform. I closed my eyes and let her lead me to the car. At the last moment, I pressed the keys into her hand. 'Just get us out of here and head for the M25.'

Vicky had the good grace to wait until we were on the main road and had lit two cigarettes before opening her mouth. 'You do realise, don't you, that you were beaten up by one girl and that you had your arse saved by another?'

'Noted. It was my fault, and I won't be so arrogant next time. Thank you, Vicky. Thank you very, very much.'

'I don't know whether you're brave or stupid, Conrad. I wouldn't have done what you did.'

'Because you're too clever. You can keep rubbing it in, or you can tell me why you think she didn't finish us off.'

'I think she recognised me. If anything happens to me, even if I've gone off piste, the King's Watch would be down on her like a ton of bricks. Clockwise or anti-clockwise?'

She was referring to the M25. 'Anti-clockwise. I think we're going to Sussex. Take it steady: I need to look at this stuff, but before I do, how come your blast knocked her back? I thought she was protected.'

'I didn't blast her, I blasted you. You're *not* protected.'

'Oh.' I checked the photos first. There were three images of Keira and an older woman. Now that I could look at her properly, I don't think Keira can be over thirty. No wonder she was so fit. In another picture, the older woman had her arm around Abbi Sayer: it must be Abbi's mother, Deborah. There was one final image that intrigued me – Keira taking an older man in a very romantic clinch. I stared at it for a few seconds, then put it aside to look at the papers. We joined the M25 and I told her to head for Croydon. I was too scared to look at my left hand, and it needed professional attention sooner rather than later.

I finished looking at the papers, and had a question for Vicky: 'Does the name John Deans mean anything to you?'

'Ooh, it's sort of familiar. Why?'

'I think he's Abbi's father. These papers are a report from a genetic laboratory confirming that the supplied samples, male and female, are the parents of a second female sample. I think this is a picture of Keira and John together.'

'Wow. That makes sense.'

'There's another paper, too. It's a short email from John to Keira, saying that he'll see her next week, only his screen-name isn't Deano or anything obvious, it's *Moloch*.'

Vicky nearly crashed the car when she swerved. '*Moloch*! Please tell me you're lying.'

'How could I lie about something that means nothing to me?'

When she'd corrected her course, Vicky put her foot down, either consciously or unconsciously. 'Howay, man. This is serious.' She beat her hand on my steering wheel. I flinched in sympathy. The throb was getting worse.

'There's this thing called *The Rite of Moloch*, OK?'

This might have been the most stressful situation Vicky had ever been in. Perhaps getting her to drive wasn't such a good idea.

'It's OK, Vicky. Just take it one step at a time. Who's Moloch?'

She took a deep breath, and took the exit for the M23 towards Croydon. 'You can find the original Moloch in the Christian bible, but that's not who I'm worried about.'

'Should I be worried about him?'

'In a way. There was an Alchemist who lived in the fourteenth century, and in those days they all used to take mythical names – sort of a combination of boasting and secrecy. He called himself Moloch of Wessex, and he worked out that he could rejuvenate himself. Completely.'

'Bloody hell, Vicky. That sounds more valuable than the Philosopher's Stone.'

'It would be, if you didn't have to sacrifice a Witch to do it.'

'Oh.'

'And not just any Witch, she has to be your daughter.'

'Hang on, Vicky. To make yourself younger, a man has to murder his daughter. Are you sure this isn't a metaphor for child abuse?'

'Well, it could be. In the story, Moloch of Wessex ran away to Europe, but his son pursued him, killed him and burned the only copy of the ritual.'

My mind baulked. This was a step too far. 'No. Surely not. It can't be true – that's beyond evil.'

'Believe me, Conrad, there are worse things you can do with magick.'

Before Vicky could say any more, the car was filled with the sound of an incoming call. The screen said *Miranda*.

'Mr Clarke?'

'Yes.'

'I know I made you a promise yesterday, but I've had a phone call from Keira.'

'Oh?'

'She rang me first thing this morning, and she told me that you two had had some run-ins together.'

'Why would she tell you that? As far as she knows, you and I have never met.'

Miranda coughed. 'She asked me if you'd been in touch, and I couldn't lie to her. I told her that I believed you to be an honourable man, and that you should talk. Once she realised that you'd been led astray by the Sisters, she agreed. She wants to meet next week.'

'When, next week?'

'She said that she'd send you her address via me on Tuesday, so that you could meet up on Tuesday evening.'

Vicky was having difficulty keeping her trap shut, and was trying to mime some question I should ask. I shook my head to Vicky and said to Miranda, 'That sounds like a sensible idea. It'll give both sides some time to cool off. I look forward to hearing from you.'

Before Vicky could start off, I interrupted. 'That confirms it.'

'Confirms what?'

'Turn off here and get me to the hospital. I'll explain it all when I've been patched up. While I'm in A&E, I need you to do some shopping.'

'Oh, aye?'

'Yes. Find a branch of Mountain Warehouse and get yourself some proper outdoor gear. Shoes, not boots, though.'

'You have to be joking.'

'And lunch. Get lunch, too.'

There's no point trying to pull rank or jump the queue in casualty; it's a question of take your turn. At least I was ahead of the rush, and wouldn't be requiring a bed. One and a half hours later, I was patched, anaesthetised and looking forward to a new scar, this one running right along my palm. I wasn't supposed to stretch the hand for at least 48 hours. The punch in the face was just a bruise, and I wondered if the cracking sound had been one of Keira's fingers breaking. I could only hope.

Unlike Keira, Vicky had gone for baggy in the outdoor wardrobe department. Well, Keira does have the figure for Lycra, I suppose. In fact, when I'd had my close encounter with Keira this morning, I felt nothing but muscle and sinew. She must spend hours running every day.

'Right,' said Vicky as we munched a sandwich in the car park. 'What's gan' on?'

'John Deans is being set up.'

'You what?'

'He's Abbi's father, I don't doubt that, but I bet he's never met her. Look at it this way. First, Keira had a bag packed this morning. Second, before we arrived, she made a phone call offering to give up her address *in three days' time*. Third, she could have torched the sitting room and destroyed these papers. Fourth, have a look at this photograph.'

I passed her the image of Keira puckering up. 'It looks genuine,' said Vicky. 'The shadows and lighting are all even. I think.'

'I'm sure it is genuine, but she's kissing him, and he's looking at the camera. Where's his left arm, and what does that say on his tee shirt?'

'You're right. His left arm has been cropped out. I think it's a rainbow on his shirt. Lots of magickal associations with rainbows.'

163

'He lives in Brighton. He's got a rainbow on his shirt. He's chosen not to snog Keira, even when she offers it up on a plate. He's gay, Vicky.'

'Bet you he's not.'

'How much?'

'Eh? It was a joke, man. Give over and put the postcode in the Satnav. I'd give you me Focus to look him up, only you can't do Keyways yet.'

I started to enter the postcode. 'You mean I might do one day? Good. What's a Focus?'

Vicky drove out of the hospital, following the Satnav back to the A23 and the long slog to the South Coast. 'Sorcerers need a Focus to work properly.' She coughed. 'The traditional focus is a crystal ball.'

'Really? A crystal ball?'

'Yes. I use a tablet computer. Does double duty as mundane and magickal fount of all knowledge. Anyway, if he's innocent, why are we going to see him?'

'Because he's at risk. I think Keira planned to get rid of him as a diversion.'

'I still don't think he's gay.'

I shook my head. Crystal balls to the lot of them. It was time for a nap.

John Deans is gay, loud and proud. When we stopped near Brighton to get a coffee, Vicky looked him up: she quickly found his wedding photo from last year, featuring two grooms. John's husband is a lawyer and his motto is *All the best lawyers wear wigs!* I rested my case.

Between the happy couple was a small boy of oriental extraction, who turned out to be their adopted son.

'What does John do?' I asked.

'We know he's a Mage,' said Vicky, 'because he donated his sperm to one of the Circles. Whatever it says here, it'll be a cover story. Aah, here we go. It says he makes bespoke clocks. He must be an Artificer.'

'Good. We need one of those.'

'What for?'

'Wait and see.'

'No chance, Conrad. After the last time, let me do the talking.'

It was John's husband who answered the door of their ground floor flat. David Gillette was younger than John, and very camp, even unto eyeshadow. He ignored me, and ran his eyes over Vicky.

'Dressed like that you must be Dykes R Us or the police, and I'm guessing the girls in blue.'

Vicky turned round to give me the most venomous look before flashing some sort of ID. 'Can I speak to Mr Deans, please.'

David dialled down the camp levels a fraction. 'Are you with the Ministry of Magic?'

I straightened up, my mind jumping ahead to when I might be living with Mina. If John Deans could have an Ungifted partner, so could I.

Vicky looked ready to kill someone. 'I'm an officer of the King's Watch, sir. There is no Ministry of Magic in real life. This is an urgent matter, and we believe your family is in danger.'

The front door opened fully, and David stepped back, waving us in. 'John! Get up here now!'

A man about ten years older than me, who looked five years younger, sprang up the stairs from a basement level. Their adopted son appeared from the living room.

We crowded into the hall, and Vicky showed them a picture of Keira and Debs. 'We believe that one or both of these women intend to harm you. Have you met either of them before?'

The men looked at each other. John pointed to Keira. 'That one paid twenty quid for a kiss at the last Pride event. What's this all about?'

I looked at David and the boy. They didn't need to hear this, so before Vicky could launch into an explanation, I showed John the paperwork from the lab. He cottoned on straight away, though he clearly had no idea what the implication might be.

'Why?' he said, utterly bewildered. Both of them had turned their attention to me, now, and I wasn't going to waste any time.

'You're only at risk for a couple of days, and only as a diversion. Pack a bag and get on the train. Preferably Eurostar. Take the boy to Euro Disney until Tuesday. We'll give you a lift to the station.'

David's brow furrowed. 'You can't order us out of the country. Tell me what's going on.'

I shrugged. 'If you're a lawyer, I assume your wills are up to date. If you're going to argue, we'll just leave.'

John stepped forwards. 'David, just go. Go and pack. Now. I'm sure we'll get an explanation when we get back.'

'Of course,' said Vicky.

'Can you give David a hand?' I said to Vicky. 'I need a word with John. Please.'

She nodded mutely and the three of them disappeared.

'Who took the snog picture?' I said to John.

'Her mother.'

Odd. No way did Debs look like Keira's mother. 'Do you mean the other woman in the picture we showed you?'

'No, not her. She was older – very neatly dressed. Silver hair. Hang on, I think David took a picture of her taking a picture. I'll get his iPhone.'

'I need something from your workshop, too,' I said. 'Something that will cut a necklace chain with a Ward built into it.'

He stopped to appraise me for a second, and I lifted my bandaged hand to show him why I needed it. He swallowed, suddenly very nervous. I think it was only when he twigged how little Gift I had that he truly believed they were in danger.

I kept watch while they finished packing. John emerged with a small pair of wire cutters and a phone. I pocketed the clippers and looked at the image of Keira's mother. My heart plunged somewhere into my boots. I asked him to text it to Vicky, and I rested my head on the freezing stone pillar.

Vicky emerged just before the others. 'Don't you ever do that again,' she hissed into my ear.

I stood up straight. 'Do what?'

'Undermine me. That's the worst sort of man behaviour. I was leading in there, and you took over.'

'Sorry. I'm really sorry. I was wrong, and I won't let it happen again.'

'Good.'

Keira made no attempt to attack us while we transported the Deans-Gillette family to the station. I was no help with the luggage, and my gloomy countenance was dampening the enforced holiday mood that David was trying to create. While Vicky bustled round, I plotted a journey to Kirkby Lonsdale via Heathrow Airport and a secret address in Rutland. I also jotted down a shopping list.

Vicky drove off and had followed the first two Satnav directions before she realised that she had no idea where we were going, and why it was going to take at least seven hours to get there.

'Bank of Conrad, Heathrow branch,' I said. 'We're seriously underpowered for this trip, and I need some hardware. I keep my emergency cash in a self-store at the airport, after that we'll pay a visit to my supplier.'

'What sort of hardware? We can't get any more Artefacts, and if that massive machine gun of yourn isn't enough, what do you want?'

'It's not a machine gun, it's an assault rifle. We'll come to the hardware later.'

We were well outside Brighton, it was getting dark and the weather forecast said that an Atlantic storm was currently breaking over the west coast, and heading our way.

'You've been driving for hours, Vicky. Now we're out of town, I can drive one handed. You need a rest. Pull in at the next garage, and I'll tell you where we're going and why I've got a very bad feeling.'

'And I thought Jeffreys was a gloomy sod until I met you. Don't ask who Jeffreys is.'

We took a break, stretched our legs and topped up our caffeine levels. I asked Vicky to check her phone for John Deans' text and image.

'Who's she?' said Vicky.

'Keira's mother. I've seen her before.'

'She hasn't tried to attack you, has she?'

'No. She served me coffee on … Wednesday. God, was it only three days ago? She's a volunteer skivvy at Lunar Hall. I think the Sisters' plan to go into lockdown has already been breached.'

'Shit.'

'Precisely. Keira has been playing a very, very long game here, and whatever her endgame is, I'm convinced it involves the Sacred Grove at Lunar Hall, and that it's going to end very, very badly for Abbi.'

I pulled out of the services and got used to indicating with my left wrist. Thank the gods for automatic transmission.

Vicky sipped her coffee. 'Would Deborah hurt her daughter like that? A daughter she's only just reconnected with?'

'Yes. She abandoned her daughter when Abbi was on the verge of puberty. This business about regretting it ever since? Rubbish.'

There was a silence.

'What's your plan, Conrad? We might be too late.'

'You said that Summoning takes time. Keira might have a broken hand. She'll need to meet up with the others, get up north and penetrate the Lunar Hall enclave. It will be tomorrow night, if magick works better at night.'

'Oh yes. Mostly.' She shifted in her seat. 'I think there's something you need to know.'

'That you're in love with Li Cheng? I know that already.'

She flushed deep red. There was an awkward silence. 'You haven't seen him at his best, is all,' she said, then moved swiftly on. 'I bet you're thinking that everyone's keeping you in the dark about magick, don't you?'

'I'm not paranoid, they really are out to get me. Even you. Especially you.'

'It's not personal, man. It's … sort of magickal etiquette. You don't give the Great Work away for nothing. There has to be a reason, a payback.'

'Not what I'd call etiquette. More like a code.'

She nodded, still red and discomposed. 'It is a code. We call it the *Chymist's Code*, but all the circles and covens have their own versions.'

What she said made sense, in a way. Everyone who'd given me an insight into the magickal world, from the Allfather to Vicky, had done so in exchange for my co-operation, my help or because it was the minimum they could get away with.

'Thanks for your honesty,' I said eventually. 'It's my turn to keep secrets now. Have a look in the glove box. There's a piece of paper on top.'

She found the paper. 'What in Nimue's name is this?'

'Read it aloud. Apart from the phone number.'

She read it to herself first, then aloud. 'This is a job for JT on behalf of AS. Collect tonight. One times P226 E and spare mag. One hundred times 9mm hollow point. One times OWB Holster. Three times MK3A2. Repeat, three quantity Mike Kilo three Alpha two. End.' She refolded the paper. 'This is all boys toys, isn't it? Guns and stuff.'

I lifted my left hand in the air and turned the bandage to face her. 'You girls won't let me play with your toys, so I'll have to provide my own. If you can think of another option, please tell me.'

'If we get caught with it, I won't be able to talk us out of the situation. You could go to jail, I could get sent to the Cloister Court.' She gave me a smile. 'That's the special court for Mages. Now you know.'

'So I do. Call the number. It'll go straight to an old fashioned answering machine, so be ready to read the message. Don't worry, the guy on the other end will delete it immediately. He doesn't want to go to jail either.'

After the call, I spent some time telling her more about Lunar Hall. She nodded, and said that until she'd seen the wall, she wouldn't know how to get round the protection. After that, we took it in turns to nap.

Once clear of Heathrow, the traffic was thinning out and we started to make good time despite the torrential downpour. I told Vicky that we'd collect my shopping then stop. 'I'm not asking you to give me any secrets, but it would make both our lives easier if you at least sorted out what I call these people. For example, why aren't you a Witch?'

She mulled it over. 'All right. Everyone who can use magick, even you, is a Mage. It's a neutral description. If you learnt your trade at the Invisible College, then you're a Chymist, as in alchemist. Got that?'

I nodded.

'If you're not a Chymist, then usually you get called a Witch or a Warlock. They're gendered terms. If you're Welsh, it's Druid. If you stick to *Mage*, you'll never be wrong. Oh, and never, ever call someone a Witchdoctor. The PC term is *Ethnic Mage*. I'm gonna close me eyes now.'

So, I was a Mage. I shrugged and focused on the road.

It was still raining when we arrived at our destination in Rutland. I pulled up before the track which led to my supplier's house because I knew that he had a hidden camera at the entrance.

'You take it from here, Vicky, and I'd use a Glamour if I were you.'

'Why aren't you coming?' Her hands were shaking.

'For the same reason you've never heard of me. If this guy sees me, he'll shoot me. If he thinks you know where I am, he'll kidnap you.'

Her hand flew up to her neck. Or rather, to where her necklace was lying, under her clothes.

'Don't worry,' I said. 'You're just a courier. You know nothing, you know no one. Just hand over the money and take the box. If you try small talk, he'll think you're trying to entrap him. You can do it, Vicky.'

She nodded with a jerk. I got out of the car and dodged under a tree to keep out of the rain.

Vicky got in the car, and when she drove off, I took a sideways look at her. It wasn't Vicky driving the car, but Keira. Neat.

She was back in good time. When I got into the passenger seat, she slammed her foot on the accelerator and nearly crashed on the next bend.

'You're mad, you are,' she said. 'Fucking mental doesn't cover it. That was the creepiest guy I've ever met in me life, including the Druid of Blaenau-Gwydir.'

'Slow down. I don't want to die in Rutland.'

She pulled up to a junction and took a deep breath.

'Well done,' I said. 'That was good work. There's a pub only ten minutes from here, and we both need some proper food. There's still a long way to go.'

'And what do we do when we get there?'

'Bath. Sleep. Hearty breakfast. Oh, and I might need you to perform an intimate service.'

'I might regret this. Go on, tell us.'

'If I want a bath, I'll need you to tie a plastic bag over my left hand.'

She shook her head. 'In a minute, I'm gonna wake up. Where's this pub?'

13 — Unlucky for Some

The thought of a cooked breakfast was too much for Vicky, who'd grabbed a croissant and met me at the car, looking even paler and wanner than usual. I tried to be positive.

'I like what you've done with your hair, if you don't mind me saying. Very practical.'

Her hair is long, but not extravagantly long. She'd bound it into some sort of loose plait. Quite a feat on your own, I'd have thought, not that I know much about hair.

'It's a Goddess Braid,' she said, swinging the end round and examining the knot. 'A sign of respect in case we need brownie points with the Sisters.'

I was learning, slowly, what is and what is not an acceptable question in magickal circles – *Do you worship the Goddess?* is not an acceptable question.

'Every little helps,' I said, and we splashed off towards Wray through the enormous puddles left behind by Storm Feargal.

I wasted ten minutes driving round the village looking for a blue Renault: Susan was a possible source of intelligence on the situation behind the wall, and we'd parted on friendly enough terms. No such luck.

When we headed up towards Lunar Hall, I pointed to the damage that Keira had inflicted on the farming infrastructure, now secured with sheep-proof netting.

'Bloody hell,' said Vicky. 'She does pack a punch.'

I didn't say when we were approaching the turn-off, because I wanted to see if Vicky would spot it on her own. When I swung the car towards the entrance, she screamed and slammed her hands on the dashboard.

'For fuck's sake, Conrad. Don't do that again.'

'Just testing. Don't Sorcerers have special powers to see through things like that?'

'No.'

I drove slowly into the fake turning circle and pointed to the fence. 'That's another Glamour, and quite a strong Ward.'

Vicky unlocked her Focus and stared at the magickal barrier. She consulted her Focus, scratched her head and played with her hair. 'Wow, that's strong,' she concluded. 'And it's been here for at least two, mebbees three hundred years. I can't even begin to unpick it. Not without a few Artefacts and stuff.'

'*And stuff.* Is that a technical term?'

'Aye, now how are we gonna get through?'

'Close your eyes and grip your seat.'

The sound of machine guns echoed in the air, fainter than last time. As we approached the cattle grid, Vicky jerked in her seat and raised her arms.

'Revenant!' she screamed. 'Nooooo....'

The sound of gunfire ceased, and I slammed on the brakes. Vicky was hyperventilating and staring through the windscreen at some inner horror. She had said that Hannah had faced a Revenant, and had had her skull caved in. I sincerely hope that I don't see one of those for a long, long time.

'Are you OK, Vicky?'

Her breathing slowed down, slowly, and she blinked, then scrabbled in the pockets of her brand new waterproof for her fags. 'I'm not going through that again without a Keyway,' she said. 'I certainly couldn't do it on my own.'

'The good news is that it only works one way – we can get out easily enough.'

'Good. Are there any more surprises?'

'Only the wall itself.'

The mystery of Susan's car was solved when we reached the Hall: it was parked outside. If her car was here, I suspected that she'd be inside. I went over to have a look, and found a carrier bag pinned underneath the windscreen wiper.

'Are there any traps?' I asked Vicky.

She peered at the bag and shook her head.

I retrieved the damp plastic and opened it. Inside was a ziplock freezer bag, the sort of thing you'd use for storing your home-made soups. Inside that was a note, in Mother Julia's handwriting.

Conrad, if you find this, stay away. If you can't stay away, remember the view from the bench. J.

'Let's have a look at the wall,' I said to Vicky.

We started with the gates. On the gravel in front of them was the huge padlock and chain which had previously secured them. It had been unlocked and dropped where it lay. Vicky examined the padlock, and I looked at the gates.

'This has been opened with a Keyway,' she said.

'And these gates have been welded shut,' I added. 'I've seen professional welding, and this is terrible. Basically, they've just been melted together.'

Vicky kicked the padlock. 'Keira's mother,' she said.

I kicked the gates. 'And when they'd got in, Keira welded the gates shut behind them. I'll leave you in peace to do your thing.'

The hotel had filled my flask with decent coffee, at a price. I poured myself a cup and watched Vicky work her way up and down the wall, the gates, the door to the lodge and finally the wall again. I poured her a cup as she started to come back.

'Hledjolf would be proud of that,' she said, clutching the mug to warm her hands.

'Not good, I take it.'

She shook her head. 'No. They've woven half a dozen Works into the fabric of the wall, including a song.'

'A song. I thought I could hear women's voices when I looked last week.'

'Aye, that's right. It means the defences can tap into the Grove to draw energy. Trying to breach that wall would be like trying to blow the national grid with a battery.'

I sipped my coffee. Like Vicky's enthusiasm, it was rapidly cooling. 'Given enough time, could you find a way through it?'

'Me? No. I know a couple of guys who could. Given enough time.'

I left her to drink her coffee and opened the package from my supplier. Sitting on top, in pride of place, was a brand new SIG P226 Elite pistol. I liked the idea of brand new – the rifling signature wouldn't be on any law enforcement database.

Vicky wandered round as I was stripping the gun and loading the magazines.

'The Occlusion round Lunar Hall will keep the sound in, won't it?' I said.

'If you shoot that at the wall, it'll bounce straight off and hit you,' she replied.

'I'm not stupid, Vicky. This is a new gun, and you don't trust a new gun until you've fired it.'

I confess. I did show off a little when I test fired the gun, shooting a couple of rocks off the top of a fence post. It worked perfectly.

I slipped the gun into the OWB (outside the waistband) holster and buckled it under my coat. The P226 is the longer version, and not so comfy to wear or so easy to hide. It is, however, more accurate over longer distances. I wanted to keep as big a distance between the three renegade Witches and myself as possible.

Vicky was looking dubiously into the box at the MK3A2s – black metal cylinders, about the size of a very chunky aerosol. 'What are those things?'

'Smoke grenades,' I lied. 'Let's go for a walk.'

I led her further round the wall than she had been herself, following a natural rise in the ground. I stopped at a spot on the other side of the wall from the bench where I'd stood to examine the Sisters' enclave.

I closed my eyes and tried to recall the layout: what had I seen that Julia wanted me to remember? And then it came to me.

'They said the Maginot line was impregnable,' I announced.

'You what?'

'Before World War Two, the French built a series of forts along the border. Everyone reckoned it was impregnable, and they were probably right. So the Germans just went round the edge, through the Ardennes. Next stop: Dunkirk. Come on, we're going to get a different perspective.'

We drove back through the Ward, and Vicky flinched at the memory of what we'd seen. Once we were through, she turned to me.

'There won't be any gaps in the wall. They're not that daft.'

'Not a gap, no. Their site is well over eighty acres, and it's on a slope. What would happen if they surrounded it with a wall?'

'How should I know?'

'It would flood, right at the bottom, where their sacred grove is. All that rain last night would run down the hill and form a lake against the wall. I'll bet you a handbag that there's no wall against the river.'

'What river?'

It was my turn to stare at her. I slowed the car and pointed to the valley on our left. 'We're on a hill. That's a valley. Of course there's a river.'

She shrugged. 'Geography was never me strong point.'

I set off back to Wray, and took the first left turn after the bridge over the Roeburn. We climbed a similar ridge to the one we'd just left, and I chose a farm at a point just opposite Lunar Hall. We were too high to see anything from here.

'Can you do a Glamour on the car?' I asked.

'Aye,' she said, perking up. It was the first time in a while she'd been able to do something positive. She got out her rugged tablet computer. 'What do you want? Li Cheng's wrote an app for this.'

'Tell me you're joking. A magickal app?'

'Of course. He got his doctorate for magickal software. It doesn't actually do the Work, it acts as a channel and focus. Makes it much easier.'

'Good for him,' I said. Mentally, I moved Major Li a notch up in my estimation. 'I don't want anything fancy, just a new number plate and a big Environment Agency logo on the side.'

'Will do.'

It took her less than thirty seconds, and most of that was spent searching for the EA's logo. Of course, she had no idea who or what they were. 'I'll leave you to do the talking this time,' she said with a grin.

I drove into the farmyard and blew the horn. A man stuck his head out of the farmhouse. I'd probably interrupted his Sunday dinner.

'Just going to take a look at the river,' I shouted. He waved us towards a path and retreated into the warmth.

I turned around in the farmyard, so that I could reverse down the track. I went as far as I thought the ground would support the car.

'Time to see how waterproof your new shoes are,' I said.

Vicky looked longingly at my hands. 'Have you got any spare gloves?'

I dug out a pair and passed them over. She shoved her hands right in, and asked me to fasten the cuffs of her jacket over the gloves. Otherwise, they'd fall off.

It was a long, wet trudge down the hill to the riverbank, or where the riverbank would be if it hadn't flooded the pasture. Neither of us looked up until the water stopped us in our tracks.

'My life, I've never seen anything like it,' said Vicky.

Across the now raging Roeburn, evergreen trees jostled for position next to the water. Even with my limited Gift, I could sense the magick swirling about them. Being evergreens, they hid the Grove from view, so I backed up a bit.

'What's that?' I asked, pointing to the air above the trees, right where the clearing was located.

Vicky joined me. 'I have no idea, but it's discharging the Lux from the Grove at a rate of knots. Something serious is happening in there.'

I stared at the river. This was the point of no return for me. If I acted now, I'd have to keep on to the bitter end.

'I'm going in,' I said.

'How?' She stared, aghast, at the swollen river. 'Hang on, never mind "how", *why* are you doing it?'

'I've nearly been killed three times. If I walk away now, I'll have to take another job and start from scratch. Besides all that, I made a promise to Mother Julia. No one would hold me to it, but everyone, including me, would know I hadn't kept it. A Clarke's Word is Binding. End of.'

'Say that again.'

There was a look on her face that I hadn't seen before. She was staring at me in a way that went deeper than scoping out my (lack of) magickal ability.

'Say what?'

'About your promise.'

'What? *A Clarke's Word is Binding*? Learning that lesson was one of the hardest parts of growing up. It was the only time my father ever hit me.'

She pulled her lip, stretching her face and looking horsier than ever. 'I can see why the Allfather picked you. There's a very, very faint strain of magick going back generations. If I had to bet on it, Conrad, I'd say that no Clarke has broken his word since… Maybe before the Reformation.'

That was both flattering and quite a legend to live up to. It was also distracting. 'I'd love to know how you can tell that, but some other time, eh?'

'Fair enough. Back to "how"?'

'Across the river.'

'You can't swim that. Not with your leg. It's madness.'

'I agree. I'm going to ride over. On a horse.'

She shook her head violently. 'No. No way. I cannot go in there, and definitely not on a horse. No chance, Conrad.'

We turned to face each other. 'Good,' I said. 'You've saved my life once, Vicky. We're quits. I wasn't going to take you, anyway.'

It took her a beat to realise what I'd said. She quickly got on her high horse – a beast she was happy to ride. 'Why not? Are you saying it's too dangerous for a woman?'

'No. I hope you know me better than that.'

The look on her face said that she didn't.

'Vicky, I need you to do two things. Both are very, very important.'

'Now you're patronising me.'

I tried not to get annoyed. 'Hear me out, OK? This is my fight, and if I win, I want the prize.' That brought a smile. 'But what if I lose? There's going to be a hell of a mess, and you're going to have to clean it up. True?'

She blew out her cheeks. 'True enough. One of us does need to live to get help if it all goes tits up.'

'Good. And if I die, I want you to go to Alain. He knows you, and he knows who my girlfriend is. I want you to go and tell her what happened.'

She stood open-mouthed. '*Girlfriend?* You've got a girlfriend?'

The combined mockery and outrage in her tone was like a slap in the face, only much more painful. 'Is it so impossible?' I said. I'm afraid that I couldn't keep the hurt out of my voice.

She started walking back up the hill, muttering to herself, and got to the car well ahead of me. 'Where are we gonna get this horse from, then?'

We drove out of Wray heading for the Fylde Equine Research Centre, and I told Vicky the headlines about my relationship with Olivia Bentley and her late father.

'What if she gets a shotgun?' said Vicky. 'You can't come this far and get shot for what you did in the past.'

'Good point. Unfortunately, I don't know where else I can get a big horse around here.'

She sighed. 'Pull in and let me ring an old pal from school.'

She made the call, pausing in mid flow to ask if the Volvo had a tow bar. It does. When she rang off, she promised me that she could get a horse from a stables over the border in Yorkshire and that we'd be back before dusk.

We didn't spend long in the Wensleydale stables; just long enough for me to see another side of my travelling companion. Vicky's old pal was exactly what you'd expect a rich farmer's daughter to be (I should know – I've been out with enough of them), and there was real affection when they met up again, but neither had a clue what to make of the other now that they weren't united by school ties. Give an ex-miner's daughter a Gift, send her to a all-girl boarding school, then this Invisible College place, and it's no wonder that Vicky sometimes struggles to find her grown-up identity.

We only just made it as the sun was setting. I drove past the farm where we'd impersonated the Environment Agency, reversed the trailer into a field and dumped it. It was a detail we could sort out later.

Vicky was very nervous of the horse. Even I was nervous of the horse, a huge gelding called Rover's Boy who'd had a moderately successful career over the jumps. Standing in the dying light, saddled and snorting, he was an impressive sight.

'What now?' said Vicky.

'You take the car and go back to the other side of the valley. Drive down to the cattle grid, where the Ward is, and wait. You might want to fill the flask up first.'

She nodded. 'I've been thinking. Give us your phone.'

I handed it over. She touched it to her own device, and did something magickal.

She passed it back. 'This should work. That wall is cutting out any electro-magnetic transmissions, so you'd be on your own big-time in there. I've entangled our phones, so you can call me, but no one can call you because the network doesn't know where you are. Good luck, Conrad. I'll be waiting.'

I held out my hand, and she put her arms round me. 'Take care, Conrad.'

I had to stand on the ramp to mount Rover's Boy. He fidgeted around at first, then he settled down and we were off.

The Roeburn had retreated a little during the day, but not much. Rover's Boy was not keen to get his hooves wet, and shied away from the water twice. He left me with no option but to go up the hill and put him into a gallop. Underneath, he's still a racehorse, and with enough head of steam, he'd carry on into the river rather than risk injuring himself. Besides, if I was going to be the metaphorical cavalry, riding in to sort things out, why not be the literal cavalry as well?

Rover's Boy didn't let me down. He plunged into the water and scrabbled for a footing, not sure whether to run or swim. I dug my heels into his flanks and urged him on. You could say that I spurred him on, only spurs are illegal. It did the trick.

He surged out of the water on the other side and reared up violently as we both hit an invisible wall of magick. It was all I could do to fall off without trapping my feet in the stirrups.

His hooves crashed down near my head, and he whinnied loudly, torn between the push of magick and his fear of the river now that I wasn't there to drive him through. After a second, he found a small margin between wood and water where the magick faded, and I got up gingerly, checking for damage. No broken bones. Not yet.

I left Rover's Boy to munch the grass and turned to face the trees. The Ward protecting the Grove was strong, but not dangerous. It was designed to make people (and horses) want to be somewhere else, so I gritted my teeth and pushed aside a yew tree.

The branches snapped at my face, and nearly pushed me back into the river, but I grabbed on to them and hauled myself past the leafy barrier. With a twang, I was through the Ward and tripping over a root to fall on the ground. I'd done it. I was inside the Grove.

'Blessed is the night, for it brings amongst us the Goddess,' said one of the trees.

Shit. The trees are talking. I fumbled to get my rucksack off and unship the torch. This was not a place to go mad and have a happy ending.

'Do not listen to men, my daughters,' said another tree. 'They will lead you into misery.'

'Shut up,' I said. The torch was shaking in my hand as I flicked the switch.

Fat trunks leading up to bare branches loomed above me. I trained the beam where I'd heard the voice, and saw only bark.

'The night is long in winter. You must gather your store in summer,' said the tree. It didn't grow a mouth, it spoke straight into my head, but I knew that the voice had come from the tree.

I started to move forward, skirting the tree and flicking my torch about to look for a path. My leg was aching from the ride, and I tripped. I couldn't stop myself braking my fall by putting a hand on one of the trees.

'A man! A man amongst us! Cast him out, Sisters!'

The wood burned against my hand, the bad hand already wrapped in a bandage. I snatched it away, and slipped on some sodden leaves. I had to roll to avoid another of the trees, and dropped my torch.

I curled up into a ball, frightened of touching anything that grew in here. Perhaps that was why the Ward by the water wasn't that strong – the Grove itself was one huge Ward. I let my breathing calm down, and slowly reached for the torch. I got to my knees and thought about where I should be heading. Something was happening in the clearing. Something powerful. It would make sense to avoid that until I had more intelligence.

Shining the torch about, I plotted a course through the biggest gaps between trees. I made sure it was heading in the right direction, and counted the trees I would have to pass. Six, to start with.

'Down there. To your right,' said a gnarled oak. The way looked more straightforward, and much easier to navigate, so I took the tree's advice. I was about to emerge when I heard a whinny from Rover's Boy. Damn. That bloody tree had led me back to the river. Damn and blast.

I thought of approaching it like Odysseus and the Sirens – stuffing my ears to avoid the song, but these voices were in my head already. It was now dark, very cold and I was no further ahead.

I turned off the torch and got out my fags. When I went to use my lighter, the magickal spark was ten times brighter than normal. Of course – there was Lux running through every branch and twig. That amplified my Talent, and if I had a Talent to see things clearly, that should be amplified, too.

Keeping the torch off, I let my eyes adjust, and a sliver of moon broke through the cloud. In its light, the tree trunks separated themselves from a single mass into individual shapes. I knew the way, I had a destination, and I could make a path from my thoughts. One step at a time, I set a course for the bench high on the hill.

'Watch the brambles,' said a tree. 'Thorns will bind you, thorns will cut you.'

'She's right,' said a holly bush. 'It's easier if you go round me.'

'Shut up, ladies,' I said. 'Or I'm coming back with a chainsaw. I mean it.'

'You wouldn't watch us bleed in life, but you'll watch us bleed now we're dead? Shame on you.'

I skirted a silver birch, took two more steps, and my foot went *thud* not *splash*. I'd found the path, and waiting on it was my teenage crush, Cindy Crawford, wearing a bikini. She looked exactly like the picture of her I'd kept hidden under my bed. Definitely an improvement on talking trees.

She played with her hair, thrust out a hip and looked down at herself admiringly. 'Good choice,' she said.

My teenage self would have been in ecstasy at the sound of that voice, and my teenage self wouldn't have noticed the lack of American accent. Like the Ward on the cattle grid, this Spirit had the knack of pulling things out of my head. I was not amused.

'If you're hoping I'll lend you my jacket, tough,' I said.

'I'm just waiting for my cue,' she replied, white teeth glinting. 'In a short while, I'm expected on stage.' She gestured to her left, towards the clearing. If I'd been in any doubt before, I was now certain that this apparition had nothing to do with the Sisters.

'Are you here to stop me?' I asked.

'I'm here to make you an offer. When Deborah has finished, I'll be at one with Abbi, and I can't wait to manifest myself again. If you give up now, I'll give you my word that I'll be your servant for a year and a day. Now isn't that a tempting offer?'

'No,' I lied. It was a very tempting offer.

She shook her golden locks. 'I wouldn't be your servant for sex, though that would be pretty mind-blowing. You don't have to betray your true love for me. Unless you want to, of course…'

I gritted my teeth.

'With Abbi's Gift and my abilities, together we'll be unstoppable. For a year and a day, I'll serve you and make your name in the world of magick.'

'I don't think so, Miss…?'

'Call me Helen, as in Helen of Troy.'

Oh dear. Poor Abbi.

'If you'll excuse me, ma'am, I'll be getting on. Don't take it personally, but I made a promise.'

The apparition looked genuinely concerned. 'No, I won't take it personally, but you will. When Keira sees you, she'll kill you, and that would be such a waste. I'd rather have you on my side, but if you want to play the hero…'

'I'm not a hero. I'm just a tradesman who keeps his word.'

'Then goodbye, Connie. You'll see me in your dreams, no doubt.'

The image of gorgeousness vanished in a dazzling burst of light. I shook my head to clear away the afterglow, and when I looked up the path, I could see smaller lights approaching. I turned on my torch and found Mother Julia and Sister Theresa waiting for me at the edge of the Grove.

'Got any soup?' I said. 'It's been a long day.'

My capacity for weirdness has grown exponentially since Christmas, but it nearly blew a fuse when I saw that the Sisters were chained together at the waist. A long, delicate silver chain, but a chain nonetheless.

Sister Theresa saw me staring at it. 'No jokes, Mr Clarke. Neither of us finds it in the least funny.'

I snorted, then I burst out laughing.

'We can take it off if we're locked in the same room,' said Mother Julia with very pursed lips. 'Such as when sleeping, for example.'

'For example,' I said.

'Not that we've slept much,' said Theresa.

She's a game old bird, is Theresa, and a powerful Witch, but she is getting on. I could see exhaustion creeping in around her eyes.

'Come,' said Julia. 'We'll go to the Lodge.'

'One moment,' I said, getting out my phone. I text Vicky: *Inside. Going for a Council of War with the Sisters.*

'How did you get that to work?' asked Julia, staring at the phone.

'I've got a friend outside. She's quite good at this stuff.' We started walking, and I asked, 'What's the situation? And why the chain? I wouldn't have picked you two to be inseparable.'

They stole a glance at each other, and Theresa spoke. 'The First Sister held us jointly responsible for our situation. She said that we must sort it out together, and act as one. The silver rope is her way of enforcing it.'

'Oh. Okay.'

Julia picked up the thread. 'Between Friday and last night, we did what we could to prepare. Before you say anything, Conrad, our prime concern was not to save our skins but to deny Deborah access to the Grove.'

I didn't believe her, but I'm sure that what she said was part of the truth.

'Then last night, the gates were breached,' she continued. 'The first we knew was when we felt our Sister die.'

'Who's dead?'

'The Eleventh Sister,' said Theresa. 'She was keeping watch through the night in the Heart of the Grove. By the time Julia and I had run down there, the barrier was up.'

I noted that she had used Julia's first name. Proximity had brought them closer together, if you see what I mean. Either that or grief.

We arrived at the Lodge, and I was quick to take off my waterproof trousers. Susan appeared with a brush to get the crap off my coat, and I whispered in her ear. 'Thanks for the note under the windscreen. It was a big help.'

'We only had twenty minutes warning of lockdown. I said that I needed something from the car.'

The three women eyed my SIG with distaste, but none of them made any comment. Food was served, and I started by asking if they knew what was going on.

'Do *you* know?' asked Julia.

'Well, as I understand it, Keira…'

'…Who's Keira?' said Theresa.

'The ringleader, I think. She's the one who's masterminded the whole thing. She was the one who tried to kill me, and she was the one who set up all the false trails. And it was her mother who opened your gates with her Keyway.'

Theresa bit her knuckles, and seemed on the verge of tears. Julia put her arm around Theresa's shoulders, and pulled her in for a hug.

'We've all been betrayed,' said Julia to Theresa. 'And the First Sister most of all. Carry on, Conrad.'

As I said before, there are going to be a lot of questions to answer after this. I ignored the betrayal and resumed my thesis. 'Keira is assisting Deborah in some sort of Binding; Abbi is a willing or unwilling victim in this. I actually met the Spirit involved on the way through the Grove.'

Theresa pulled herself away from Julia's embrace. 'You met the Spirit? How did he manifest himself?'

'Herself. It was most definitely female. She dug out an image from my unconscious, somehow, and offered me a deal if I gave her a free pass on the Binding business.'

'You did well to resist her. I don't suppose she told you her name.'

'She did, actually, but only her stage name. I've no idea what her real name is. She calls herself Helen of Troy, would you believe?'

The Sisters looked at each other in horror. 'Merciful Goddess, preserve us,' said Julia.

'Not good news, I take it.'

Julia placed her hands on the table, to stop them shaking. 'If they complete the Binding, and if Helen takes all the Lux from the Heart of the Grove, then the world of magick is in serious trouble. As is the mundane world. She really did start the Trojan War, you know.'

There was some soup in the bottom of my bowl. I mopped it up with some fresh bread and chewed over the idea that there had really been a Trojan War, and that a real person called Helen had started it. As far as I could remember, the gods had a lot to do with it, but ancient Greek ideas of Fate and Free Will were a little too much to swallow right now. I'd stick with the central idea: Helen betrayed her husband while Penelope stayed faithful to Odysseus.

'Why are you smiling, Conrad?' It was Susan who spoke.

I rose from my chair and kissed her. 'Because your food is gorgeous. Come on, Sisters, let's make a recce down to the Grove.'

14 — The Fourteenth Sister

We made an odd grouping – the two Sisters, chained together, and me behind, limping and cursing. Julia led us straight down to the Grove, past the Hall itself and over their beautifully manicured lawn. As the woods came in to view, I remembered going through them.

'I nearly didn't get here,' I said. 'Can either of you shut up those talking trees?'

Theresa stopped dead, the chain yanked on Julia and she slipped on the wet grass. Her Sister helped her to her feet, then rounded on me.

'Those "talking trees" are my life's work, Mr Clarke. That's what a Memorialist does, as you clearly didn't know. They won't interrupt us.'

'Good,' I said. I was none the wiser, but happy to know that our approach to the Heart of the Grove wouldn't have a running commentary from the undergrowth.

The Sisters followed a path through the Grove until I could feel the magick prickling all around me, centred on a space ahead of us. I struggled to make out what we were looking at until Julia turned on her torch.

The reflection dazzled me for a second, then resolved itself into an image of the three of us, perfectly reflected in a curved wall.

'What the fuck?' was my intelligent contribution.

'Dodgson's Mirror,' said Theresa. 'As in Charles Lutwidge Dodgson, better known as Lewis Carroll. *Alice through the Looking Glass* is a joke, because nothing goes through this mirror.'

'Nothing?'

'No light, no sound, no force and no object can penetrate from either direction. It is an utter and total barrier. Until you appeared, our plan was to wait until it comes down and deal with them. Now that you're here, you can wait with us, and bear witness if necessary. There's nothing doing until then.'

I stared at my reflection, then looked away because I'm not a pretty sight. I lit a fag, and neither of the Sisters objected.

'It must come down soon,' I said, because Helen said she was waiting for her cue. Unless she pops out of another dimension.'

'There are no other dimensions,' said Julia. 'It's complicated, but Spirits exist alongside us. Helen will enter the Heart of the Grove from above.'

'There's no top? Why didn't you tell me?'

'It extends upwards for about a hundred yards,' said Theresa.

I checked the time: seven o'clock. 'I know some people from the mundane world who could help.'

Theresa was withering. 'Help how, Mr Clarke?'

'There's an RAF Typhoon Squadron in Lincolnshire. If I pulled the right strings, they could be here in half an hour and carry out an air strike.'

'Don't be stupid,' said Theresa. I'm going to give her the benefit of the doubt, and say that it was guilt and frustration that was making her so unpleasant. On second thoughts, no. She just didn't like me.

Julia gave me a smile. 'He's not being stupid; he's made a sensible suggestion, the first actual one we've had since Lika was murdered last night.' She turned to face me. 'Thanks, but no thanks, Conrad. For one thing, it would kill Abbi and destroy the Heart. Even bound to Helen, she'll still be alive, in a way. For another thing, it won't work unless you're on the plane. No Ungifted pilot will be able to see the target, will they?'

Damn. I should have thought of that. I tried to wrap my head round the idea of Dodgson's Mirror. 'Would a lot of Lux, in a focused spot, make a small hole? Big enough to jump through?'

Theresa was slightly less scathing this time. 'No. The nature of the Mirror is absolute: it reflects all energy. Even the Goddess herself and all her Spirits could do nothing. It's like multiplying by zero, no matter how big the multiplier, the answer is always zero.'

I got that, and took the thought a stage further. 'Is it a superconductor?'

Theresa's eyebrows shot up with unexpected respect. 'No, otherwise it would be permanent. It's a Charm, a special Charm, but a Charm nonetheless. It needs a constant draw of Lux to remain in place.'

'So it can't be perfect. Somewhere, there is a connector, a place for the Lux to be fed in.'

'Yes, there is. The Mirror extends underground, and it has roots, just like the trees, and at about the same level. The Mirror draws Lux from the Grove. Not only that, a Witch must keep part of her mind on it constantly. That would be Keira.'

Eureka. I had a plan.

'Let's go, Sisters,' I said. 'I need to make a call.'

I almost bounded up the path to the Pendle monument. I sat down, where all the Novices had sat to write their poems and paint their pictures. My response to the Grove was going to be rather different from theirs.

Keeping my fingers crossed, I made the call. Five minutes later, I had a proposal for the Sisters.

Putting my call on hold, I said, 'I can get agents into the Heart of the Grove and disrupt Keira's concentration. At a cost. I don't understand what it means, but the price is 36oz Troy. Is it anything to do with Helen?'

Both Sisters drew in their breath. Julia spoke first. 'That price is a weight of Alchemical Gold, on deposit with the Dwarves. Like a bank.'

'It's more than we have,' said Theresa. 'The Daughters at Glastonbury would stand surety, though. Most of our wealth is here, tied to the Grove.'

'But how?' said Julia. 'This sounds impossible.'

'It's not guaranteed,' I said. 'And the price is only payable on success.' I waved the phone. 'My associate says take it or leave it, but decide now. If you can think of a better way...'

'I propose we take it,' said Theresa firmly.

'I agree,' said Julia. 'Tell your associate we have a deal.'

'Oh, there's one more thing,' I said. 'You'll have to kiss goodbye to your lawn. Probably for a couple of years.'

'Our lawn?' said Julia. 'Whatever, but no more conditions.'

I retrieved the call and gave him the go-ahead, then stood up. 'Right. We need six sisters, standing on the lawn, at exactly 60 degree intervals, holding a Charged Wand, whatever that is. And we need them in position asap.'

The women looked both bewildered and energised. 'What on earth for?' said Julia.

'Never mind that,' said Theresa, 'let's just do it. We're going into the Hall, Mr Clarke. Still no-go for you, I'm afraid.'

'I'm going to the Lodge,' I responded. 'Once this starts, we play to the end, and I'm going to get myself ready; you should do the same. And bring a big cloak, big enough to fit me. When the Mirror fails, I don't want to stick out too much. We're going to be standing by the Heart, waiting for them.'

As they moved off, I heard Theresa muttering. I think she said *He'd stick out anywhere, like a ruddy great lamp post.*

Charming.

Susan made me a cup of strong coffee while I refreshed myself, then joined me in the covered passage while I had a smoke.

'Did you know the Eleventh Sister?' I asked.

'Poor girl,' said Susan. 'She was an identical twin, the older by seven minutes. The other twin, Anna, is the Twelfth Sister. She's in bits.'

There was nothing to say to that. Odin said there was no afterlife on offer with him: I wondered what the Great Goddess offered. It would be no consolation to Anna.

'They're Polish,' said Susan. 'The first non-British Sisters ever to join the Coven.'

A light came into the garden: Julia, separated from Theresa, and accompanied by a stooped figure in a snow-white robe.

I heard an intake of breath from Susan, and saw her bow very low. 'First Sister,' she said. 'In the name of the Goddess, welcome.'

I gave a respectful nod to the white figure, who nodded back and lowered her hood. The First Sister was old, very old, and her fingers were gnarled with arthritis. Her hair, as white as her robe, was silky and tied in a Goddess Braid.

She coughed, and I could hear the strain in her voice. 'Blessings of the Goddess, Susan. Your wait will soon be over, if it is willed. And a blessing to you, Mr Clarke. There's something you should know.'

'I know so little, Sister, that my ignorance is visible from space.'

She smiled. 'Julia was right to trust you, and I was wrong to doubt her. You may not succeed in preventing this … tragedy from reaching its conclusion, but you are right to try. What you need to know is that Keira is my granddaughter. I had no idea she was capable of this, and no idea that Augusta would aid and abet her. That's all, Mr Clarke.'

That's all! I was still digesting the information when the First Sister raised her hood.

'They're ready,' she said. 'Julia will take you.'

The First Sister headed up the path towards the bench, well away from the action. Julia pointed down, towards the lawn.

A *Charged Wand* is a sort of magickal beacon, I discovered. It even has a light on top. If you get lost in the marsh, you make one, hold it up and wait for rescue. Something like that.

The light on top made it easy for me to stand in the middle of the lawn and move the six Sisters into exactly the right position. Satisfied, I left the stage and joined Julia, Theresa, Rose (the medic) and a distraught kid by the Monument. I'm guessing the kid was Anna.

'Are you bringing in a helicopter,' said Julia. 'You used to fly them, didn't you?'

'Very sharp, Mother,' I said, 'but wrong direction. I'm expecting help from below.'

Rose looked alarmed, and gathered Anna into her cloak.

I sent a text, and walked to the edge of the lawn. 'Right, everyone. On my mark, plant your wands firmly in the ground and step back. Three, two, one, now!'

Six Sisters planted their sticks and retired to admire the circle.

'Now we wait,' I said. 'You might want to sit down.'

Ten minutes into our wait, Theresa turned round. 'Look at the sky over the Heart of the Grove.'

We craned our necks to look up, beyond the top of Dodgson's Mirror. A new glow had entered the sky, sparkling diamonds of light danced and swirled around the tube of magickal glass.

'Helen is getting ready to manifest,' said Theresa. 'We've got about another hour.'

We watched the light show until one of the six Sisters let out a small scream. In the middle of the circle of Charged Wands, the ground was moving.

It moved some more, and other bursts of soil around the lawn showed that something was happening underground, then the centre burst open. Help was at hand, or rather, help was at paw. His Worship, the Lord Mayor of Moles, is about the size of a bull. His henchmen were rather smaller, about the size of a dog. That's still rather large, for a mole. Four of them emerged in the middle of the Moleish Star, and started to nose their way around the grass.

'Game on, Sisters,' I said, rather too enthusiastically. Only Theresa seemed to share my joy.

Julia pulled herself together. 'Will this work?'

'Yes. All we have to do is make a small sculpture of Keira.'

'What on earth for?' said Rose.

'We can't tell them to attack the one with brown hair, can we? They're blind.'

'Oh.'

'Leave it with me,' said Julia.

I ventured onto the lawn to meet our allies, and let them nose me all over. His Worship had said that he could transmit an Enhancement all the way to Lancashire, given enough power, and I had believed him. He didn't use the analogy himself, but I reckoned that these fellows were about as intelligent as dogs, as well as being the same size.

Warily, Julia approached us, carrying a small object.

'It's a living tree,' she said. 'If the tree agrees, you can take a branch and mould it. Will this do?'

It was a perfectly formed statuette of Keira, right down to the ponytail (which was *not* a Goddess Braid). I left it on the ground for the moles to get acquainted. They nosed around it in turn, then held up their snouts until they sensed the enormous discharge of Lux in the Grove. One by one, they scuttled off down the path.

'Who's coming?' I said to the company. 'We need to be quick: those moles won't hang around when they get digging.'

'Theresa and I,' said Julia. 'Here's your cloak.'

I took one of the MK3A2s out of my rucksack, took off my coat and put on the cloak, holding it roughly closed so that I could drop it quickly.

'Let's go, then.' I let Julia lead the way. Theresa was now walking with a stick.

'I hope you've borrowed a Persona,' I said to Julia, 'or this won't work.'

'Yes.'

'Good. The three inside the Mirror won't be expecting me. The plan is simple: we form a staggered triangle with me at the back. Hopefully, they'll just think I'm a tall Witch. You two need to provide as much distraction as you can – and stay as safe as possible while I go for Keira. This will all be over very quickly.'

'Wait,' said Theresa. We stopped. 'Look up. See? Helen has begun her manifestation. It will take a while to complete, but I suggest you change your tactics, Mr Clarke.'

'Why?'

'Once Helen has manifested in the Heart of the Grove, Deborah will be able to restore the Mirror *and* finish the Binding. You need to deal with her first.'

It sounded very dubious to me – Keira was the trigger happy one. I didn't fancy leaving her on the loose.

Julia took my hand. 'Theresa knows what she's talking about. Trust her. I do.'

I nodded, and we resumed our pace. There was no sign of the moles when we got to the Mirror. I put Julia front right, Theresa middle left, and I took the centre rear.

We stood still, waiting. I practised counting to four with the magickal wire cutters gripped in my teeth and the MK3A2 gripped in my hand. It's not a smoke bomb, it's a concussion grenade. It delivers more blast than any other hand-held weapon – about 950Kj. Unfortunately, it delivers it over a very short range.

My heartbeat was slowing as the waiting got longer. I was ready. I'd even started thinking about a cigarette when the Mirror came down.

My eyes raked over the clearing, the Heart of the Grove. My torch was in my left hand, and I dropped it when I saw that the clearing was well lit. To the right was a white statue, and in front of it an altar. Abbi was lying on it, flat on her back.

At the opposite end of the grove was Deborah, arms outstretched, her head wreathed in light. That left Keira. She was to Deborah's right, and she was being mauled by moles. One of them was already dead. I gripped my cloak and ran forwards, starting to move to my right. For this plan to work, and for me to tell the tale, I needed Keira between me and Debs.

Dodgson's Mirror had left a trench around the clearing, a clear enough mark to see and jump over. Julia was first, but to my left, Theresa was struggling to get across. That trench would be several metres deep.

As I jumped over, Keira finished off the last of the moles and became aware of us. Julia put on her best playground-clearing teacher's voice and shouted, 'NO! Stop!'

I dropped the cloak and took another step, moving towards Julia to get Keira in position, and then I tripped on a fucking mole hill. A blast of air ripped over me, sent by Keira, and something wet landed on my face. Julia screamed.

Keira helped me out by moving to protect Debs, who was only now turning to see what the fuss was all about. Her step to the left gave me enough time to stand up. She realised who I was and was raising her arm to attack me when I pulled the pin, released the safety handle and took two steps forward. Keira hesitated, then stood and watched as I bowled the grenade over her head with my best googly.

A grenade is not a cricket ball, but the principle is the same. Keira had no way of knowing what it was, but knew it was dangerous. She fired at the grenade and missed, fooled completely by the spin. The internal fuse reached the TNT core just over Deborah's head, and the clearing was filled with light, sound and death. The explosion blew Deborah's head off.

Keira's Ancile saved her life, and mine. The blast blew her backwards; the vacuum pushed me forwards, close enough to pile into her. It wasn't very dignified after that, if there's any dignity in combat. I smacked her broken finger, she screamed. I put my knee on her left arm, she tried to kick me in the balls. Again. This time I was ready for her.

I slammed my left forearm across her windpipe and ripped open her top. Before she could lift her magick hand, I'd cut the chain on her necklace, and it was over. I smacked her head on the ground to stun her and stood up, drawing my gun. I braced myself, aiming at her chest, and said, 'One word, one move and I fire. No second warnings.'

Her head fell back on to the ground, and I could see tears welling up. I bet they weren't for Lika.

Behind me, I could hear laboured breathing and small cries. Good – Julia must be alive. The heavy breathing would be Theresa. I hoped she knew a Charm for first aid.

The problem was not Keira, it was Abbi. I heard a groan from my right, and then a scream: 'Mummy!'

I kept my focus on Keira. If you fly choppers, you do get the knack of concentrating your gaze on two things at once. I saw a shadow flit in front of me as Abbi staggered to her mother's body, then another shadow as she stood up.

'You bastard,' she said. I'm guessing she meant me. I increased the pressure on the trigger, ready to dispatch Keira and deal with Abbi.

'No, child,' said Theresa. 'It was not him. The Goddess guided him, as she guides me.' Leaning heavily on her walking stick, Theresa interposed herself between Abbi and me. 'It's time to mourn, child.'

I heard Abbi begin to sob, and a rustle as she collapsed on the grass. Theresa turned to face me.

'Can you immobilise this creature?' I said. 'It's that or I finish her off.'

Theresa hobbled up and withdrew the silver chain which had bound her to Julia. I stepped back and Theresa bound Keira's hands, a surge of magick sealing the knot. Now it really was over.

I holstered the gun and turned to Julia. The Mother had gone white, which was not surprising because her left arm had been blown off at the elbow. Theresa had already applied a tourniquet, and some sort of Charm which was keeping shock at bay. For now.

'Well done, Conrad,' said Julia. She nodded at her severed arm. 'This is going to make gardening something of a challenge.'

I squatted down next to her. 'Thank you, Julia. Thank you for trusting me in the end.'

'I should have trusted you sooner.'

'No regrets, Mother. Are you up to making a quick phone call?'

'Help me up.'

I levered her into a sitting position and she pulled out her phone. 'Who do you want me to call?'

'Just a quick one. Ring Susan up at the Lodge and tell her to get straight up to the cattle grid and escort my partner through the Ward. Please.'

She nodded, and thumbed her phone awkwardly. I sent a quick text to Vicky: *Over. Alive. Someone coming to open Ward. Get down here asap. C.* I hesitated, then added an *X*.

Theresa was comforting Abbi, while keeping her gaze locked on Keira. I first retrieved the cloak they'd lent me, then went over to the prisoner.

'Mine, I think,' I said to Keira. I bent over her, and she flinched back. 'Sit still,' I told her.

Her necklace had unravelled into her chest. Carefully, I retrieved the ends and lifted the broken chain and all its Artefacts, trying not to catch the little pendants on her bra. I put the whole lot in the pocket on my thigh, then covered her with the cloak, making sure her hands were exposed.

'Why did you do it?' I asked. 'You're not stupid, you couldn't imagine that you'd control that monster once she was inside Abbi.'

She raised her chin. 'We did it for Cassandra's Bowl, one of the most powerful Artefacts of the ancient world. With that, Debs and I would have been made, and Abbi would have joined herself with one of the greatest Spirits alive. Helen is not a monster.'

'You're blind, Keira. More blind than those poor moles you slaughtered.'

I turned my back on her, and went to do something even I found distasteful: remove the necklace from Deborah's headless corpse.

Theresa grimaced when she realised what I was doing, and turned Abbi's face away. Before picking it up, I saw that the chain had a clasp. I fumbled for a second, then it clicked open. I slid off the Artefacts and left the chain on the body for Abbi to collect, if she wanted it.

Lights flickered on the path as the rest of the Coven warily approached us. When they saw me, they broke into a run, scattering to help Julia, Theresa and Abbi. I kept a close eye on the prisoner, just in case. One of the Sisters brought my coat and rucksack, and I was glad to cover up. It was getting parky down by the river. The last figure to appear was Anna.

She walked up to Keira. 'Is this the one?' she asked. I nodded, moving my hand towards my holster in case Anna wanted to get revenge for her twin.

Anna pointed at Keira, and said something loud and violent in Polish, then she spat in Keira's face and walked away. Keira was beginning to realise just how lonely she was going to be for the rest of her life.

The Heart of the Grove was a magickal place, of course. It was also magical – a beautiful haven of nature and of life, though currently a little battered. A few of the trees would now be silent, smashed into pieces as Dodgson's Mirror encircled the clearing. Inside, there were only two human creations visible, both made of limestone. One was the altar, and the other was the statue. I stared and stared at it. I'd seen it before, or variations of it, in Catholic churches and cathedrals all over Europe: it was the Virgin Mary. What's that all about?

'Don't tell anyone,' said Theresa, pointing to the statue. 'Seriously, it's our little secret.'

'I wouldn't know who to tell or what to tell them.'

'I was thinking of your new employers.'

'Aah. About that ... she's on her way now.'

Theresa rolled her eyes and went to speak to the Sister I now knew was Dawn, the Occulter. I could hear Theresa muttering about *Just as I was getting to like him.*

Susan appeared, showing Vicky where to go, and I was so glad to see them that I nearly ran over and gave Vicky a hug. She came straight up to me, and we had the hug anyway. A quick one.

'You're a lucky bastard, Conrad,' she said.

'Luck had nothing to do with it. It was all planned.'

'Aye, blokes always say that. No, I meant you're a lucky bastard because you don't have to do any of the paperwork. It's gonna take me weeks.'

'You can start by arresting this one.'

'Fair enough.' She fished the little pickaxe from under her top and showed it to the prisoner. 'Keira, I am arresting you for breaching the King's Peace and you will be arraigned before the Cloister Court. With the authority vested in me by the Peculier Constable, I place you under an order of Silence. Sic Fiat.'

Keira struggled for a second, then went limp. Now the tears really started.

'Mr Clarke?' said a voice from behind me. It was one of the sisters whose name I hadn't learnt yet. 'Shall I put this creature out of its misery?' She pointed to one of the fallen moles.

I bent down to look — there was a big gash on its side, and it was clearly in pain. Then I noticed its undercarriage. It was male.

'No, Sister,' I said. 'Take care of him, heal him and look after him. In the spring, your efforts may well be rewarded.'

She raised her eyebrows. 'If you say so.'

I noticed over her shoulder that the statue of the Virgin Mary had become a statue of some Greek goddess. I was wondering what to do next, when I received a message from the Allfather: *Come to the First Sister. Alone.*

No one noticed when I slipped out of the Grove.

15 — *Favours given, Favours received*

It was a long walk up the hill to the bench, and I was breathing heavily by the time it came into view. The First Sister was slumped forwards, her small body looking even tinier next to the Allfather. For this manifestation, my Patron had gone all Gandalf – long white beard, bejewelled eyepatch, that sort of thing, except for the spear. Gandalf doesn't do spears. I stopped before him and bowed low. 'My Lord?'

'You have discharged your duty, and you will get your reward. It is a fair thing, Conrad.'

'Thank you.'

'And I have paid my debts – to the Dwarf and to the Goddess. It is time for you to be released from your bond to me.'

That was a shock. 'I had expected it to be for life.'

Odin shook his head. 'You are already asking questions: did I manipulate you into this mission? Did the Goddess put extra spin on that grenade?' He laughed. 'Did I put that molehill there for you to trip over?'

He was right. The more I looked, the more I found it hard to draw the lines between coincidence, free will and divine intervention.

'You cannot function like that,' he said. 'You would begin to doubt your own existence if you did. For now, the truth: I chose you for this mission, yes, and I gave you the Enhancement you needed to begin on the path of magick. After that, I did nothing that you did not see with your own eyes. To my knowledge, the Goddess does not play cricket. Yet.'

He raised his arm, the one not holding the spear. 'I will release you with an answer, a boon and a gift. The first two, you may take as you wish, the gift you can take now.'

'Forgive me, my Lord. What's a boon?'

'A favour. Choose it carefully. Do you wish to be released?'

I didn't think about it long. 'Yes, my Lord.'

'Give me your hand.'

I held out my right hand, and he took it in a firm handshake. I felt the rune on my back tingle, then vanish; a tiny weight lifted from my shoulders. When he released my hand, a gold band had appeared on my right ring finger, yellow gold with a tiny spot of light glowing on it.

'It's a special version of the Troth ring. It makes visible your old family saying. Wearing this, the whole magickal world will know that a Clarke's Word is his Bond.'

I bowed again, and was about to launch into a speech when he placed his hand on my shoulder.

'Go well, Conrad,' he said. 'I will leave you, but there is another who would speak to you.'

The Allfather disappeared, and the First Sister jerked awake – only it wasn't the old lady looking out of those eyes. I was now in the presence of the Goddess. I bowed very low, lower than for Odin. That's what you do around her.

Her voice, when it came, was stronger and sweeter than the First Sister's had been, but it was still the voice of an old lady.

'We are one,' she said. 'The First Sister has surrendered her life and joined with me. She knew that she could not continue here, and I accept her sacrifice gladly. Will you grant me a boon, in return for my blessing?'

Dealing with the Allfather had been easy in comparison. I got the sense that much, much more was being held back here, and that there is an enormity to the Goddess which I couldn't fathom. I had to lick my lips and swallow hard. 'Of course, my Lady.'

'Carry me down to the Grove and lay me on the altar.'

'Of course, my...' I stopped speaking, because the Goddess had gone, and the Coven was down to ten Sisters. Eleven, if Abbi still counted.

The First Sister's body was tiny, and the path was downhill, but I was exhausted. I got the feeling that putting her down for a rest was not an option, so for the final time today, I had to grit my teeth and put one foot in front of the other, step by step down to the Heart of the Grove.

When I got to the trench where Dodgson's Mirror had been, I nearly lost it completely. I was standing, swaying, in front of the gap when the assembled women saw me. A hush fell over the crowd.

'Help?' I said, rather more pathetically than I intended.

Vicky reacted first. She scouted around, and found a pile of raw planks which they must use as benches. She grabbed Susan, and they put it over the trench. They stood back, and the Sisters, all eleven of them, formed a guard of honour to the altar.

When I laid down the body of the First Sister, her hand brushed against mine, and I felt a tingle. The wound caused by Keira's necklace had healed completely, except for a scar, and I somehow knew that my tiny little Gift had just got a little bit bigger. Not much, barely noticeable to someone like Vicky, but it mattered to me. I bowed my head and gave a quiet *thank you*.

Vicky touched my arm. 'Come on, Conrad. We're done here. Julia says we can use anything we find in the Lodge to make ourselves comfortable for the night. They'll be here until dawn, cleansing and mourning.'

'All of them? Including Abbi and Susan?'

'Aye, all bar Keira. She's coming with us.'

When I stepped over the trench, I didn't look back.

Vicky told me that she'd struck Keira deaf and dumb, so we pushed her off in front and walked slowly up the path behind her.

'Can you cook?' I asked Vicky.

'Nah.'

'Do I have to do everything round here? Fourteen women, and the only bloke is the one doing the cooking. Where's the justice in that?'

'Welcome to the brave new world of magick, Conrad,' she laughed.

Back at the Lodge, Vicky put Keira in the chintzy sitting room and locked the door with a Work. I got to grips with the kitchen.

I filled her in on the details over a vegetarian fry-up (eggs, but no bacon), and she told me that the Deputy PC was coming up tomorrow to take over the investigation, and to take custody of Keira.

'I am in so much shit,' said Vicky.

'Why? What did you say?'

'Nothing, really, but how can I talk me way out of this?'

'Don't. You've had my back, Vicky, and I've got yours. Just say I called you in – I'll deal with the rest.'

She looked dubious, but gave me the go-ahead to try. I started working on a story with suitably plausible deniability.

Over coffee and a last ciggy in the garden, we talked about tomorrow. I said that I'd start by returning Rover's Boy to Wensleydale. Vicky looked relieved to be excused that duty.

'I'll be going to Preston in the morning,' I continued, 'and I need you for an hour in the afternoon, to do me a big favour.'

'No problem. What do you want in Preston? A rocket launcher? Land mines?'

'Land mines are illegal. No, I need to go shopping for make-up.'

She shook her head. 'You know what, Conrad, the sad thing is that I believe you. Goodnight.'

The wire mesh outside HMP Cairndale was a shock to Vicky. She'd never been to a prison before.

'Why am I here?' she asked.

'Captain Robson RMP is here to interview a prisoner. With their co-operation. I phoned ahead and told them you'd be coming – all legal and above board.'

She gave me a dark look. 'There is no planet on which this is a good idea, except Planet Conrad. I'm not sure I've got me interstellar passport with us.'

'So long as you've got your Army ID, we'll be fine. Come on.'

I led a reluctant Vicky through the Official Visitors' entrance, and guided her through the formalities. She reserved her astonishment for the moment when I announced that I was the prisoner's legal representative for this interview. While we waited for a gate to open, she hissed in my ear, 'Every time I think you can't get worse, you get worse.'

'Says the woman who goes clubbing with a Glamour and no cash.'

'Not any more.'

Outside the interview room I asked for a minute with my client. Inside, Mina ran into my arms as soon as the door was closed. We took full advantage of the privacy for as long as we could.

'What is this, Conrad?' said Mina. 'Why didn't you just visit me normally?'

'I was in the area, and I want you to meet my new colleague. I passed the test.'

She sighed. 'I wish I could be more enthusiastic, but prison makes you selfish. Inside, I'm thrilled. You know that. You also know that I will now have something else to worry about.'

'This might cheer you up,' I said, and handed over the makeup.

Her face lit up as she took out the goodies and lined them up on the table. 'How did you know what to get?'

'Mr Joshi.'

She gave me that *Don't be silly* look.

'I asked him if he had a friend at the Preston temple, he did, and his friend introduced me to his daughter-in-law. We went shopping. Simple.'

I retreated and opened the door. Vicky stepped in, and her brows knitted together like Velcro when she saw Mina and the parade of cosmetics.

'What's gan'on?' she said sharply.

Mina looked up in shock, clutching a vivid nail polish.

'Mina, this is Vicky Robson. She saved my life over the weekend. Vicky, this is Mina Desai.'

Vicky looked from me to Mina and back again. 'Are youse two…'

Mina put down the nail polish. 'As much as we can, in the circumstances.'

'This is one story I've *got* to hear,' said Vicky.

'I'll tell you on the way back to Lunar Hall,' I said. 'For now, I need a favour. Can you explain to Mina what the Great Work is. With demonstrations. If I do it, she'll think I've gone mad.'

Vicky put on her serious face. It didn't really go with her outsize fleece, rugged trousers and Goddess Braid. 'Are you sure, Conrad? It might not go like you think.'

I coughed, and I could feel the red creeping up my cheeks. 'I promised Mina that I'd never lie to her. Things will get awkward if she doesn't know the truth. I'll wait outside. I'm afraid we've only got twenty minutes left.'

Nineteen and a half minutes later, Vicky emerged, leaving me to say goodbye to Mina. My true love's eyes were almost on stalks when I went to kiss her. We didn't waste time talking.

On the way back to the car, Vicky kicked me in the bad leg.

'Ow! What the bloody hell was that for?'

She gestured to her clothes. 'For this. You didn't need me to tell Mina about magick, you just wanted me lookin' me worst so she wouldn't get jealous. I've a good mind to tell her she's too young for you.'

'She knows that already. I'm not counting my chickens with Mina until she's been released and found her feet again.'

'Yeah, well, she's a canny lass, right enough. Sharp as a knife. And very worried about you. You really are a lucky bastard, Conrad.'

I unlocked the car. 'I know. Let's get going: I've got a story to tell you, and then I'm going to leave you with the Deputy PC.'

'Are you going down to London to claim your reward?'

'Not yet. There's time for that later. I'm going home to Clerkswell. There's a pint of bitter down there with my name on it.'

Conrad and Vicky's story continues in The Twelve Dragons of Albion, Second book of the King's Watch, available now from Paw Press. Turn over to find out more.

The Twelve Dragons of Albion

The Second Book of the King's Watch
By Mark Hayden

How do you tell the difference between a Ghost and a Spectre? Give up?

I'll tell you: Spectres are much better looking. Well, that's what my eleven times great grandfather said, and he should know – he's the Spectre haunting my house...

You'd think that staying alive and saving the girl would be enough for now. But no...

After proving himself in a desperate magickal battle, Conrad is admitted to the King's Watch to regulate the world of magick.

And what does the world of magick do? It laughs in his face.

At least Conrad now has a partner with some serious magickal firepower. Vicky Robson joins him on a mission to investigate rumours of a Dragon's egg, and to get him through his magickal entry test for the Invisible College.

And then Conrad discovers that the Invisible College won't let him keep his ammunition, and that the Dragon's egg is all too real.

So what does he do? He grits his teeth and reminds the world of magick that he who laughs loudest laughs last...

Available in Ebook and paperback from

PAW PRESS

www.pawpress.co.uk

Author's Note

Thank you for reading this book; I hope you enjoyed it.

The King's Watch books are a radical departure from my previous five novels, all of which are crime or thrillers, though very much set in the same universe, including the **Operation Jigsaw** Trilogy that Conrad himself refers to as part of his history.

If you've only just met Conrad in this book, you might like to go back the Jigsaw trilogy and discover how he came to be on the M40. As I was writing those books, I knew that one day Conrad would have special adventures of his own, and that's why the Phantom makes a couple of guest appearances.

A book should speak for itself, especially a work of fiction. Other than that, it only remains to be said that all the characters in this book are fictional, as are some of the places. Merlyn's Tower, Lunar Hall and Hledjolf's Hall are, of course, all real places, it's just that you can only see them if you have the Gift...

And Thanks...

This book would not have been written without love, support, encouragement and sacrifices from my wife, Anne. It just goes to show how much she loves me that she let me write this book even though she hates fantasy novels.

Although Chris Tyler didn't get to see the draft this time, his friendship is a big part of my continued desire to write.

Finally, thanks to my wonderful cover designer, Rachel Lawston. She put up with a lot on the way to getting here, and I am eternally grateful.

Made in the USA
Columbia, SC
13 July 2020